Death in the Downline

MARIA ABRAMS

QUIRK BOOKS
PHILADELPHIA

Library of Congress Cataloging-in-Publication Data
Names: Abrams, Maria, author.
Title: Death in the downline : a novel / Maria Abrams.
Description: Philadelphia : Quirk Books, 2025. | Summary: "Having lost her dream New York City journalism job and her boyfriend, Drew returns to her hometown and runs into an old friend, who recruits her into a multi-level marketing scheme. When a distributor dies suspiciously, Drew begins to investigate and discovers dangerous secrets about the whole organization"—Provided by publisher.
Identifiers: LCCN 2024028017 (print) | LCCN 2024028018 (ebook) | ISBN 9781683694144 (paperback) | ISBN 9781683694151 (ebook)
Subjects: LCGFT: Detective and mystery fiction. | Novels.
Classification: LCC PS3601.B738 D43 2025 (print) | LCC PS3601.B738 (ebook) | DDC 813/.6—dc23/eng/20240624
LC record available at https://lccn.loc.gov/2024028017
LC ebook record available at https://lccn.loc.gov/2024028018

ISBN: 978-1-68369-414-4

Printed in China

Typeset in Adobe Caslon Pro, Brother 1816, and Bennet

Designed by Elissa Flanigan
Cover illustration by Kelly Llanos
Production management by Mandy Sampson

Quirk Books
215 Church Street
Philadelphia, PA 19106
quirkbooks.com

10 9 8 7 6 5 4 3 2 1

TO MOM AND DAD

From the Podcast *Pyramid Scream: Inside the LuminUS Murders*

Episode 1: How Did Someone Like Her Fall for This?

Before I begin this podcast, I have a message for my listeners.

Joining an MLM doesn't make you stupid. Some of the smartest, most educated women I know, like the ones you'll hear about this season of Pyramid Scream, *have been duped. Corporations like LuminUS are expert scammers. They know exactly what to say and how to say it with the sole purpose of convincing you to ignore your better judgment and join them.*

I have the utmost respect for those who have joined and made it out the other side. I think those in MLMs are some of the hardest workers out there. As much as the companies promise flexible work hours (fit LuminUS into the nooks and crannies of your busy #momlife!), it's a 24/7 job. Time away from the hustle equals missing out on a sale.

I don't, however, have respect for predatory CEOs like Dixie LaVey who know the damage they're causing and do it anyway. Or for those #bossbabes who tell their downlines to take out another line of credit to support their own glamorous lifestyles.

One of the more troubling aspects of this story—apart from the murders—is that here we have this educated, successful woman, Drew Cooper, who by all accounts should have known better. And yet, she still got sucked into this scam. That's how charismatic these LuminUS "huns" are. They can convince you to go bankrupt selling their bogus products. They can make you refinance your home, sell your assets, take out loans you can't afford to pay back, and borrow money from family, all to buy more and more inventory despite not moving any.

How do they do it? Is it their charisma? Their enviable, social-media-ready lifestyles? Their promise of a built-in sisterhood? Or is it the brainwashing tactics they learned from the LuminUS handbook? Whatever it is, it was enough to persuade someone like Drew Cooper to put aside her common sense, as well as the gnawing feeling that this was too good to be true, to become another puppet in Stephanie Murphy's downline.

Hijacking your finances is the easy part. Once they have control over that aspect of your life, the areas their influence can reach are limitless. They can control your relationships, your social life, your shopping habits, and your appearance, and they can even upend your sense of morality.

As you listen to this season of Pyramid Scream, *put yourself in these women's shoes, and ask yourself, "How far would I have gone?"*

Let the LuminUS ladies in—crack the door open even an inch—and they will never leave. Not until they get everything they want, whatever the sacrifice.

LuminUS Recruitment Post Template

Hey, babes!

If you had a magic wand, what would be your perfect HOME 🏠? What would be your perfect VACATION 🌴? Your dream CAR 🚗? What would be your perfect LIFE 💃?

Psst . . . I have a secret. I can make your dreams come true.

I'm looking for new members to join my team!

Must be:
☞ Hard working
☞ Always hustling
☞ Energetic
☞ Loyal

Must NOT be:
☞Lazy
☞ Easily burnt out
☞ Shy
☞ Squeamish

Do you have what it takes to change your life?

Message me NOW!

#BossBabez #SheEO #LuminUS4Life

Chapter 1

How did I end up here?

It was the singular thought that looped in my brain since leaving New York, one that never let up.

It was 2018. The world was busy playing with fidget spinners and watching teens eat detergent pods online. I was busy being torn from the city I loved even though I'd done everything right. In the end, it didn't matter.

This is what I kept thinking—*But I did everything right*—as I stared blankly at the shelf. Boxes of dried pasta were squeezed together, side by side, competing to be the focal point. Buy me! No, buy me instead!

My shoulders went limp. Was this what my life had become? Spending a weekday afternoon shopping for cheap noodles instead of doing literally anything else? I picked the first one I saw—store-brand linguini—having forgotten which kind my dad asked for. As if on cue, my phone buzzed with a message.

DAD
Potato.

I rubbed the space between my brows, right over one of my deeply set frown lines and to the left of a new pimple budding below the surface of my skin. *This is what my life has become*, I thought. Newly thirty, newly single, no job, no money, and living at home with my father who only recently learned how to text.

DREW

DAD
Bag potato.

I didn't respond. I knew what he meant: A bag of russet potatoes that he forgot to include on the shopping list he scribbled on a sticky note that morning. A bag that would sit in the back of the dark pantry, forgotten, until sprouts grew from their eyes.

My dad wasn't a chef. Neither was I. My mom hadn't been either, but she was the one who always cooked, and despite her being dead for fourteen years, my dad still insisted on using her old grocery list. Some people get stuck in a moment and never grow out of it. My dad was one of those people.

I hadn't lived with him in over a decade, but he hadn't changed much. Sure, his hair and mustache had turned gray, his skin had become saggy and spotted from sun damage, and I swore he had shrunk an inch, but his essence stayed the same. As did his culinary palette.

I had left my family home, this small town, right after high school, vowing never to return. It wasn't my dad I was trying to get away from. He tried his best, despite not knowing how to raise a teenage daughter as a single father.

I harbored no hard feelings toward my father. It was the town I wanted to escape: Clearfield, and everything it represented. A suffocatingly small town in central New Jersey wasn't where I was supposed to be. I was meant for more.

Where did it all go wrong? I had done everything right: Admission to Columbia straight out of high school. An easy transition to the School of Journalism to get my master's degree. A brief stint interning at the *New York Times*. And then a full-time job at one of the most well-known media companies. Okay, I was writing listicles for BuzzFeed, but a job's a job. And it was a news outlet people immediately recognized by name.

Yet there I was. Staring at a row of cheap, watery pasta sauces, missing Zabar's like crazy, and feeling sorry for myself. Not to mention nursing a major hangover.

I grabbed two jars of plain marinara and threw them into the cart. They landed on the bags of potato chips that lined the bottom, protecting the glass jars from the impact. No one had ever accused a Cooper of being a healthy eater. I ate healthier in New York, but had become so depressed I no longer cared if my nightly diet consisted of a pint of brownie ice cream with a side of diet Dr. Pepper.

New York, I thought with a pang in my gut. Brassy but beautiful, cultured, never boring New York. Each time I remembered the city, I also remembered how I was ripped away from it, kicking and screaming like a petulant child. I could pinpoint the exact moment it all went wrong: Sitting in the apartment I didn't own and barely chipped in for rent on. Bryan, my boyfriend—correction, ex-boyfriend—walking in, chewing his lower lip. About to drop the bad news.

I shook away the memories. The quicker I could finish my shopping, the quicker I could return to my dad's home—correction, my home. And the quicker I could crawl back into bed and rewatch bad nineties sitcoms.

Life, as I came to realize, had other plans.

It was the kids I heard first: high-pitched begging for bags of fun-size Snickers followed by promises that they wouldn't ask for anything else ("Mom, we swear!"). I heard her next. A woman's voice, low but stern, telling the kids to keep quiet and reminding them they had already performed this routine in the cereal aisle.

Was it her? I wondered. Oh, please no, it can't be her.

Despite the hushed tone, the voice sounded familiar. I hadn't heard it in years, but she was someone I could never forget.

She was also someone I didn't want to see. Not there, in the pasta aisle, not ever. I darted into the housewares aisle and ducked behind a display of packing tape. No one bought housewares at the grocery store. I thought I would be safe.

I was wrong. She turned her cart into my aisle as we locked eyes. It took her a beat to recognize me, but when she did, her lips spread into a smile, and she quickened her pace.

"Drewww!" she called out, waving one hand while the other steered the full cart. One of her children tugged at the bottom of her shirt, but she brushed him away. "Oh my God! It's been so long."

"Steph," I said half-heartedly as she raised her arms to give me a hug. There was no escape. I went limp in her arms. She squeezed me tightly and I could smell her strong perfume: a mix of citrus and something sharp like industrial cleaner. Her platinum hair—which I knew was naturally chestnut brown—was pinned back into a messy bun that was made to appear effortless, and she wore a white cotton shirt tucked into her dark khaki shorts. Her makeup, albeit too heavy for my taste, was impeccable, and gave the illusion that she hadn't aged a day since high school. I tucked more of my body behind the display, hoping to hide my ratty leggings and old charity 5K T-shirt.

At the sight of her, memories began flooding back. I thought of our summers together, when the days were long, and there was no better feeling than having a best friend, no school, and parents who allowed you the freedom to wander so long as you returned before sunset. But those days were long gone.

"What brings you back to Clearfield?" Steph asked. "Visiting your dad?"

There it was: the question I had been dreading, asked by the person I wanted to hear it from the least.

"I . . . uh . . ." I trailed off. Steph watched me with her piercing green eyes as I awkwardly toed at the floor tile.

"Mom! Can I please get this notebook? It's for school." One of the kids waved a colorful book in Steph's face. She took it from him, a bit too forcefully, before catching herself and saying, "Why of course you can. Anything for school. Grades are number one!"

I was saved. For now. "Are these your kids?" I asked, wanting to change the subject. Didn't parents love talking about their kids?

"They sure are. Jax over here is eleven, and Rob Junior just turned nine."

"Rob Junior?" I asked out loud. I thought of Rob Senior, otherwise known as Rob Murphy, otherwise known as the reason Steph and I stopped being best friends.

"Wow, it really has been a long time!" she trilled. Jax, or the one I presumed to be Jax based on his height, walked toward the end of the aisle. "Where are you going?" Steph asked.

Jax huffed and said, "I'll be by the ice cream."

"Ice cream's not on the list, sweetie," Steph told him. Jax ignored her and walked around the corner. "You can get sorbet! The natural kind! No sugar added!" she called, but he was already out of earshot.

Steph forced a giggle. "You know how boys can be at that age," she said.

I didn't. The closest I came to knowing about children was spending the occasional brunch with my boyfriend's niece. Ex-boyfriend, I reminded myself. Ex, ex, ex. Our separated status was so fresh my brain hadn't had a chance to fully process it. Neither had my body. A bolt of sadness shot through me, making my muscles feel weak.

"We really need to catch up," Steph said. "Are you going to be in Clearfield long? I know how busy you must be in New York City working for that big newspaper of yours."

"Actually." I sighed, preparing myself for the next statement. "I'm here to stay. For the time being, at least. Once I find another job in the city, I'll move back. Shouldn't be too long." I didn't believe the words coming out of my own mouth.

Neither did Steph. She turned her attention to her younger son. "Rob, why don't you go help your brother." Rob nodded and ran off, the squeak of his sneakers hanging in the air.

Steph approached me. I stepped back, smacking my back into a wall of lightbulbs.

Her face seemed pleasant—she was smiling, her eyes soft—and yet, it felt predatory. Like a vulture approaching a bloodied deer.

Here it comes, I thought, preparing myself to get what I deserved.

"You know, Drew," she began. I held my breath. "I'm so glad to bump into you. I've thought about you a lot over the years, and I think we should have coffee. Talk things out, you know? We've been through so much together. It would be a shame to let all that history die. Especially since you plan on staying."

I let out the breath. "That would be amazing." It wasn't the speech I expected from Steph. I expected a verbal lashing. Maybe a slap. Instead, I got an olive branch. And I was more than happy to accept.

I too had thought of her often over the years. How can you forget your childhood best friend? The sister you never had? No matter how sour things went in the end.

We exchanged phone numbers and planned to get coffee the very next day. Steph again told me how excited she was to see me, and for a moment after she left, I was equally as excited—not to mention relieved. Steph didn't seem angry with me, and while I couldn't be certain, it sure seemed as though she had forgiven me.

I was also excited to have a friend. All of my friendships in New York were surface level. We shared texts, visited the occasional thrift store together, and gossiped about our coworkers during happy hours, but there were no true bonds made—nothing that survived my move out of the city, anyway. Once I crossed state lines, I became a ghost.

Having a friend would make Clearfield more bearable. And Steph and I had been so close, inseparable from grade school through high school. We hung out every chance we had. And when we weren't together, we were talking on the phone. There were no secrets between us. Not back then. The secrets came later.

But here she was, back in my life and looking better than ever. When I thought of her, I had pictured an unhappy housewife, frumpy and permanently exhausted. Instead, she was a vision. Tanned and toned, with a complexion so clear I couldn't find a single pore. Meanwhile, I barely had the motivation to wash my greasy reddish hair or put on a pair of actual pants. Not to mention my face resembled a pepperoni pizza, marked with active zits and healing red spots. My face was so cratered it made the moon feel better about itself.

Still, the meetup would be a good thing, I told myself. A step in the right direction. My elation carried me down the cereal aisle, where I grabbed two boxes of generic frosted bran flakes. The sugar would trick my dad into eating the bran part.

As I finished shopping, I rehashed the conversation with Steph.

Despite my excitement, something about the encounter made me uneasy. My nerves had blocked it at first, but when I thought back, Steph seemed . . . off. Her movements stiff. Her words rehearsed. It reminded me of a movie I once saw where the department store mannequins came to life. They were shaped like humans, sounded like humans, but they watched you with those flat, painted-on eyes. Dead eyes.

Before I could second-guess the coffee date, my phone buzzed.

STEPH

Hey grrl! 😊 Awesome seeing u again!
Tomorrow's going 2 be so much fun 😊
Yayyy!

My thumb hovered over the keyboard. If I knew then what I know now, I would have replied with a giant HELL NO. Instead, all I said was, "Yay!" Seconds later, she replied.

STEPH

We have SO much to talk about!

Chapter 2

Plastic bags cut into my wrists as I lugged them from the trunk to the front door of my dad's 1950s brick ranch. The screen door was propped open with a garden stone, which I was grateful for despite it letting the flies in.

"Do you need help with the bags?" Dad asked me the moment I walked in. He sat in the kitchen, going through a stack of mail alongside a checkbook and a calculator with buttons the size of domino tiles.

"I can manage," I told him while hoisting the bags onto the counter. I hadn't bought much. My brain was still wired for city shopping and getting only what I'd eat for the next day or two. "Except for the potatoes. They're still in the car."

Dad nodded and stood.

"I'll get them," I said quickly. "I didn't mean you had to. Go back to your work. I got it."

"No, no. It's the least I can do since you went out and did the shopping." Without waiting for my rebuttal, he walked out the door.

"But you paid for it!" I called, but he was already out the door.

This was the awkward dance my dad and I had been doing since I moved back. Actually, it was the same one we'd been doing since I was sixteen, right after my mom died. She had been the buffer between a burgeoning young adult and a man past middle age. Without her, my dad and I didn't know how to be a family unit. He wasn't a bad father. Not in the slightest. But he didn't know how to raise a young woman. Tampons and frilly bras made him nervous. I had gone to my mother for everything, and wasn't used to relying on my dad for emotional support. So we drifted apart, each of us choosing to grieve on our own.

When I went off to college, our communications dwindled to the obligatory weekly phone call and the occasional email. Enough communication to make sure the other was alive, but not enough for any real substance. Once a year, Dad had visited the city, where he spent a weekend day with me before catching the train back home. Eventually, even those had stopped and morphed into mere promises of visits.

I never went back to Clearfield, afraid that if I left New York I would be sucked into the sleepy town and trapped there, like some sort of *Twilight Zone* episode. I had promised myself I'd never move back, and here I was: unpacking groceries in my dad's kitchen, my only plans for the evening to watch television and swig a cap full of NyQuil so I could pass out at nine.

"You didn't buy the store brand?" Dad asked as he plopped the heavy bag of potatoes onto the counter. They landed with such a *whack*, I thought the tiled counter would break.

"I didn't notice. It was the first bag I saw."

"That's how they get you. They put the more expensive bags out front, so you grab them first. You gotta search for the cheaper ones toward the back," he said.

"Sorry. I'll remember that for next time," I told him, not wanting to say that the price difference was a dollar, if even that much. Who was I to argue about saving a few pennies? It was my dad's credit card I used to pay for the groceries while I watched my own checking account balance plummet. Not having to pay rent was a huge help, but between student loans and phone bills, I was a month or two away from being in serious trouble.

Wanting to distract myself from my dark thoughts, I blurted out, "You'll never guess who I bumped into at the store."

Just then Dad's mangy old cat, Captain Milton, trotted through the open doorway and brushed up against his shins, leaving wads of orange fur behind. I didn't wait for him to guess. "Do you remember my friend Steph?"

"You're joking, right?" Dad said. "Of course, I do. You two were inseparable. How's she doing?" He sat back down at the table to sort through the rest of his bills.

"Fine, I guess. She's married, has two kids, and looks really good." *Really* good, I thought. Like a walking filtered photo, except it was all real. "She asked me out for coffee," I added.

"I'm surprised you haven't kept in touch," Dad said, bending down to stroke Captain Milton. "You two were joined at the hip back then. If I saw one of you, I'd see the other. Not that we ever saw either of you much. You were always in the garage, blasting the same song over and over."

It was a memory I hadn't thought about for ages. In high school, Steph was obsessed with NSYNC, especially Justin Timberlake with his curly frosted tips and penchant for oversize LA Lakers jerseys. We used to try to re-create the dance moves from their music videos.

Dad broke my stroll down memory lane by asking "Whatever happened between you two, anyway?"

I didn't have an answer. At least not one that I wanted to share with Dad. The truth was, I wasn't ready to face why we had stopped being friends in the first place, not when Steph was still happily married to a major part of that reason.

Rob. The star of the wrestling team, with wavy brown hair, blue eyes, and muscles that burst from the surf brand T-shirts he used to wear. Rob, the straight-C student whose family went to church every Sunday. He always had the latest cell phone and brand-name sneakers. I felt betrayed by both Steph and Rob. The three of us grew close once they started dating. Steph insisted she and I were a package deal, and Rob wasn't one of those clingy partners who demanded constant alone time. In high school, he was a catch. In college, he became Steph's biggest mistake. Or so I felt.

Our very last conversation was toward the end of our first college semester. I was in another state, but we talked on the phone every night. That night, Steph had a big announcement. She was dropping out of college to marry Rob. Her excitement quickly faded as I told her she was throwing her life away. Our talk turned into a fight, which turned into the end of our friendship. Steph always promised me I'd be her maid of honor, but in the end, I hadn't even been invited to her wedding.

Instead of talking to my dad like a mature adult, I shrugged, mumbled "I dunno," and shuffled into the living room. I plopped down on the couch and turned on the television, flipping through the channels before settling on an old episode of a trashy reality show where families swapped mothers.

Pulling out my phone, I automatically opened a job-hunting app. Every free second of my time was spent poring through job listings, each one of them located in New York. The faster I could get out of Clearfield, the better for both my mental health and bank account.

At first, I had focused on writing jobs, specifically in my field of journalism. On paper, my background seemed impressive if you didn't look deeply enough: an MA in journalism, a prestigious internship, and a position at BuzzFeed as an associate staff writer. No one needed to know that I was technically a contractor or that my job was no more than scouring Amazon for trending products and writing quizzes called *What Type of Bread Are You?* Your favorite color's purple? Congrats! You're a pumpernickel.

And no one needed to know that I had been fired through a group email along with 90 percent of the other contractors. No severance, no vacation back pay, not even a goodbye party. Only an informal message addressed "To whom it may concern."

My search for journalism jobs had yielded about six roles, all of which required much more experience than I had, so I expanded my scope to include copywriting, technical writing, and grant writing. Zero interviews later, my search now included everything from retail to food service to overnight security shifts at department stores. I was a handful of rejections away from considering becoming a bicycle messenger even with my crippling fear of city traffic.

I Kwik-applied to each new position, which I could do with the single press of a button, and propped my feet on the coffee table. On the TV screen, an ultrareligious wife who sewed her own clothes was having an emotional meltdown.

"What do you want for dinner?" Dad asked from the other room.

"I could cook something," I offered.

"Only if you want to," he said. "I know you're probably spent from going to the store."

Here we go again.

"What if we ordered in?" I asked. "Is Sal's Pizza still open?"

"They closed last year. We have a frozen one I can pop into the oven. Five cheese and no delivery fee."

"Works for me."

I checked my phone. No new positions within the last five minutes, but two new rejections, both of which thanked me for my interest and let me know that despite my "impressive background," they had found other, more experienced candidates to pursue. I deleted the emails.

I then opened my note-taking app and stared at the list of random links and late-night musings I had jotted down. After losing my job, I planned to finally finish the true crime book about the murders in the Pine Barrens I had started in college. A pair of college students went missing, only to be found in pieces months later. Rumors swirled that the Jersey Devil was responsible, which was ridiculous, but added another layer of intrigue to the case. The murders were never solved, but I suspected the students' philosophy professor, and felt that if I did enough research and interviews, I could close the cold case.

I always wanted to write long-form crime journalism, but never had the time. I had nothing but time now, but my desire to sit down and write was about as strong as my desire to mow the lawn, so I closed the app. I was willing myself to get up and grab a pint of triple caramel chunk ice cream when my phone buzzed.

It wasn't an interview request, but it wasn't bad news either.

STEPH
Get excited!

STEPH
I'll pick u up at nine tomorrow. After I drop the kids off at school.

I began to type "Need to reschedule. Sorry" before deleting it. What else did I have going on? I would spend another four hours watching garbage television before eating dinner, still in front of the television, while my dad and I watched a garbage movie. In silence.

I texted her back.

DREW

From the kitchen, the oven door slammed, followed by a loud grunt. The smell of burning cheese and paper filled the air.

"Everything okay in there?" I asked.

Another grunt. Followed by "I left the damn cardboard on the bottom. I think I can pick most of it off. A little extra fiber never hurt anybody."

I sent Steph another text.

DREW

Can't wait.

Chapter 3

The next morning, I awoke to the sound of my phone vibrating crazi-
ly on my bedside table. I bolted upright and unlocked the screen with
shaking fingers. Was it the *New York Times*, calling to offer me a job?
Or even Bryan, begging me to take him back? Not that I would, but
it would be nice to hear him grovel.

But it was only Steph, who had sent me a barrage of texts and
emojis about how excited she was.

STEPH
Heyya! Rise and shine ✧

STEPH
Can't wait to get our java on!

STEPH
Boys are driving me CRAZY this AM! 😵

After a long shower and shaving parts of my body that hadn't seen
a razor in ages, I spent too much time choosing an outfit. It needed

to be cute, but casual, and make me seem as though I hadn't obsessed over how to clear my skin in twelve hours and ended up picking my face to the point of needing to use a triple antibiotic ointment.

I had struggled with my skin since I was thirteen, trying every treatment on the market: creams, serums, chemical peels, wipes, and even oral medication that I quickly stopped taking because it gave me heart palpitations. The stress of moving home had made it worse. My usual scattering of whiteheads were accompanied by painful, deep cysts.

Most of my clothes were still in boxes, so the only pieces that worked were a stretchy pair of black jeggings and a flowy yoga top. I never ended up taking the class I'd bought the top for, so at least it had never been soaked in sweat.

I had only ten minutes to spare when I ran downstairs.

"Look at you! You look so nice," my dad told me in a tone that was trying too hard to be supportive.

"Meh. This was the best I could find." I spread out my arms to show him the outfit.

"Well, I think you're beautiful." He leaned in and started to open his arms for a hug before changing his mind, scratching the back of his head, and turning toward the living room.

As I walked outside, swatting a mosquito away from my face, a car pulled into the driveway: a bright metallic-blue Mercedes SUV with an emblem the size of a dinner plate on the front grill. From the driver's seat, Steph smiled and waved wildly. Too much energy for this early in the morning.

"Oops, let me scoot my bag," Steph said when I opened the door. A giant leather tote emblazoned with *L*s and *V*s sat in the passenger seat. Steph carefully moved the bag to the back seat, and I wondered if she had left it there on purpose to show off her designer purse.

Steph had always been more interested in labels than I was, although back then it was all about Hollister and Coach. Her family was wealthier than mine, and it showed. Her house had a second floor and a hot tub, while mine was a brick ranch with two cramped bedrooms and a single tub that was avocado green. Steph hadn't invited me over for dinner much, preferring to spend time at my house, even with my green tub. "Your parents are so chill," she'd told me. "They let you eat in front of the TV, and you can use as much ketchup as you want."

I didn't say much as we drove down my street. Steph did most of the talking. She was always the more talkative one. I was the introvert adopted by the extrovert, and there had been many times I'd leaned on her social nature to conceal my awkwardness.

According to Steph, her morning was a parental nightmare. Her sons had slept in, spilled oat milk all over their school uniforms, and dropped their world history project, sending pieces of a Chichén Itzá diorama skittering across the floor.

"I'll be finding tiny clay Mayans around the house for the rest of my life," Steph joked. Then, she asked the question every woman begins hearing incessantly the day she turns thirty: "Do you have kids?"

"God, no. No offense," I added. It wasn't that I didn't like kids. They were okay in small doses, but I didn't want any of my own. The thought of being a slave to a drooling, shitting ball of snot and tears made me shudder. I could barely take care of myself, much less a tiny human who lacked the strength to hold its head upright.

She frowned and said, "Aww," stretching out the word. "Maybe someday, though?"

Maybe never.

"Sure," I said.

"Are you still dating that gorgeous hedge fund guy?" she asked in a sultry voice.

"Bryan? How do you know about him?" I wondered how she knew about Bryan but not that I was child-free.

Steph shrugged. "He was in a bunch of your photos, so I assumed you were together."

Steph must have been stalking me on socials. I didn't blame her. Part of me was flattered. In between job applications and doomscrolling, I also snuck peeks at Bryan's pages. He was already with *her*. The woman he left me for: Tall, shiny black hair, and cheekbones that could cut diamonds. Julianna. A twenty-two-year-old club promoter. Even her name was gorgeous.

"We broke up," I told her.

"Ah, well, you're better off. To be honest, he looked like a douche."

She was absolutely correct. Only a douche would invite his girlfriend to a Michelin-starred restaurant, then wait until dessert to tell this girlfriend, who stupidly thought she was being proposed to, that he wanted to see other people. He tacked on a "Hey babe, I would love it if ya stuck around" to soften the blow. He even had the nerve to ask me to meet Julianna. I told him I would see them in hell.

Steph and I drove through downtown Clearfield, which was a generous description since Clearfield had one main road, cleverly named Main Street. As we took a right off Elm and onto Main, the first thing I noticed were the boarded windows. What was once Dot's Diner and Pete's Hardware had become a wall of plywood. An old FOR SALE sign flapped in the breeze. Graffiti marked the brick exteriors with tags that read TWEAKFIELD.

"What happened?" I asked. "Everything is so grim." Trash overflowed from the garbage bins, littering the once quaint streets with Dunkin' Donuts cups and napkins.

"It's changed, hasn't it? I guess you haven't visited in a while,"

Steph said. "There was a battle between us and Pinecrest over who would get the big box stores, and Clearfield lost. Once the Walmart went up, no one wanted to shop local anymore," she explained. "Then the drugs moved in."

"Since when does Clearfield have a drug problem?" I asked. The hardest stuff that was passed around our school was the stem-filled marijuana that someone's uncle grew in his basement.

"Someone hasn't been keeping up with the *Clearfield County Herald*, I see. There's a story about an OD every month."

"Pills?" I asked.

"Pills, heroin, meth, whatever synthetic is out there. It's scary. That's part of why Rob and I moved to Pinecrest. I didn't want to raise my kids here."

"Where are we going?" I asked as Steph blew through Main Street. The diner we used to get midnight coffee and fries in was boarded up too.

"The Starbucks in Pinecrest," she said. "Probably not as fancy as the coffee shops you're used to in the city, but I'm only five points away from a free flat white."

"That was my nickname in high school," I joked, but Steph only gave it a forced giggle.

As we pulled onto the highway, Steph talked about her wonderful home life and I zoned out. The boys were perfect, Rob was perfect, his business was thriving, they spent every night braiding each other's hair and weaving friendship bracelets, blah, blah, blah.

Finally we pulled into the Starbucks parking lot. Steph grabbed her giant purse and pulled out a reusable tumbler that was bright blue with her initials decaled in an ornate font. Underneath that, a logo I didn't recognize: a silver lotus flower.

She held the cup in front of her steering wheel and took photos, moving her manicured long nails in various poses, before telling me, "I'll post these later. Let's go in."

The store was as expected. Well decorated but sterile. It made me miss the coffee shop on my old block so much it hurt.

We waited in line. Steph tapped away on her phone, posting her riveting hand-holding-a-cup photo, and it was the first time that day that I really looked at her. Even under the corporate fluorescent lights, Steph looked amazing. She had actually accomplished what I was trying to: casual chic made to appear thrown together. Tight gray jeans were rolled up on the ankle to show off her brown calfskin boots, and her white T-shirt was just tight enough to show off her abundant chest and thin waist. Her blond hair was pulled back in a high ponytail with the ends curled. How did she manage to bleach her hair without a hint of damage? Or a single dark root showing?

Steph didn't notice as I ogled her. I glanced down at my own ensemble and suddenly felt the urge to hurl myself into the display of bagged ground coffee.

Without reading the menu, Steph ordered something called a "grande hot white mocha, three pumps, with sweet cream foam and low-calorie caramel drizzle." The barista, a clearly annoyed twenty-something with neon-yellow hair, asked me what I wanted.

"A small coffee. Black." Even that was three bucks.

"Oh, come on now! Get something more than that," Steph encouraged. "A black coffee is so boring."

"I'm good."

Ignoring me, Steph said, "She'll have the same as me," and whipped out a blue credit card before I could argue.

"Let me pay you back," I told her as I searched through my wallet for a ten-dollar bill I knew wasn't inside.

Steph slapped away my hand. "Stop it. It's on me, and I won't hear otherwise. Now let's get a seat and finally catch up. I need to know about everything you were doing in New York! I bet it was so glamorous. Like *Sex and the City*. Bet you're a Carrie."

My first thought was that she was trying to flatter me. I was a Miranda, and everyone knew it. My second thought was, *Uh-oh, here it comes*. Another moment I had been dreading: I would have to tell Steph the truth about why I had slunk back to Clearfield with my tail between my legs.

I still could hardly admit my failure to myself, much less to someone else. Especially after I had just spent a twenty-minute car ride listening to how Big Rob just got a pay raise, Little Rob was accepted into a prestigious architecture summer camp, and Jax won honorable mention at the state science fair. I wouldn't be surprised if she told me their dog just received its doctorate from Stanford and was joining the Space Force.

"I'm in between jobs right now" is all I could muster.

"Is that why you moved back in with your dad? I was worried he got sick." She took a sip of her thick drink. It got stuck in the straw before making a loud slurp. "Weren't you a columnist for that big newspaper before BuzzFeed? Could you get your job back with them?"

"Hardly. You're thinking of my internship at the *Times*, and I was far from a columnist. Glorified lunch fetcher was more like it."

"But what about your work at BuzzFeed? Surely that experience will get your foot in any door. I've seen your name on so many of their columns."

"I hope so," I told her. Steph was the only one impressed by my previous work. BuzzFeed sounded glamourous, but it was too goofy to be taken seriously by the news outlets I wanted to work for.

"I love taking their quizzes. They're so much fun. Last night I took one that guessed my age based on my favorite dog breeds. They guessed twenty-four because I kept picking the flat-faced ones. Isn't that hilarious?" Steph crinkled her nose as she laughed. "Did you ever write those?"

"Sometimes. Most of my work was more research-focused," I said, not bothering to clarify that the extent of my "research" was scouring the best-reviewed items on Amazon for articles such as "50 Trending Accessories That Deserve Their Own Wing in the Louvre!" and "Drop What You're Doing (and Your Pants!) and Buy This Bidet!"

"What happened?" she asked. "You were always such an amazing writer."

"I . . . uh . . ." I took a sip from my drink. My mouth filled with creamy sugar that instantly made me feel nauseous. Skipping breakfast had been a bad idea. "Layoffs. I was technically a contractor, so once their budget became tighter, I was one of the first to go."

"Do you think they're going bankrupt?" Steph asked, suddenly more interested.

"Nothing that extreme, but they weren't making any profit. Instead of taking a pay cut himself, the CEO decided to fire 15 percent of the staff. The freelancers are always the first to go. I lost a job, and the executives got fat bonuses." The anger in my voice was palpable. I had only recently learned about the true reason for my firing thanks to a *Forbes* article, and was still salty about it. The CEO, a former rich kid who thought he was the smartest guy in the room, planned to save money by crowdsourcing content from readers. He realized people would write for free just for a crumb of clout.

"Rob's company almost went under a few years ago when Clearfield's economy was declining and new construction stopped. No one was spending money on landscaping. That's when we had to move our operations to Pinecrest," she admitted.

I scratched at a chip in the table's wooden veneer and asked, "How *is* Rob?"

Steph eyed me cautiously, wondering if it was a loaded question. "He's wonderful! We're wonderful," she said.

"I'm glad to hear it. I really am."

I must have sounded as genuine as I felt, because Steph relaxed and put her hand over mine and gave it a squeeze. "I need you to know that I'm sorry," she admitted.

"Sorry for what?" I asked, surprised by how easily the apology had come. And that I was even getting one. Shouldn't *I* be the one apologizing, not Steph? Wasn't it my fault that our friendship ended?

I still remembered our last conversation like it was yesterday. I was at the Columbia School of Journalism, while she was majoring in biology at Rutgers on a full scholarship.

"Rob asked me to marry him," she'd gushed. That was bad enough, and then she added, "I'm leaving school. Rob's going to take over the family business, and we're going to move back to Clearfield."

I should have tried to reason with her, approach her with maturity and a constructive argument that would allow her to see what a terrible idea it was. Instead, I yelled. I told her she was making the biggest mistake of her life. She was giving up on her dream of being a doctor, a pediatrician. She loved babies, and it had been the motivation behind all her hard work. Steph was throwing it all away, and for what? *Rob*? The guy who peaked in high school and would be smoking weed in his mom's basement if it weren't for the safety net of his dad's business?

And what about *our* plans? Steph had wanted to move to New York, too. She was supposed to be the head pediatrician at Mount Sinai while I was the head beat writer at the *Times*. We'd meet for lunch in the park, where Steph would scold me for eating too many street pretzels while I made fun of her Buddha bowl. That's how life was supposed to be, until we retired to a ranch in Connecticut where we'd run an animal rescue for senior dogs.

By marrying Rob, I felt she was giving up on not only her dreams, but mine. Steph was destined for so much more than being a townie.

But I was in no position to judge. Not back in college, and especially not that morning at Starbucks. Because there I was, back in Clearfield, unemployed, acne-ridden, and deep in debt, while Steph was thriving and happy in her marriage.

"I'm sorry for never reaching out," Steph said, her voice quavering. "For being immature after our big fight. For not even inviting you to the wedding. You were just trying to look out for me—I know that now. I missed you so much for so long, and instead of giving you a call, I did nothing. I was afraid that you would tell me to lose your number." Steph pursed her lips. Her eyes glistened, on the verge of dropping a tear.

I slid my hand out from under hers. Was I ready to forgive her? After all the years of resentment I had held on to, despite telling myself I had moved on? It felt like she had chosen Rob over me that night. All that time, I had wondered how such a strong bond could have been broken within seconds.

I was about to tell her I needed time to think when I heard a squeak escape her lips, high-pitched and barely audible. It was Steph's tell that she was trying not to cry. I had heard it so many times after my mother died. Steph had wanted to be strong for me, never letting it slip that she too was devastated by seeing her friend in so much pain.

As though she had wrapped a wool blanket around my shoulders, I felt the familiar warmth of my feelings toward Steph return, melting the iciness in my heart.

"I felt the same way," I told her, sliding my hand back under hers.

Steph beamed, gripping my hand even tighter. "I'm so sorry I called you a brainless twat."

"I'm sorry I called you a grub-faced know-it-all."

"What's a grub face, anyway?" I asked.

"Who knows?"

We laughed so hard that tears fell down our cheeks. Steph repeated, "Stop, stop, don't make me cry," dabbing her fingers under her eyes to make sure her mascara didn't run.

At that moment, a decade-long dam broke, allowing the waters to run free. I had my friend back. My *best* friend: the one I never allowed myself to realize how much I missed until then. Our memories, the experiences we shared—first periods, first boyfriends, first heartbreaks, the death of a parent, whispering secrets under the covers at sleepovers—made me who I was. Steph had been there through it all.

"Is it weird if I give you a hug?" she asked.

We rose and held each other. The end of Steph's ponytail slapped against my cheek as she rubbed my back. She smelled of expensive floral perfume with hints of vanilla, different from the one she had worn at the grocery store.

When we finally pulled apart and went back to our seats, I couldn't wait to catch up. For real, this time. There was so much lost time between us; time that needed to be made up for.

Steph held her phone in front of her and opened the front-facing camera. She used her long index nail to dab at her under eye.

"I have to tell you that you look stunning," I said. "You were always pretty, of course, but how have you managed to avoid a single wrinkle? Or acne scar?"

Steph slapped her phone down and exclaimed, "First of all, thank you so much! I'm so glad you asked!" She slid her purse onto her lap and rummaged inside. "I use a range of products that, I kid you not, have worked miracles. No one believes I'm thirty when I tell them—much less a mom of two boys. Heck, I still get carded everywhere!" As she spoke, she pulled out a series of bottles, all different sizes but each one bearing a bright-blue label with a large logo: an ornate *L* crowning a lotus flower in shiny, silver ink. It was the same logo that was on her coffee thermos. Once she had finished, six bottles stood in a row on the table like chess pieces, ready for war.

Steph took one of the bottles and unscrewed the dropper top. She lifted it to her nose and took in a big whiff. "Mmm, you *have* to smell this one. It's one of my favorites. An overnight vitamin C under-eye serum with coffee extract and peppermint. Smell!" She held the tip of the stopper to my face. I pulled away. Even from a distance, the peppermint stung my eyes.

"What are you doing?" I asked. And what was up with her demeanor? She was so heartfelt moments ago, but she'd flipped on a dime. Even her voice had changed—a high-pitched, overly excited valley girl drawl, but with too much stiffness to be believable.

"Showing you what I've been up to. These are all products from LuminUS. It's a natural beauty company focused on clean products and utilizing results from the most cutting-edge clinical findings. I'm a consultant. One of their top consultants, to be exact."

"I didn't know you were a salesperson. What stores do you supply?" I asked.

Steph giggled and opened another bottle. She took my hand, dropped a milky liquid onto the top of my palm, and rubbed it in. It formed a white film. "Yes, I sell LuminUS, but no, we don't sell to stores. We're direct to consumer. LuminUS believes it's the best way to empower its consultants and customers. What better way to connect people with product than to show them face-to-face how wonderful it is?" She continued to rub my hand. A quarter-size patch of red skin bloomed under her finger. "Check out this serum, for example. It's a daily moisturizer with hyaluronic acid and shea butter. Doesn't it feel like silk?"

It didn't feel like silk or any other type of fabric. It felt raw and was beginning to sting.

"The best part is," she continued, speaking faster now, "if you love the products, which I know you will, you can also become a consultant and share the benefits of LuminUS with others. Like me! I only have one opening for a new consultant this month, and I saved it for you despite the long backlist of people *dying* to join."

That's when it hit me. Like a speeding Mack truck slamming a load of iron girders directly into my chest. This meeting wasn't an attempt to rekindle a lost friendship. It wasn't a way to make up for lost time. We weren't going to hug and sing Jack Johnson songs while apologizing to each other behind floods of happy tears.

This was a goddamn sales pitch.

"I need to leave," I said as I shot up from my seat, leaving my untouched coffee behind. "I'm not going to be roped into some sort of pyramid scheme."

"Pyramid schemes are illegal!" Steph said brightly. "This is totally different! It's an exclusive multi-level marketing opportunity."

I walked around the table and made for the door.

Steph didn't say sorry or try to explain her actions. She called after me, still hollering on about Huminus or Moominus or whatever her bogus company was called.

"Give it a chance! It's only eighteen hundred to join! It'll change your life! Drew!"

An empty promise I didn't believe. No amount of vitamin C or serums or acids would change my life. I was a loser. I had lost my job, my apartment, my boyfriend, and, now, my only friend.

It Pays to Be a Winner: The LuminUS Guide to Success

What Do I Say When . . . ?: Winning Scripts for Common Sticking Points

Q: What do I say if someone asks, "Is LuminUS a pyramid scheme?"

A: You laugh it off! This person is clearly regurgitating false information they've read somewhere online. The good news is that they are interested in learning more about LuminUS! Take this time to educate them. Say:

"First of all, pyramid schemes are illegal. LuminUS is a direct-sales company with multiple levels. The only pyramid I believe in is the one that puts God first, my family second, and LuminUS third."

Q: What do I say when my husband tells me no?

A: Men are nervous creatures. They're not as ready to jump into an opportunity as we are! They also like to be the ones making the decisions. Speak to their doubts. Turn the tables so they feel as though it was their choice to allow you to sell LuminUS. Say:

"You're the boss! And I know you can tell a solid deal when you hear one. That's why I wanted to bring you this opportunity. With LuminUS, I have the chance to make thousands of dollars a month! And I can even work from home and choose my own hours, which means I'll still be taking care of the family like I am now. What do you think? Can I tell you more?"

Chapter 4

My feet slammed against the pavement as I marched out of the coffee shop and into a gym across the parking lot. I didn't want Steph to follow me, and the last place she'd expect me to be was inside of a gym.

I opened Lyft and it virtually laughed at me. There were no drivers nearby. Pinecrest was more developed than Clearfield, but it wasn't dense enough to warrant an active rideshare app, which meant I had only one option: I needed to call my dad.

I knew I should have driven, I scolded myself as I waited for my dad to answer the phone. Wasn't that rule number one of awkward coffee dates? Have an easy way out and never, ever get into the other person's car, even if it has buttery leather seats.

My dad was more than eager to pick me up despite having to cut his lunch break short. He had been tripping over his feet trying to be helpful, and this was the first time since letting me move in that he could do something other than pay for groceries.

When I got into his car, it was obvious I was upset. My cheeks were red, and I bit my lower lip. I had never been able to hide my emotions, which was ironic considering how terrible I was at sharing them. I also had a tendency to cry when I was angry enough. And right then, sitting in my dad's car with my arms crossed, I was beyond angry.

"Are you okay?" he asked. "How was your meetup?"

Terrible. Catastrophic. The equivalent of a marble-size kidney stone without painkillers. "Fine," I said.

My dad could see through my lie but didn't press the issue. He turned up the radio volume as an NPR segment discussed the newest advances in mycology.

Suddenly, I felt fifteen all over again, brooding in my dad's beat-up sedan as he rubbed the sides of the steering wheel with his thumbs. A nervous tick. Unlike when I was fifteen, I couldn't come home and immediately run to my room to call Steph.

What a bitch. Trying to use me to sell her shitty beauty products. Had she held on to a grudge this entire time? Waiting until I was down on my luck to jump in like a hungry vulture? Or was our friendship so meaningless to her that I was nothing more than a potential customer? Or an easy mark?

My phone buzzed incessantly. Steph was calling and texting, but I ignored it.

STEPH

SOOOO sorry 🙏

STEPH

Please let me explain.

I turned off my phone and slid it into the cupholder.

Steph always made me feel less valuable than her, even if she wasn't trying to. Her father owned a successful insurance company while mine worked in manufacturing at the local pharmaceutical plant. She was gifted a brand-new Nissan Maxima for her seventeenth birthday while I worked nights bagging groceries at the ShopRite to scrape together enough money for a used Jeep Wrangler.

It wasn't all material wins, either. Steph had always been prettier, thinner, more athletic. More popular. Steph could fit into any group. She waltzed between the jocks and book nerds with ease, while I was stuck in a clique limbo, not popular but not a pariah either. Just forgotten and ignored.

Still, despite her natural gifts, Steph always chose me. She said no to party invites with the other popular kids to watch bad rom-coms and eat gummy worms with me. She had stuck up for me when Lenny Coppola asked why she was "wasting time with that sad weirdo."

"Because she's my best friend, and you're a dork who uses his mom's pink Bic to shave his balls," she retorted. She had learned that tidbit from Vanessa Shaughnessy, who had walked in on him in the bathroom during a pool party.

Steph had always had my back. No matter how moody or insecure I was.

When we pulled into our driveway, I thanked my dad for the ride and locked myself in my room. Thirty years old and acting like a teen.

How did I end up here?

I sprawled on the bed and applied to more jobs, expanding my search past the city and into the Connecticut and New York suburbs, purposedly avoiding New Jersey. I needed to get out of here, more than ever. Clearfield was nothing but a black hole full of betrayal and grief.

Four hours later, fed up with being in my room and starving, I pushed down my pride and went into the living room.

My dad was on the couch, stroking Captain Milton's head, who made airplane ears at me—the feline equivalent of giving me the middle finger.

"If you're hungry, I'm defrosting some beef. I was going to make sloppy joes, but I can do burgers if you want."

I saw a soggy plastic bag of ground meat sitting in the sink. No matter how many times I told my dad I was a pescatarian, he refused to absorb the information. Even if I did eat meat, it wasn't a good idea to fill my body with globs of beef fat. My skin couldn't handle it.

"I'll have some cereal."

"Suit yourself. I'll leave you a patty in case you change your mind."

My dad looked up and fixed me with an uncharacteristically perceptive look. I had been turning toward the kitchen, but his expression froze me in place.

"You know," he said as he lowered the volume on the television, "I always liked Steph. I thought she was a solid influence on you. She always offered to clean up the dishes after dinner." He paused for a moment, his eyes watching the screen but his mind elsewhere. "And she was so strong for you. After your . . ." He didn't finish, but I knew what he wanted to say.

After my mom died.

It was breast cancer. She was diagnosed on a rainy January day after feeling a hard lump in the shower.

"It's nothing," she had assured us. "A swollen lymph node or a cyst. I'll be fine."

She died ten months later, in November of my junior year. A week before Thanksgiving. It happened in such a blur, I barely had time to register that my mom was gone. Gone forever. We had been immensely close, and she was always the other person, besides Steph, who I went to with my problems.

I missed everything about her. The way she was a terrible cook who loved sauteed mushrooms that filled the house with the stench of earthy fungus. How she smoked light cigarettes outside, even when it was freezing, because she didn't want to stain her beloved floral wallpaper.

When she died, I was in a state of shock and despair. And Steph was by my side through it all. She slept over nearly every night for an entire year. She helped me with my homework, often doing it herself and putting my name on it so I wouldn't fall behind. She even helped cook meals for both my father and me, though her culinary skills were wasted on us. Steph was a wiz in the kitchen, but she was relegated to mostly macaroni and cheese from a box thanks to our childlike palates.

Steph was the reason I didn't give up. I desperately wanted to disappear, let myself fail, but she wouldn't let me. Without her, I would have never been accepted to Columbia. Steph forced me to sit down and complete my applications, even reaching out to the guidance counselor for copies of my transcripts. She practically wrote my essays, dictating what I should write as I typed.

And there I was, brooding in the living room, ready to cut her off forever. And for what? Because she tried to sell me some skincare?

It wasn't like I didn't need it. My skin *did* suck.

"I was looking through some old financial papers and found this in one of the files," Dad said. "Must have fallen in by accident."

He handed me a four-by-six photo. It was faded, the colors muted, but showed Steph and me on Halloween when we were six. I was ketchup and she was mustard. We had made the costumes ourselves using red and yellow T-shirts and paper hats that were supposed to look like bottle tops but instead made us look like coneheads. In the photo, we beamed. Two kids unable to contain their excitement to collect as much chocolate and candy as humanly possible. And more importantly, to proudly show everyone that they were very best friends.

Life was a hotdog, and no matter how time had separated us, Steph was the mustard to my ketchup.

"Be right back," I told my dad. "I need to make a call."

Steph answered on the second ring.

"Drew! Listen, I am *so* sorry, I—"

"You don't have to be sorry," I cut in. "I overreacted. Big time."

"I shouldn't have sprung it on you out of nowhere like that," Steph said. "We were having such a great time, and I messed it up." Her sincere voice had returned. She no longer sounded like the busted Stepford robot I left at Starbucks. "Let me make it up to you."

"I was the ass. Not you," I told her. "You don't owe me a thing. But I wouldn't mind getting together. Trying again. A fresh start."

"Yes!" she exclaimed into the phone. I moved it away from my ear. "That's precisely what I was thinking. I want to invite you to a party I'm throwing tomorrow night."

"A party?" I asked, unsure if I was up to the challenge of socializing with people I didn't know. Reconnecting with Steph was one thing—we had a history, and when we weren't fighting, she was easy to be around.

"It's not a *party* party. More like a relaxed happy hour," she breathed into the phone. "Full disclosure, it *is* a LuminUS event."

"Seriously?" I groaned.

"But wait! I *promise* you don't have to buy anything or talk about the products at all. I'm inviting you because I think you'll have an awesome time. Besides, I organized it last month, way before I knew you were in town. A bunch of other LuminUS ladies will be there."

I groaned again.

"Oh, stop it. You'll like all of them, I promise! Plus, Jenny Fitzsimmons will be there. You remember her, right?"

"I do." Jenny was a classmate in high school, one of the few whom I liked. She was sharp, her humor as dry as mine. She had gotten suspended for giving out free ear piercings in the girls' bathroom after she "borrowed" the piercing gun from Claire's in the Hamilton Mall. Needless to say, I thought she was pretty cool.

"I really *really* want you to come. It won't be the same without you. What do you say?"

I waffled, unsure whether to hang up or agree.

Steph added, "There's going to be a cheese tray."

She knew me too well. "I'm in."

From "At the Bottom of the Pyramid: Stories from Ex-LuminUS Distributors"

First published in *New York* magazine

"God, the parties were the worst. We were told they were optional, but it was nearly impossible to sign anyone on to your downline without pressuring them in person. I always felt like a used car salesman, but not a legitimate one. The kind at one of those 'Buy Here Pay Here' places where everyone gets approved for a loan and the cars are all lemons. I spent $400 on each party. I was lucky to make $15 back in sales."

—Lisa Jennings, active in LuminUS 2017, Silver level

"They told us to smile. Smile! Always smile! When people ask why you're always so happy, tell them, 'It's because I get to sell LuminUS!' No one can smile that much. I felt like I was constantly on stage at a pageant. At one selling party that lasted six hours, I smiled so much I sprained my jaw. I couldn't chew hard food for two weeks.

"I did lose fifteen pounds, though."

—Krista Lowry, active in LuminUS 2015–2018, Ruby level

"I'd rather drink Lysol than go to another one of those fucking parties."

—Anonymous, active in LuminUS 2016–2018, Gold level

Chapter 5

Steph had moved out of Clearfield and into a planned residential community in Pinecrest named Cortland Ranch, where, according to a billboard I saw before the turnoff, I was promised a lifestyle of sophistication and carefully crafted amenities surrounded by a picturesque setting. That's right, folks, Cortland Ranch: where the American dream comes true.

The houses *were* nice. Stone foundations crowned by horizontal siding and large windows—clean, modern lines without too many unnecessary architectural flourishes. Nothing like the McMansions that plagued the country in the early 2000s with their gaudy turrets and fake balconies.

Steph's house, in particular, was stunning, a sprawling modern farmhouse with white siding and black shutters. Her long driveway was filled with parked cars. Shiny Lexuses, Teslas, and Mercedes overshadowed my dad's ten-year-old Toyota sedan with the missing hubcap on the rear driver's side tire. I parked it behind a white SUV that was shaped like a storage container and knocked on the front door.

Steph opened the door holding a glass of chilled white wine. She wore a bright pink cocktail dress with tiny yellow flowers. Her hair was tousled in beachy waves that framed her face.

"Hiiii!" she exclaimed, giving me a one-armed hug. I tried to hug back but ended up patting her shoulder like I would a cute puppy. *Atta girl.*

"Love, love, love that top!" She squeezed the material between her fingertips. It was just a wrinkled cranberry button-up—the nicest thing I had that wasn't in storage. "Can I get you a glass of wine?"

"Yes, please," I answered, trying not to sound too eager.

"Come on back. The girls are outside by the pool house. I can't wait for you all to meet!"

Steph gave me a tour as we walked, leading me through the main living room, kitchen, and dining room. "Mind the mess. With two kids and a husband, this place is a pigsty."

There was no mess. Nothing was out of place. I didn't see a single toy or half-eaten pudding cup or anything indicating the house was occupied by living humans. I *did* see a built-in pizza oven, which made me insanely jealous. Her decor was all ecrus and beiges with silver accents. Every square inch of wall was plastered in shiplap. Bryan, who knew things like this, would have called the style modern French country. If it weren't for a bowl of bright yellow lemons, I would have thought we were inside of a tooth.

"Where are the kids?" I asked. It was suspiciously quiet.

"Downstairs with the sitter. Rob offered to watch them, but I wouldn't let him miss the party." I noticed a giant family portrait above the electric fireplace. Everyone wore matching white button-ups with khaki pants on a pristine beach at sunset. Rob was still handsome. His wavy brown hair was thinner and peppered with gray, but he still had that chiseled chin and strong Roman nose. His puppy dog eyes were now creased at the edges with thin lines.

We stopped in Steph's kitchen. Above the sink, a distressed wooden sign read LIFE IS SHORT, LICK THE SPOON! Steph pulled out a bottle from her wine fridge and poured me a glass. I sipped it carefully, resisted the urge to gulp it down.

We made our way to another living room—*how much living were these people doing that they needed two living rooms?*—which led to French doors that opened onto the backyard.

The large pool was lit from below with soft lights that made it glow blue. The paved area around the pool was strewn with string lights and paper lanterns and ringed by standing tables decorated with blue floral centerpieces. Women mingled around the tables while uniformed staff passed out finger foods and glasses of wine. Steph had lied to me: This wasn't a casual, happy-hour type of gathering. This was a full-out soiree.

Each woman was better dressed than the last. It was a sea of five-inch heels and bodycon dresses that showed off fake tans and even faker boobs. *So much blond*, I thought. I couldn't find a brunette in the bunch, not to mention anyone who wasn't white. I used my free hand to smooth out the wrinkles in my top as Steph led me to a table where two women were nose-deep in their phones.

"Girls!" Steph chirped, getting their attention. Their heads turned toward me, smiles sparking onto their faces like a light switching on. "Mackenzie and Bre, I want you to meet my best friend, Drew. She just moved back to Clearfield. Mackenzie and I are both in Leah's downline—you'll meet her later—and Bre's in mine."

Mackenzie Russo was the first to introduce herself. She was a petite woman with a long face and features that would be alien on anyone else but worked on her: wide-set blue eyes and lips so round they formed a permanent *O*. Her icy-blond hair was styled in two long French braids, and around her neck was a golden crucifix crusted with diamonds.

Mackenzie told me she also lived in the community, only two streets down. "I'm on Pacific," she said.

"They have a corner lot, too," Steph added.

Bre, short for Breanna, did not live in the community, which was a fact that Mackenzie was quick to point out. "Bre's the only one not in Cortland Ranch. She lives in—oh, what's the name of your apartment complex?" Mackenzie snapped her fingers. "I always forget."

"Terracina Village," Bre said, shifting her weight from one stiletto heel to the other. She fiddled with one of her silver hoop earrings.

Bre had close-set eyes and a wide nose she'd tried to slim down with brown contour too dark for her orange complexion. She wore a hot-pink blazer purposely buttoned low to show off a corset-type bra.

"That's right. I knew it sounded Italian," Mackenzie said.

Bre took a bite off her plate.

"You're not eating a macaron, are you?" Mackenzie asked Bre.

"It's only one. And it's filled with fruit. Strawberry." Flakes of pink pastry flew out of Bre's mouth as she spoke.

"It's filled with butter and creams. Come on, Bre. You know better. How do you expect to lose those last ten pounds if you don't have any self-control?"

I watched, biting my tongue with my front teeth as Bre put down her plate and pushed it away. Had Mackenzie tried coming between me and a fresh pastry, I would have shoved the whole thing down her push-up bra.

I saw Steph eyeing me. She could tell I was uncomfortable.

"The conference is just around the corner," Mackenzie reminded Bre. "You know how many photos we take there. Don't you want to look your best?"

"Conference?" I asked.

Bre jumped in. "It's the annual LuminUS sales conference! It's called LuminSANITY, and it's a ton of fun: three days in Utah in a beautiful hotel in the mountains, where we learn about upcoming products and new recruiting tactics. Plus, we get to meet a bunch of other LuminUS ladies, from Platinums to Silvers and everyone in between."

"It's the biggest event of the year!" Mackenzie chirped.

I had nothing to offer. None of these terms made sense to me. Platinum? Silver? LuminSANITY?

"Leah's here!" Steph gasped, with the excitement of someone who had just seen Beyoncé. She hurried toward a middle-aged woman with a severe blond bob and gave her two air kisses on each cheek.

And just like that, I was left alone with the two strangers.

"So, Drew, what do you do?" Bre asked. That dreaded question.

I shifted from one foot to the other. "I'm a writer. Journalist. Or, I used to be. I'm, uh, taking a break." My voice cracked.

"Ooh, a writer?" Bre said. "That sounds interesting. Mackenzie used to be a licensed social worker."

"Technically, I'm still licensed," Mackenzie added. "No longer practicing, though."

"Why's that?" I asked.

"Glad you asked! I no longer need to practice. I started my own business with LuminUS, and it's going so well that I quit. I walked in one morning, looked the senior clinical director in the eye, and told him it would be my last day. It was such a freeing experience. Besides, who wants to work sixty hours a week for forty grand a year?" She scrunched her nose as she laughed, revealing a row of veneers, each as white and large as a piece of Trident gum.

"She used to be a director, too," Bre said as Mackenzie playfully waved her away.

"Oh, come now. Drew doesn't need to know my entire life story. I left that life in the past on purpose. Everything I have now I owe to LuminUS."

Here comes another sales pitch, I thought. If Steph couldn't persuade me, these strangers had a fat chance in hell. I politely told the two I needed to get some snacks and beelined to the food table. As I piled my plate high with cheese crackers and skewers of cherry tomatoes with mozzarella balls, I couldn't help but overhear some of the conversations. The word *LuminUS* was repeated over and over in tones ranging from hushed to excited to reverential. Was that all these women spoke about? I understood this was a LuminUS-themed event, but there had to be other topics of interest besides how well snail mucus hydrates your skin.

"Drew?" a woman's voice came from behind me. It sounded familiar. "Wow, I haven't seen you in ages!" I turned.

"Jenny?" It was Jenny Fitzsimmons, Ms. Free Ear Piercings—but if it weren't for the scar above her eyebrow from being bucked off an irate pony during our fourth-grade spring carnival, I wouldn't have recognized her. The once-edgy girl who dyed her hair jet-black and wore baggy jeans covered in chains was now blond. She wore a pale pink lace dress and nude wedges. "You've . . ."

"Changed?" she asked as she swished the bottom of her dress from side to side. "I've lost a little bit of weight."

"A little bit? You're tiny!" Jenny had always been a bigger girl who was proud of her curves and enjoyed showing off her thighs and ample chest. Now, I could see her clavicle.

"Thanks," she said, although it wasn't a compliment. "To be honest, I hate this dress. The color reminds me of a nursery. But Steph picked it out and insisted it would look good against my cool skin tone." Along with the weight, Jenny had lost her confidence.

"I didn't know you were friends with Steph." I didn't know anything about Steph. Not anymore.

I knew Jenny from newspaper club, which had been one of the few activities I did without Steph. She had planned on joining, but was too busy with Spanish club.

"We reconnected last year," Jenny said. "Bumped into her at the mall and have been close ever since. She's the one who introduced me to LuminUS."

"Do you use the stuff? Tell me honestly," I asked, lobbing a ball of mozzarella into my mouth. Jenny was honest to a fault. When we worked on the newspaper together, I wrote the weekly news beat, boring articles about administration and funding. Jenny did student profiles. Each week our editor had to remind Jenny to be more positive and not refer to the football players as "meatheads who smell like jock itch spray."

If anyone could give me the real scoop on LuminUS, it was Jenny.

"It's a miracle product. It's worked wonders for my skin," she replied in a flat tone.

"Really?" I pressed.

Jenny eyed the cheese moving from my plate to my mouth, salivating. She took a swig of her wine, and suddenly I noticed how much she resembled Steph: same hair color, same copper eyeshadow and taupe lipstick, same dainty accessories. But everything was just a little bit off. The fake eyelashes were too heavy for her eyes, her highlighter was overdone, and her hair was more brassy than platinum. If someone had to draw Steph from memory, the picture would look like Jenny.

"I love LuminUS," Jenny said stiffly. "Their nutrition supplements have been literal game changers."

"I thought they only made skincare," I said.

"No way. LuminUS has an entire line of SkeleSlim shakes for appetite control and metabolism boosters. It's how I lost eighty pounds." She coughed. "They're yummy, too."

"Well, you look great."

She didn't. Jenny looked tired. And hungry. I offered her a puffed mushroom pastry, but she waved it away.

Jenny and I didn't get a chance to speak further. She was whisked away by the older blond with a bob who insisted Jenny show her friends her before and after photos.

I stood by the food table, alone, picking at the hors d'oeuvres that no one else was interested in. Every few minutes, I checked my phone. I eventually got so bored I spent twenty minutes applying for jobs. Normally this would be uncouth party behavior, but no one cared. Most of the other women were on their phones, posing and posting, typing messages, or scrolling through news feeds, their acrylic fingernails clacking away at the screens like pecking chickens.

Occasionally, I saw a familiar face—girls I knew in high school but never had a relationship with. A small group of husbands huddled around the open bar. I recognized Rob, who looked bored out of his skull. I also noticed a blond man with a sprinkling of blond stubble, equally bored, who had been following Mackenzie around. I assumed he was her husband.

One of the husbands was older than the others, with graying red hair and eyeglasses. Of the bunch, he was the only one who seemed to be enjoying himself. He noticed me watching and waved me over, but I limply waved back and pretended to take a phone call.

After an hour, I decided to leave. Steph was nowhere to be found. I didn't owe her a goodbye, anyway. She had invited me to a party and dumped me like she used to do to her younger brother when her parents insisted he tag along with us. This time it was my turn.

This was supposed to be a do-over from the coffee date. A chance to reconnect, for real this time. I tried not to be upset. This was a party she had organized well before I returned to Clearfield. My invitation was an olive branch, not a promise of quality time.

Still, she could have at least spent five fucking minutes with me.

I finished my second glass of wine and filled my canvas crossbody bag with puff pastries, desserts, and veggies from the crudité platter, wrapping everything in napkins. No one else was eating them anyway.

I made my way back into the house without being noticed. I had almost made it to the front door when I felt someone grab my elbow.

"You're not leaving already, are you?" Steph asked.

Where had she come from? "It's getting late, so I figured I should go."

"It's seven thirty."

"I want to make sure my dad's okay. We're supposed to watch a movie tonight. Gerard Butler's in it." I tried to think of more excuses as Steph blinked at me. "But I want to thank you for the party. It was, um, a lot of fun." She eyed my bag. The top of an asparagus head poked out, and I quickly pushed it down. "I hope you don't mind if I take some food."

"Not in the slightest!" She kept hold of my elbow and led me back into the house. I was afraid she was taking me back to the party, but we stopped in the kitchen. "In fact, before you go, I want to give you something."

Steph opened a drawer which was filled with different LuminUS products, rows and rows of blue bottles of all shapes and sizes. She took out a large one full of vitamins. "Here. This is one of my faves. It's a hair, skin, and nail supplement that I think will be perfect for you."

I read the label out loud. "LuminUS BeautyBoost. Find your beauty within. Six thousand mcg servings of biotin in each capsule."

"It's vegan too!"

"Thanks," I said. "But I can't afford it." While finding ways to keep myself occupied during the party, I'd glanced at a LuminUS catalog. A complete collection was being offered as a door prize. The least expensive item was a sample of nighttime face jelly, cherry scented, and even that cost over $25 for an ounce.

"No, no, it's a gift! They're usually $64 retail, $58 with the distributor discount. I'm telling you, girlie, this will clear up your skin in a flash." She snapped her fingers as I stroked my cheek. Was my skin that bad? Okay, I knew it was, but was it *that* bad that Steph needed to give me medication for it?

"Don't be offended," she said. "You've been battling with your skin for as long as I can remember. Remember how we tried covering your face with toothpaste freshman year?"

"My skin dried up and smelled like peppermint for a week." I touched the newest cyst bubbling on my chin. I was willing to try anything that could stop it in its tracks.

"I know these vitamins will help," Steph assured. "I use them myself. Haven't had a breakout since."

I eyed Steph's skin—not a bump or blemish to be found. Not that she had ever had bad skin. Still, I put the bottle in my bag.

She gave me a hug and said, "I know we didn't see much of each other tonight, but I'm so glad you came. Let's get together this week. Only you and me this time, okay?"

I agreed and she asked me to text her when I got home safely.

I drove home with the pills rattling on the seat beside me. I hadn't meant to, but I caught a glimpse of my forehead in the rearview mirror. Most of my makeup had sweat off. The skin beneath was the texture of an avocado peel.

With one hand, I opened the pill bottle and swallowed a Beauty-Boost. The capsule got caught in my throat and I began to hack. For a moment, I couldn't breathe. I felt the edges of the pill scratch against my windpipe as I tried to cough it out.

The car wove in the lane as I punched my chest with a balled fist. I clenched my diaphragm as hard as I could and gave a final, guttural cough. The pill flew out of my mouth and pinged against the windshield. My eyes watered and my nose ran as I gasped for air. At the first opportunity, I hurried to park the car along the shoulder.

I should have taken it as a sign. I should have rolled down the window right then and there and thrown the bottle into the darkened pines of the New Jersey forest. I should have finished my drive home, watched the movie with my dad, continued my job search—as fruitless as it felt—and forgotten all about LuminUS.

Instead, I wiped the snot from my nose and popped a new pill, making sure to throw my head back. That time, it slid down with ease.

I was never one for being content with my situation. I wanted more.

I would start with fixing my skin.

From the LuminUS.com Product Page for BeautyBoost Supplements

Acne is caused inside of the body. Time to fight back!

Time-released BeautyBoost capsules kill pimple-causing bacteria on a cellular level. Containing dermatologist-grade ingredients along with natural ingredients such as tea tree oil and oregano extract, users reported a 99% reduction in their blemishes!

With regular use (1-3 capsules per day with meals) skin will appear smoother, brighter, and post-inflammatory hyperpigmentation will decrease.*

Retail Price: $64.00

LL Price: $58.00

Cautions: Avoid excessive sun exposure and UV rays during use. Women who are pregnant or could become pregnant should limit their daily dosage to 1 capsule.

* These statements have not been evaluated by the Food and Drug Administration. This product is not intended to diagnose, cure, treat, or prevent any disease.

Chapter 6

A burst of sun lasered through the side of my curtains and woke me. I wasn't ready to get up, so I turned over and threw another pillow over my head to block out the light.

It didn't work. I had a massive headache and dry mouth and couldn't get comfortable no matter how hard I tried. I'd only had two glasses of wine at the party, but it must have been enough to give me a mild hangover. Outside my door, I heard my father clinking mugs in the kitchen. The smell of burnt coffee traveled into my room. It turned my stomach, but I yearned for caffeine, so I rolled myself out of bed. Shuffling into the bathroom, my legs heavy, I took a washcloth and soaked it with cold water so I could drape it over my throbbing head.

My skull hammered, but when I looked up and saw my face in the mirror, the pain no longer bothered me.

My skin was . . . better. Not perfect, far from it—I still had a scattering of bumps—but some of it had cleared. Plus, there were no new eruptions, and the balloon on my chin hadn't grown like I'd expected it to.

I wiped my face with the cloth, expecting more makeup to come off and reveal my true, blemished skin underneath. But I wiped and wiped and nothing changed.

Racing into my room, I pulled the bottle of BeautyBoost from my bag.

What was in this stuff?

I read the label.

Radiate from within with LuminUS's BeautyBoost. Formulated with quality ingredients that are guaranteed to make you runway ready with shiny hair, glowing skin, and strong nails.

Ingredients: Dermatologist-grade vitamins and LuminUS's proprietary blend of essential extracts.

Take 1–3 capsules daily with a meal.

I took another dose—without a meal, but I figured with how much I gorged myself the night before it was probably fine.

Maybe Steph wasn't bullshitting me after all. Maybe these pills worked. I had tried nearly every over-the-counter treatment available—wipes, creams, gels, masks, oils, cleansers—and nothing worked. BeautyBoost's ingredients weren't clear (what the hell were "essential extracts"?) but it couldn't be any worse than salicylic acid or benzoyl peroxide, could it?

I flipped open my laptop and began to research.

The LuminUS website had a clean, modern layout, with its bright blue and silver lotus logo prominently displayed. Women's smiling faces held bottles toward the camera on staged sets with rows of products in the backgrounds.

Its ABOUT US page included their mission: *To empower women to live their best lives and follow their dreams through the power of revolutionary health and beauty products.*

I read the bio of the company's founder, Dixie LaVey. It was accompanied by a glamour shot of her resting her head on her fist and sporting a silver lotus brooch against a blue blazer. She was older than the models on the site, mid-sixties, with a puffy halo of blond hair, bright red lipstick, and the kind of button nose only possible with multiple rhinoplasties. Her bio included a personal message in which Dixie spoke about her breast cancer diagnosis being a springboard for her foray into beauty products.

Breast cancer. It hit close to home.

I remembered how my mother looked during her treatments. Doctors had warned that any kind of treatment would be a Hail Mary, but we had to try. She went through chemotherapy for a few weeks coupled with radiation and fistfuls of daily pills.

Nothing worked. We stopped treatment. Any fragment of life my mother had was drained in such a short time. A once vivacious woman was reduced to a withered husk of her former self. As much as Dixie LaVey using her diagnosis to sell face creams should have turned me off, I understood. Had my mother survived, as Dixie had, one of the steps to recovery would have been looking like her best self again.

While she lay in the hospital bed, too exhausted to move, she still made me paint her nails. She always had beautiful nails, naturally long and strong. The treatments had made them short and brittle, the consistency of tissue paper, but I painted them her signature color anyway: dusty rose. Afterward, I helped raise her arm to her face so she could see the work. She smiled, revealing her rotting teeth, and told me she felt beautiful.

I stroked her cheek, the skin cold under my fingertips, and said,

"Yes, Mom. You are beautiful."

My phone buzzed as I shut the laptop. My eyes were watering, and I couldn't stand to read the words *breast* or *cancer* for another second.

I tucked my messy hair behind my ears. Flipping on the camera, I snapped a quick photo and sent it before I could change my mind. As much as I scrubbed my face before bed, the mascara had still dyed my under eyes. I looked like an exhausted Nosferatu.

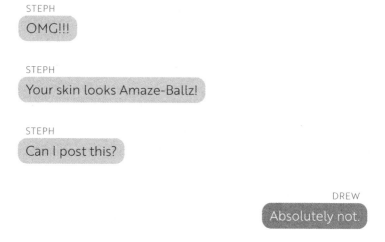

STEPH

Boooo

My skin *was* improving, but that didn't mean I wanted anyone else to see it. Especially not in the harsh light of the morning sun.

STEPH

If you change your mind, check out my links: @SMurphy_LuminUS_NJ

I clicked on the link. It opened my Instagram app and brought me to Steph's profile. Her grid was photo after photo of her posing in different outfits, a LuminUS product prominently displayed in every one of them. She was posing by a brick restaurant; a wall full of succulents; a pink neon sign that read BELIEVE IN YOURSELF; a snow-encrusted tree. She wore tight ripped jeans, maxi dresses, mini dresses, crop tops, halter tops, tube tops, denim jackets, and beige felt hats. Her profile photo was her holding her LuminUS tumbler while she threw her head back in a laugh.

I recognized the most recent photo as the one she had taken with me in the car. She posed with the plastic tumbler, the Mercedes emblem displayed prominently in the background. I read the caption: "MONDAY Vibez. Currently obsessed with this hot white mocha with sweet cream and caramel drizzle. Gotta have my STARBZ! What's your fave coffee? Comment below!"

There was no mention of me or catching up with an old friend. Or that the cup was empty. Or that she barely drank her super tasty "Starbz" because it was 900 calories.

There was another ping from Steph.

STEPH

I'm going live on FB if you wanna check it out!!

Her message was accompanied by a link to something called a "live selling party." I clicked it.

A message appeared on the screen: "Get ready. We're about to go live! In five . . . four . . . three . . . two . . . one . . ."

The video began. Steph was in what looked like her office, a room I hadn't seen in person. Her walls were painted LuminUS blue, and behind her, she had shelves upon shelves groaning under the weight of hundreds of products. A framed quote hung above it all: WAKE UP. BE A BOSS. REPEAT.

"Hiya, ladies!" she screeched. She was alone in front of the camera. What kind of party was this?

She told everyone she was ecstatic at the large turnout, but was expecting many more. I read the viewer count. Over two hundred. Seemed big enough. If even half of those people ordered a cream, she would have a solid profit.

Steph held up bottle after bottle, spinning them in front of the camera and spouting off their ingredients and benefits. Whatever problem you had, LuminUS had a cure.

Fine lines and wrinkles? Try YouthDefend with retinol, vitamin C, and kelp!

Dry skin? Try DrownMe with hyaluronic acid, peptides, and red algae!

Struggling with sagging skin? Firm up that flapping flesh with GravityLift, containing ceramides, vitamin E, and sea buckthorn oil!

Steph asked the audience if they had been feeling overwhelmed lately. If stress had been weighing them down.

"Stress can be a killer on the skin. Trust me, I know. With two kids and a husband to take care of, I need to be careful or else my face becomes dull—lifeless. Good thing I have SunGlo! With glucoside, caffeine, and crushed pearl essence, it will instantly make your skin radiant."

She instructed the viewers to leave a comment with the word *GIMME* to add a free mini tube of SunGlo to their order.

Comments poured down the screen. GIMME!! GIMME! GIMME!!!

Fourteen products down; who knew how many left to go. The viewer count was up to over three hundred.

I closed the app. Maybe I shouldn't have been so fast to judge. Clearly Steph was doing well in this endeavor—she was making sale after sale, and the least expensive product on the docket was $36.

My business acumen was poor, but if there was a markup of 20 percent on each order, a typical reselling cost, and a hundred women made an order with an average cost of $100 . . . I gave up trying to do mental math, but I estimated the profit to be in the low thousands. Not bad for an hour of work.

As Jenny would have said, "That's stripper money." And Steph was in her element. She worked the camera like a pro, holding viewers' attention with ease.

Scrolling down her page, I recognized some of the women she tagged in her posts. Many of them had been at the party—the real-life one.

Curious, I clicked through to a few profiles. Each page was nearly identical to Steph's, littered with carefully posed selfies in front of various locations with long captions that usually ended with a question.

LuminUS was everywhere. In the photos, in the captions, in the profiles. Each woman listed her occupation as LuminUS Independent Consultant along with a blue heart.

There was no mention of who the women had been before joining

LuminUS. I knew Mackenzie had been a social worker, but there was nothing on Facebook about her past. Her bio only described her as "LuminUS Independent Consultant, Ruby Level. Wife to Chase Russo and mother to three littles: Brynlee, Kinslee, and Hadlee. <3"

I looked her up on LinkedIn. It was an older photo, but I recognized her. Her hair was darker, more unruly, and her eyes looked smaller without the lashes, but it was Mackenzie. The page hadn't been updated in some time, but it showed that Mackenzie had graduated at the top of her class from Rutgers with a major in social work and a minor in child development. Shortly after becoming licensed, she joined the New Jersey Division of Child Protection and Permanency, where she became a director six years in.

Rutgers University? The youngest director in the office's history? It was an extremely impressive CV—which she had abandoned for LuminUS.

On Facebook, I found the middle-aged woman who Steph had been focused on at the party: Leah Monroe, LuminUS Independent Consultant, Platinum Level. Proud wife to local Lutheran minister, Aaron Monroe—who I recognized as the man from the party with the genuine smile—mother to Aaron Junior, Anthony, and Luanne, and grandmother to Aaron III, Oliver, and Julie.

There was Bre Santos, LuminUS Independent Consultant, Emerald Level. Wife to Dennis Santos and mother to two fur babies: Chester and Croissant.

Finally, there was Jenny Fitzsimmons, LuminUS Independent Consultant, Silver Level. Wife to nobody. Mother to no one.

Jenny's profile shocked me. Not because she was single or childless, but because of the photos she had never deleted. The ones that were dated over a year ago showed her old self, the Jenny I remembered: Healthy and gleaming, wearing black crop tops that showed her full tattoo sleeve of botanicals. Her smile was genuine, her eyes naturally sparkling—not from supplements, but from happiness.

Who was this new Jenny, and why had she changed so much? No longer was she hanging out at music festivals or drinking Blue Moons at hip dive bars. Now she was sipping chunky smoothies the color of swamp algae with fake lashes so heavy they weighed down her eyelids. Her new photos weren't as polished as the other women's. The lighting was dull, the perspective either too close or too far from her face. You could see she was trying to match the others, but came up short.

Whatever identity Jenny had had before was washed away, kept covered, like her tattoos. Behind the plastered smiles and captions explaining how "G R E A T F U L" she was, I could tell she was miserable. I wondered about all the other "LuminUS ladies" I had met.

Who had they been before LuminUS? And what was so powerful about the company that it made them willing to change completely?

From the Podcast *Pyramid Scream: Inside the LuminUS Murders*

Episode 3: The "LuminUS Lady"

If you've been listening to this podcast, by now you've probably done a little cyberstalking yourself. Have you checked out the women's old profiles?

Of course you have, and you've likely gone down the same rabbit hole I did when I began researching this story. One profile includes a photo tagged to another, and you continue down the MLM tunnel until you lose track of what woman's profile you started on.

You've noticed it, haven't you? That a LuminUS lady is easy to spot. She has a certain look, a certain way she carries herself that lets you know, at first glance, that she's a LuminUS lady.

So, what makes a LuminUS lady?

Based on leaked internal messages between previous employees, this look was not only encouraged, it was practically forced upon distributors.

According to the documents, "A LuminUS Lady needs to be made in Dixie's image: blond or lightened hair (preferably long and voluminous), fingernails in a short to medium almond shape (painted in nudes or reds, no artwork unless it's LuminUS branded), and weight shouldn't exceed a BMI of 18 (the lower the better!)."

This didn't include LuminUS's equally demanding wardrobe requirements, which specified that "A LuminUS Lady needs to always be put together. When assembling an outfit, ask yourself, 'Is this appropriate for Church?' Always maintain a modest but classy look."

It's clear Dixie was assembling her "army of women," as she enjoyed frequently saying, from the inside and out.

Chapter 7

"You're home early," I said as my dad walked in.

I was at the table eating a plate of pizza bagels. It was only noon, and I hadn't been expecting him until six, when he usually returned from work. I had microwaved the bagels on a paper plate, and they had cemented themselves to it. With each bagel, I also ate a tab of paper.

My dad said nothing. He reached into the fridge and cracked open a can of Keystone Light. He wasn't much of a drinker. The six-pack had sat in the back, untouched, for who knew how long. I knew it was a gift from our neighbor, Frank, who insisted every home contain his favorite beer brand on the off chance he stopped by for a visit.

"Everything okay?" I asked, suddenly concerned.

He sat next to me and rested his head in his hands. Everything was not okay.

"I lost my job," he said from behind his fingers.

"*What?* How? You've been working there for . . ."

"Over forty years. Since I was eighteen. It was my first job after high school." And the only job he'd ever had, not counting part-time positions during summer breaks.

He'd started as a quality control inspector at BioNa Labs, making sure no capsules were broken as they rolled down a vibrating ramp and into the bottling area. Over the years, he'd climbed the ranks to become a manufacturing technician.

"Did they give you a reason?" I asked.

He shook his head and sighed deeply. "Budget cuts. They told me my position was terminated."

"I thought the plant was doing well. Didn't they make, like, a billion dollars a couple years ago?" BioNa wasn't as big as the major pharmaceutical plants, the Pfizers and the Mercks of the world, but it made a killing manufacturing generic OxyContin. During the last month of my mother's life, she had eaten them like Tic Tacs.

"The company did. But our plant reported some of the lowest numbers. It's because our machinery was never updated. For years, I put in requests to upgrade the mixers. The agitators would stick and not mix fast enough. They ignored me, telling me they needed to pour their resources into the bigger New York and California plants."

"Did they give you any severance, at least?"

"Only two weeks' worth."

Two weeks. It was *nothing*. I was stunned, but I tried to stay positive for him. "You'll figure something out. You have so much experience, I bet you'll find another job in no time," I said, parroting back the same speech he'd given me when he found out I'd been fired. "BioNa can't be the only manufacturer in town."

"That's the issue," Dad began. He scratched the skin on the side of his face next to his ear. It was his tic. The one he did compulsively when he had bad news.

"BioNa cut my hours a few months ago. I was making barely enough to pay the bills, and lost most of my benefits. Since then, I've been looking for a new job, but no one will give me a shot. Not even in Pinecrest. They don't say it outright, but I know it's because I don't have a college degree."

"What are you trying to say?" I asked. He was rambling to avoid being direct. Another one of his tics.

He took a deep breath, held it, and released it in a long sigh. "I'm selling the house," he said. "I've been in this house since your mom and I bought it when we found out she was pregnant with you. Thirty years I've been here. Thirty years of memories, good and bad."

He scanned the kitchen. The room was filled with memories of my mom. From the apple-themed backsplash tiles that matched the apple-themed towels and potholders my dad had never replaced to the ceramic chicken cookie jar. My mom had been going for a country kitchen motif. It would have worked if not for the Italian chef statues that held bottles of wine.

I couldn't look at an inch of the house without thinking of her.

I sensed my dad's grief and tried to bury my own. "Maybe it won't be the end of the world," I said brightly, my voice sounding false, even to myself. "A fresh start and a smaller place will be a positive change for you. Less space to clean, lower heating and cooling bills—maybe we can find a condo where they do most of the upkeep."

"Actually . . . I already found a place. It's the Shangri-La Apartments off Atlantic Ave," Dad said, but he didn't sound excited. "It's not a house, it's an apartment, but it's in my price range and the utilities are included."

"Sounds great. When do we move in?" I wasn't thrilled about having to move, again, but I couldn't let my dad see my disappointment. Spending a few days hauling boxes wouldn't be so bad, and he really did need a smaller place, one without a lawn to mow every week or 1,200 square feet of cat-hair-covered carpet to vacuum.

He scratched his cheek faster. Harder. Pushing his chipped fingernail into his skin. "I don't think you're understanding. It's a one bedroom. Actually, it's a studio. *I'm* moving in next Wednesday. You're . . . um . . . you're going to have to find somewhere else to live."

There it was. The bad news. The anvil falling on my head, which was still throbbing in pain. "What the hell, Dad?" I said after a stunned silence. "Couldn't you find a two bedroom? Or a real one bedroom with a pull-out sofa I could sleep on?" I knew I sounded like a spoiled child, but I couldn't help it. Bryan had screwed me just weeks ago with the same announcement: It's closing time. Find somewhere else to go because you can't stay here.

"Not in my price range," he explained. "I'll be getting unemployment benefits and housing assistance, but that will only cover rent. Hopefully, I'll get approved for food assistance too. I can barely afford to support myself, much less two people. Frank told me he knows a buyer for the house, which is great, because I still have to pay off the second mortgage I took out to pay for your mom's medical bills." He drank the rest of his beer and wiped the foam from his lips. "Plus, you're going to find a job soon and move back to the city. I know you only came here as a last resort, and I don't blame you. Staying in Clearfield will suffocate you."

Suddenly feeling as though I were going to vomit, I pushed away the plate of cold pizza bagels. There's a kind of comfort in knowing you always have your childhood home to fall back on. I had believed it was a stable place that would always be there if I ever needed it. Parents weren't supposed to kick you out. Not when you're trying to get back on your feet.

And what about my dad? He had devoted nearly his entire life to BioNa, and they dumped him with no notice and without so much as a month's pay. Two weeks' severance? It was an insult. No one worked harder than my father. I could count on one hand the number of days he had taken off during his entire forty-four-year tenure: one when he and Mom got married at the Clearfield Courthouse, one when I was born, one to pick me up from school when I got stung by a yellowjacket during Field Day, and one for my mother's funeral.

Now he was a sixty-two-year-old man reduced to living in a studio apartment on food stamps and unemployment.

"What about Captain Milton?" I said, as though reminding my dad of his presence would be enough to convince him to think of an alternative.

"It's pet friendly."

"Well, now I can breathe a sigh of relief. I'm so thrilled you made sure to consider Captain Milton while making your plans." My tone was harsh, but I wasn't angry at my dad. I was angry at myself for not finding a job, angry at BioNa for their corporate greed, and angry at how unfair life was.

I shot up from my chair and walked outside. There was only one person I could think of to confide in.

DREW

Can we talk?

△ △ △

When I pulled into her driveway, Steph was waiting for me by the front door. I parked behind her blue Mercedes, hardly stopping to rip the keys out before rushing out to meet her.

We hugged. It was automatic. I hadn't told her the news, but she knew something was wrong.

"Come inside," she said. "Let me pour you a giant glass of wine."

"It's not even one," I told her as we went inside.

"Are you complaining?"

"No. But I still have a headache from last night," I said.

"Perfect. We'll drink red. Nothing like some antioxidants to clear that noggin."

Steph took out a bottle of red wine from her wine fridge, which was now overflowing with corked bottles—leftovers from the party.

I was never much of a drinker. Not after my teenage binging phase. At sixteen, you don't know how to cope with grief. I tried to numb the pain by sneaking sips from the dusty bottles of vodka in my parents' liquor cabinet. That worked for a little while, until the bottles were more water than alcohol, so I tried taking some of my mom's leftover painkillers. Those worked better, but when Steph caught me, she panicked and forced me to flush the pills down the toilet. For weeks, she watched my every move, making sure I didn't sneak any behind her back.

Another reason I owed Steph. She taught me how to work through my emotions even when the pain was so intense it felt like I was on the bottom of the ocean and my chest would implode from the pressure. *Never hide your pain*, she used to say. *Tell me instead*. If it weren't for her, I could have been another one of Clearfield's addicts that I kept hearing about: ignored, blamed for the town's demise, and left without resources or care.

Steph and I drank from our glasses. The wine was too sweet and too cold, and it stung going down. Steph watched in silence, waiting for me to gather myself. Hanging out with Steph felt comfortable, but different—like sleeping into your childhood bed, except the sheets are new and smell like Flowerbomb instead of teenage funk.

I explained everything: How I lost my job, how Bryan dumped me for a leggy Instagram model slash club promoter, how my dad was laid off and forced to move to the Shangri-La Apartments across the street from the abandoned Kmart. How, in one week, I'd be homeless, jobless, and worthless. For the second time.

Steph listened intently the entire time. I finished my glass, and she refilled it. She didn't tell me everything was going to work out, or that I had nothing to worry about. She knew those empty comforts would drive me crazy. Instead, she listened. The edges of her glossy lips were pinched slightly while her ocean-green eyes focused on mine, unblinking.

It's as if she knew what I was about to say next. And maybe she did. She had always known me better than I knew myself.

I wiped the wine stain from my lips, my mind fuzzy from the alcohol, and said, "I want to learn more about LuminUS."

From an outsider's perspective, nothing changed, but I knew better. I felt the shift—how a hush fell over the room, the temperature spiking a degree. I had said the magic words that freed Pandora from her box, and there was no way to shove her back in.

Steph nodded, and slowly rose from her seat. She walked out of the room. I wasn't sure whether to follow, so I stayed planted in my chair and finished the rest of my wine.

A minute later, Steph returned holding a blue cardboard box. She set it down in front of me as delicately as if it were a priceless artifact.

"I present to you the key to a brighter future," she cooed.

"The LuminUS Success Builder Starter Kit," I read out loud.

"I'm not trying to pressure you," she began, "but if you *want* to join LuminUS as an independent consultant, this box contains all the tools you'll need to build your empire."

I opened it. Within were 6 samples of LuminUS's top-selling products, a manual called "The LuminUS Guide to Success," a 30-day planner to keep track of social posts, a 200-page info booklet listing each item and what ailments they cured (yes, cured!), and an exclusive, sterling-silver LuminUS lotus pendant to show how special every brand ambassador was to the LuminUS community.

I was overwhelmed. What was I doing? I wasn't a salesperson. The one year I tried being a Girl Scout I sold the fewest cookies in the entire troop: two boxes to my parents and one to a neighbor who I later found out never paid. He did eat the cookies, though.

Steph felt my trepidation. "Remember how I told you that Rob almost had to close the business? What I didn't tell you was how bad things really were. We were living to paycheck to paycheck. I was terrified. Every night, I lay awake, wondering how I was going to feed my kids if we lost the company. Can you imagine what that does to a mother?"

I couldn't imagine. She paused to compose herself before continuing. "Taking care of the boys was overwhelming. It felt like they were outgrowing their clothes every week. I tried finding play groups or kids sports to keep them entertained, but most of the free programs in Clearfield were canceled. No one had funding anymore. Even the rec center stopped their Mini Picasso hours because they couldn't buy new paints. Rob's business was failing. Landscaping was a luxury, and if people were mowing their lawns at all, they were doing it themselves to save money. I knew I had to step in. We couldn't support our family on one income, so I searched for a job. But there was nothing. And I mean nothing. All I could find was a part-time gig bagging groceries at the Save A Lot for seven bucks an hour."

Now *that* I could imagine. I was striking out left and right in my job hunt, even for minimum wage positions.

"I was becoming frantic. Would we have to move? Sell everything, including the house? I didn't want to pull the kids out of school, away from their friends.

"But by some sort of miracle, when I felt as though I had reached my breaking point and was going to crumble into a million pieces, I met Leah when I was bagging her food. You know Leah Monroe, right? She was at the party."

"Sure." I knew Leah more from my cyberstalking than from the party. She was the middle-aged woman with the blond bob and overly enthusiastic husband.

"Anyway, we begin chatting and she tells me about LuminUS. At first, I felt the same way you did. How was *I* going to sell beauty products? I didn't know a single thing about sales. But the more I learned about LuminUS, the more confident I became. I believe in these products. They work! And because they work, they practically sell themselves. I made three thousand dollars in the first month. I paid off the car, filled the fridge with organic foods, and treated the family to a weekend at the shore. For the first time in my marriage, I was providing financially. Even more than Rob. Two years later, I'm now Platinum level, have a downline of thirty-six women, and make five figures per month. A *month*! I'm ready to retire my husband if only he would agree to it. You know how stubborn Rob is."

I had no idea what Platinum level meant or what a downline was, but five figures per month sounded awfully sweet. It also sounded unbelievable. Had I not seen these women's profiles and how successful they were, I wouldn't have believed it myself.

"I still don't know. It all sounds . . ."

"Too good to be true?" Steph asked. "I felt the same, but Leah coached me along the way, as I'll do for you. And LuminUS has every support you could possibly imagine. They have videos, online courses, training guides, you name it. Drew, I won't let you fail."

Steph leaned in, resting her elbows on the marble counter. I bit my lower lip, chewing on a piece of chapped skin.

"What do you say?" she asked. "Are you in? What could you do with an extra thousand or more a month?"

I thought of my dad and how it would feel to help him financially. I thought of having enough money to rent my own apartment, maybe even buy one outright. I thought of moving back to New York and showing Bryan he wasn't the only one who could afford to pay retail for True Religion jeans.

Still. Direct sales? Was this where my graduate degree had taken me? Was I ready to say goodbye to my dream of being a journalist?

No. It would be a stepping stone, I told myself. I would make enough to support my myself and my dad until I found a writing job. Maybe it would even free up time for me to write my true crime book. I could be my own boss at LuminUS *and* in my writing career.

Without giving myself time to reconsider, I blurted, "Fine, whatever. I'm in. Things can't get any worse, can they?"

"Wonderful!" Steph squeezed me into a hug. "I can't wait for you to get started! You can pay the $1,800 start-up fee whenever you get a chance."

"The *what?*" My mouth went dry. My headache instantly returned.

"I told you about it at coffee, remember? It's a one-time fee to cover starting expenses, but you get so much in return! Access to the training portal and videos, sales scripts, a 10 percent discount on the LuminUS website, your own landing page, a credit card swiper for *direct* direct sales, group coaching sessions, and, ah jeez, so much more."

My head spun. It *seemed* like a lot of stuff, but $1,800? My bank account was one autopay away from dipping into triple digits. "I'm not sure I can cover the cost."

"Don't worry about that. I had the same issue. What you should do is open a new credit card and borrow the money against the balance. Once you start selling, you'll pay it off in no time. Plus, you get the points. You have good credit, right?"

"I do. I think." I never missed a payment. My student loans were in good standing. I lived within my meager means.

"Then it's easy peasy lemon squeezy!" she exclaimed, grabbing one of the decorative lemons from the bowl and laughing to herself.

"I guess that sounds fine. But I still don't know where I'm going to live."

"I can fix that too!"

Steph took me back through the front door and around the beautifully landscaped garden to the garage. She led me up a flight of outdoor stairs on the side of the building. She took out a set of keys and opened the door.

It was a studio apartment: kitchen, bedroom, and living room combined. Small, but cozy, and as impeccably designed as the rest the main house. Shiplap covered the walls, the wooden furniture was whitewashed, and abstract paintings full of pastel blues and yellows that resembled sunny summer skies were tastefully arranged.

"This was supposed to be a mother-in-law suite for Rob's mom, but she decided to move to Florida instead. We tried renting it out, but didn't get much interest. Rob said we should Airbnb it, but I don't like the idea of strangers staying in my house. It creeps me out. I'd much rather have a friend use it."

"This is amazing, but I'm still not sure I can afford it. How much is rent?" I asked.

"Don't start." Steph elbowed my arm. "I'm not going to charge you rent."

My jaw dropped. "Are you serious? I can't accept a free apartment. It's too much." The place was adorable. Surely Steph could find a suitable tenant who could afford to pay. In the city, an apartment of this size and quality would be in the thousands per month.

"Watch the kids once in a while, and we'll call it even. Besides, you're about to get started with LuminUS. It won't be long before you can afford a place on your own!"

Sounded true enough. Right?

She hugged me and said, "I'm so excited for you!"

I hugged her back. For the first time in a long time, I felt an inkling of hope. I had joined a business and secured a place to live all in one afternoon. And the $1,800 starting fee was much more palatable with a free apartment thrown in. For a moment, I allowed myself to breathe. The pressure had been suffocating.

"I can't begin to thank you enough," I told Steph. "I'm going to owe you forever."

Steph howled a "Woohoo!" and waved her arms in the air. Her silver bangles clacked together. This was going to be fun—a slumber party with my best friend that didn't end the next morning.

"There's only one rule," Steph said. Sternly. Her smile tightened as she watched me with hawkish eyes to make sure I was paying attention. "You cannot go into the garage downstairs. Ever."

"That's fine," I assured her.

"I mean it. It's off-limits."

"Okay." I raised an eyebrow, suddenly curious as to why she had turned so serious.

Steph's cheerful expression returned as jarringly as it left. "Not that it matters, because it's always locked. Rob keeps his classic car in there. He would die if anything happened to it. You might hear some noises coming from downstairs, but that's just him tinkering around. Nothing to worry about."

Steph's top lip quivered. It was brief, and I would have missed it if I weren't staring so intently at her face. She walked toward me, getting so close I could smell the fruity wine on her breath. "You're officially part of the LuminUS family," she said. "Now let's get started!"

Post from Mackenzie Russo's Instagram

January 2018

So . . . I was driving Brynlee to school when she said, "I have something to tell you." 😛

"What's up, honey?" I thought she was going to say . . . I got in trouble at school. Or . . . I ruined your favorite sweater, AGAIN. Honestly, I was a bit annoyed. ☹

But then she says, "Momma, I'm going to start taking LuminUS's SkeleSlim so I can be skinny like you!"

Me: "The ones with all the yummy flavors like mint chocolate, pomegranate, and sour apple?"

Brynlee: "Yes! My favorite's strawberry banana!"

That's my girl! 🤍 🤍 🤍

#StartThemYoung #LuminLife

Chapter 8

The first thing Steph did—after all the boxes in my new apartment were unpacked—was give me a makeover. She plastered me with foundation, concealer, powder, bronzer, highlighter, and contouring. Fake eyelashes were glued onto my lids and my lips were lined beyond their natural shape. My natural waves were straightened then recurled so they could hang loosely around my face.

When Steph handed me a mirror, I didn't recognize the person staring back at me. She was a stranger. A pretty one, but a stranger nonetheless.

Then she had me take a new profile pic for my socials. Steph positioned me in the backyard so the pool would be showing in the background. She handed me a huge canvas Chloé bag that matched the airy light-blue cotton dress she put me in. I fake laughed, one hand holding the bag while the other brushed a loose wave from my face.

In the end, the picture looked fabulous. "I didn't know you were such a skilled photographer," I told Steph, impressed by the lighting and how she found the perfect angle that made my nose look smaller, my lips fuller, and my eyes larger.

"You can thank Facetune. They have a preset beauty filter that does the heavy lifting."

My profile refresh didn't stop at the picture. She also told me to change my occupation from "Columnist at BuzzFeed" to "Independent Consultant at LuminUS." That one stung.

Once we split up for the day, she emailed me a script for my first post. It sounded so cheesy my cholesterol shot up twenty points. It was filled with phrases like "cheers to becoming a LuminUS sister" and "I'm ready to begin my new life going down the LuminUS path." All I had to do was fill in the brackets with information about myself, including my hobbies, one of which was prefilled with "spreading the word about LuminUS, of course!"

I didn't want to do it. It made me feel so exposed.

I logged in to my Facebook account. I hadn't updated my profile picture in years. It was a photo of me holding a slice of pizza outside of Artichoke Pizza's takeout window. I remembered that day: I got a slice to celebrate my first day on the job as a real journalist.

I'd been so happy.

I deleted the picture.

Somehow, even from the main house, Steph seemed to be able to tell I wasn't totally on board.

STEPH
You got this! I believe in you 🖤

I uploaded the post, following the recommended template minus the grammatical errors that had somehow made it past the LuminUS copyediting team and the lame phrases I couldn't bring myself to copy and paste. I also had nothing to put in the section about "your husband and children" so I ignored it.

Hey Ladies!

My name is Drew Cooper and I'm T H R I L L E D to tell you that I joined LuminUS!

Before I tell you about LuminUS, some fun facts about me: my favorite color is orange, I won the county Halloween costume contest in second grade for my Waldo from Where's Waldo costume, and my biggest passion is giving other women the tools they need to be their best selves!

What is LuminUS? 🖤

LuminUS sells health and wellness products. From serums to supplements, it uses high quality and exclusive ingredients you'll find only in LuminUS. We have been in business for the last four years and are one of the fastest growing brands in the eastern United States!

Tell me about yourself! Comment below with a photo of your favorite breakfast food! 👇

Shop my store: drewcooper.luminus.com

#LuminUSLady #ReadyToBeginMyNewAdventure

I pressed POST and tossed my phone onto the couch. A minute later, it dinged with a notification. My dad wanted to know how my new business venture was going.

I had been nervous to tell him about shelling out $1,800 when both he and I had so little. He told me not to "beat myself up" and reminded me how much starting a business can cost.

I texted him back that it was "going great" and added a thumbs-up for good measure. Then I checked the post to see if it got any traction.

Four views, one comment. An ex-coworker had commented on my post: "Did you get hacked?"

I was about to toss my phone against the wall when my dad sent me an email. He'd forwarded a Yahoo News article about the best online marketplaces. He was trying to be helpful, but the list was full of ideas like Craigslist and eBay, none of which would help me.

I wrote back an overly enthusiastic thank-you. My guilt over reacting so badly to the move and leaving him alone in his new apartment, a rat-infested dump next to a half-abandoned strip mall, was at an all-time high.

I needed a nap. My head was killing me, and if I took another ibuprofen, I'd go into liver failure. I had just crawled under the covers when I heard footsteps on the stairs.

Steph burst in, dressed in an adorable sundress, her hair blown out.

"Aren't you ready?" she asked. "We have Leah's welcome luncheon in ten minutes!"

I groaned and pulled the covers over my head.

"If you come, I'll owe you nachos and a movie night," she said in a sing-song voice.

I threw the covers off. "Deal," I said.

△ △ △

Maybe it was because I'd made her twenty minutes late, but Steph was in a bad mood when we arrived at the Briargate Country Club for Leah's event, a welcome luncheon for the newest members of her downline. Steph didn't crack a smile when I put on a posh British accent and joked about how moist the finger sandwiches would be. When we arrived in the event space, a room overlooking the ninth hole, she immediately pulled Mackenzie aside for a private chat without so much as a hello to the others.

"What's that about?" Bre scoffed.

"Probably LuminUS," I answered. Wasn't it always about Lumin-US? Hardly a conversation occurred at these parties that didn't revolve around sales numbers and distributor levels and post counts. Rarely, someone would share a personal life event, but it was always twisted into how to leverage it to sell more LuminUS. Did your kid break his leg while riding his bicycle? Make a post showing your son's cast with a caption that says, "No matter what challenges God throws my way, it doesn't stop me from working on my business!"

Bre ran her fingers over the front button of her too-tight blazer dress, trying to shove the top of her bra down. "They've been doing that a bunch. Scurrying off into private corners. Having secret meetings. Mackenzie won't tell me what they're about, and it sounds like Steph's not telling you either."

Before I could respond, Leah clanked a silver spoon against her porcelain teacup and invited everyone to sit. She gave a gushing speech about how much growth her team had seen in a short time. She then introduced each new person on the team. Besides me, there were three others, all somehow in Leah's downline, but not in Steph's. *Downline*, I'd learned, was the word they used to describe a LuminUS lady's recruits, whose sales she got a cut of. The structure gave me a headache. Every time I tried to visualize how each woman connected to the others, it made a spiderweb in my mind, with Leah at the center. When Leah said my name, Steph elbowed me hard in the side, she and Mackenzie having slid guiltily into their seats moments earlier. I stood and waved awkwardly to the crowd as they applauded, as the other downlines had done.

After Leah's speech, I sat with my team as servers dropped off tiered trays of sandwiches and pots of herbal tea. Steph didn't say much, and I noticed Mackenzie's mood was equally sour. They looked like a couple who had been interrupted midfight and were ruminating about the things they wished they said. I was curious, but not enough to pry. If it was about LuminUS, I was already sick to death of the topic.

I was nibbling on my fourth cucumber–cream cheese tart when Leah approached me. She had been making the rounds, spending personal time with each new LuminUS lady, and now it was my turn. Bre scooted her chair away as Leah slid one next to me.

"So, Drew," Leah began as she fluffed her feathery collar, leaning in so close I could smell the Altoids on her breath. "How are you enjoying being a part of our little family? Steph tells me she has such high hopes for you. Having worked in New York for a major media network, surely you must know so many high-profile people!"

"I would hardly call BuzzFeed a *major* media network," I said thinking of papers like the *Times* or the *Guardian* or *Politico*. Places I'd kill to work for.

"Nonsense! My daughter's always forwarding me your articles."

I was taken aback. "*My* articles? Really?"

"Well, I'm not sure if they're ones *you* wrote, per se. Did you ever write recipes? I love those one-pot meals you can whip together in thirty minutes or less."

"Oh, those," I said, dejected. "Not my department."

Leah waved her hand. "No matter. I'm sure you'll be able to parlay your skills into LuminUS. Before I joined, I was a stay-at-home wife for over twenty years. Before that, the longest job I had was a summer I scooped ice cream at Springer's. I was a horrible saleswoman when I first started."

"*You* had trouble selling?"

Leah laughed loudly and said, "Everyone does! Who likes hearing 'No' or feeling like a pest? You'll get used to it. And then you'll get good at it. That's when the real fun starts." She shot a side-eye at

Bre, who was desperately trying to eavesdrop without being caught. When Leah caught her eye, she straightened her posture with a snap and leaned in toward Mackenzie, who was too busy on her phone to notice.

Leah turned her attention back to me. "You're going to love it here, Drew. With a brain like yours, there's no way you'll fail. I'll make sure of it."

△ △ △

Thankfully, Steph's mood had lightened by the time I came over for our movie night, and I was riding high on the slew of compliments I'd received at the luncheon. It had been a while since I'd had an ego boost. Lately, the only feedback I'd received was "no" and "your qualifications aren't what we're searching for at this time."

While it was nice to hear from the other downlines who fawned over my height and weight, telling me I should have been a model although I barely reached five foot seven, it was Leah's words I clung to. She was different from the others—older, steadier, more experienced, and with a classy air about her that came with age and success.

Steph kicked Rob out of the finished basement and arranged a smorgasbord of popcorn, cheesy nachos, barbecue potato chips, and Milk Duds.

"You remembered my favorites!" I said.

"The Cooper family food pyramid," she replied. Steph was dressed down in a matching pink silk pajama set. Her face was bare except for the false lashes, which she said were professionally glued on and wouldn't come off for weeks.

I sat in one of the overly stuffed leather recliners and put the bowl of chips on my lap. Steph took out her phone and tapped on the screen.

"We said no phones," I reminded her, my tone snappier than I intended. This was supposed to be a night away from LuminUS. I had met my end of the bargain. The least Steph could do was turn her phone off for ninety minutes.

"Chill," she said. "I'm streaming the movie from here. Now sit back and relax and enjoy the comedic stylings of one Mr. Adam Sandler."

"No way," I said. "*The Wedding Singer*?" Our favorite movie. We used to watch it once a week at minimum.

"You bet." Steph hit play and the movie began. We knew every line and repeated them as the actors spoke. Before long, we stopped paying attention and began chatting. There were so many topics to catch up on. Up until then, we had shared brief updates in between LuminUS talks, but nothing more substantial than "Jax is a starter on his soccer team" or "I think I've developed an intolerance to onions."

Steph asked me about Bryan. I complained about Julianna. We broke our no phone rule to stalk her profile.

"There's no way she's not editing her photos," Steph said. "No one's legs are that long."

I fake cried into a throw pillow. "They are! She *actually* looks like that."

"Well, I bet she can't recite the capitals of all fifty states."

I began singing the capital song we learned in second grade. Steph joined in at Denver. We mumbled over a few and disagreed on the pronunciation of Montpelier ("It's *peh*lier—""No, it's *pee*lier") but we high-fived over our serenade in the end.

Above us, the sounds of running footsteps banged against the ceiling.

"I swear to God, if they're playing touch football in the house again . . ." Steph grumbled. "I don't ask him for much. Watch the boys when I'm busy; occasionally pick up dinner on the way home from work. He fights me on everything like I'm some overbearing wife."

Steph wanted to vent. I had picked up on subtle clues their marriage was strained. They never kissed, not even a peck on the cheek. They hardly said good morning to each other. When I came over, Rob was either outside or in the basement, distancing himself from the rest of the family.

When they were dating in high school, Rob and Steph had been inseparable, pawing at each other like two wildcats during mating season. They were so enmeshed I didn't know where one ended and the other began. I didn't expect that sort of heat to remain a decade later, but their love hadn't warmed into a strong friendship. It had cooled off completely.

"Have you discussed your frustrations with him?" I asked.

"Not as much as I should. It hasn't been easy for a while. At first it was about his business. He was stressed about money, which meant I took the brunt. Now that we're . . ." She didn't continue. Instead, she pulled up a nacho loaded with thick cheddar and jalapeños, let the yellow string of cheese pull and break, and put it back down instead of eating it.

"If it's not about money, then what are you fighting about? Does he feel emasculated because you're doing so well with LuminUS?" Steph had commented about wanting to and being able to retire her husband. But he didn't want to give up his business.

"*Pfft*," Steph coughed out. "Drew," she began, "I . . ." Her eyes glazed and her mind went somewhere I couldn't follow. Finally, she said, "I . . . don't want to talk about this. Let's talk about fun stuff. This is supposed to be a movie sleepover night like we used to have."

"There were plenty of movie sleepover nights when we talked about serious stuff."

"True," she agreed. "How's your dad doing, by the way? After the move? It must have been hard to leave that house."

I thought about him having to give up the home where he watched my mom die—the home where they'd shared their fondest memories. I wondered which outweighed the other. Then, I thought about what he was doing at that moment while I was enjoying Steph's cushy digs and heated leather movie seats. Probably sitting on his old recliner, Captain Milton on his lap, and eating a microwaved meal. "You know what? You're right. Let's talk about something lighter."

"Okay," she said, "how about this? What game did we used to play all the time?"

"Uno?"

"Yup! Wait right here."

Steph went upstairs to grab the cards. After a few minutes, she hadn't returned. It shouldn't have taken that long. The family board games were neatly arranged in a closet near the huge flat-screen.

I heard stomping above me and muffled voices and stood on a recliner so my ear could be closer to the ceiling. It didn't help, and my feet sunk into the plush leather.

Another stomp. Two people were next to each other, and by the weight of the thuds, they were two adults. Were Steph and Rob fighting again?

When I heard someone coming down the stairs, I fell back into my seat. Steph was shaking her head and mouthing words as if she was replaying an argument in her mind.

"Everything cool?" I asked.

"Yeah, totally," she shot back with force, and I knew everything was not totally cool. I dealt the cards and after getting back-to-back draw four cards, Steph loosened up.

That night, we were having fun. The kind of playful revelry you can only experience with a person who has shared your childhood history. We didn't talk about LuminUS or sales quotas or hashtags. We bantered and joked, and I was elated to have my Steph back.

I didn't want to ruin it.

We continued playing Uno, gossiping about classmates while throwing down cards.

"I've missed you," she said.

"I've missed you too."

Two more rounds of Uno, another plate of nachos, and one romantic comedy later, I said goodnight.

I went back to my apartment with a pep in my step. Steph was back. *We* were back. I washed my face, put on my LuminUS creams, took my supplements, and went to bed. As I plugged my phone in to its charger, some texts came in.

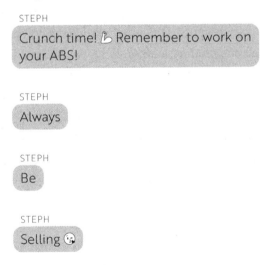

You've got to be kidding me, I thought, chucking the phone against the wall. It put a tiny dent in the coastal blue paint.

Chapter 9

The days that followed went by in a LuminUS-blue-tinted blur. Between the parties (in person and virtual), group chats, daily post goals, reminders about daily post goals, and constant commenting to boost engagement, my brain felt like mush. And it was getting me nowhere. I'd only managed to sell one product, a bottle of DrownMe to a former coworker from BuzzFeed who compounded my humiliation with her pitying message: "Hope things turn around for you soon xx." I had zero leads on potential downlines, and I'd been blocked by half of my Facebook friends. The very last thing I wanted to do at eight a.m. on a Sunday was talk LuminUS.

"You're late," Steph said as she grabbed my wrist and pulled me through the house. She had called an early morning meeting with her immediate downlines about the LuminSANITY conference, which was coming up next weekend. In the kitchen, she ripped a paper towel from the roll, wet it under the sink, and handed it to me.

"Here. You have deodorant stains on your shirt."

I rubbed the white lines that had formed on the black fabric of my top, but it only made the towel break apart, leaving me with both deodorant stains and balled-up pieces of paper stuck to them.

"Give it back! Mom! MOM!" A child ran in between us, around the kitchen island, and back to another part of the house. She was followed by two more children. All girls. All very loud.

Mackenzie came running. "Brynlee! Honey, give your sister back the doll. BRYNLEE!"

Steph pinched the bridge of her nose as Rob moved past us to get to the fridge. He wore gym clothes and ignored the chaos as he pulled out a sports drink.

"Hey, Rob, honey?" Steph asked in a sweet but strained voice. "I asked you to watch all the kids while I work, remember?"

"I was thirsty."

"We have a drink fridge downstairs."

"It only has water and ginger ale. I need my electrolytes." Neon-yellow liquid dribbled down Rob's beard as he gulped the drink. Some spilled on the floor, white marble that matched the counters. Steph watched it drip. Her eyelid twitched.

Rob avoided my gaze. He had become more withdrawn from me, no longer forcing pleasantries but instead walking away when he saw me coming.

"How's the car coming along?" I asked, trying to break the tension with a topic that interested him. I wanted to have a closer relationship with Rob if for no other reason than I lived in his house, rent free, and saw him practically every day. At night, more and more noises came from the garage. I figured Rob must have been busy fixing his classic car because he'd had to move most of his landscaping equipment to the back patio.

Rob turned, slowly, and asked, "What—"

Crash!

Glass shattered, followed by a child's wail, followed by Mackenzie yelling, "We're okay! Everyone is okay!"

Steph was on the brink of losing it. She put her hands over her eyes.

"Rob. Honey. I'm going to need you to take the children downstairs and watch them until Mommy's finished. Can you handle that? Can you do that for me? This one favor?" Her voice was both stern and condescending—her mom voice, which I imagined came out when she was really serious.

Rob threw away his drink and called for the children. They followed him downstairs like ducklings paddling after their mother.

Once they were gone, Mackenzie appeared, cradling two-thirds of a sand-colored ceramic lamp. Its cord dragged against the tile, hanging flaccidly from the broken pieces of ceramic.

"We can glue it," she told Steph. "It broke clean."

"Throw it out," Steph said.

"I'll pay for it. Even though it was technically Jax who—"

"Throw. It. Out."

Mackenzie gingerly took the lamp toward the metal trash can and tossed it.

As we followed Steph to the back room, Mackenzie whispered to me, "They're good girls. It wasn't their fault." She took a moment to check if Steph was listening. She most definitely was. Women like Steph didn't miss the sound of a fly pissing.

"Did you meet them?" Mackenzie asked, this time louder.

"Who?"

"My daughters. I'm so rude. Brynlee's six, Kinslee's five, and Hadlee's the youngest. She's four."

A baby per year. Mackenzie sure was busy between 2012 and 2015.

"Yes, and Mackenzie had to bring them all today on account of, what was it again? Canceled something or other?" Steph asked.

"Their gymnastics class was canceled. Their assistant coach has the flu."

"That's right. Heaven forbid the kids have to tumble with only one coach. Oh well. At least it's almost summer vacation."

We took our places in Steph's back sitting room. Bre had been waiting, her nose glued to her phone, most likely her social accounts. I had stalked some of her feeds. There were photos upon photos that looked nothing like her: her nose blurred to nonexistence, and the inches shaved off her waist causing the background to warp. And she shilled more than LuminUS: clothes, jewelry, nail polish, smoothie powder, essential oils, you name it.

A part of me felt sorry for her. How low was your self-esteem that you had to digitally create a new person and pass it off as yourself? My self-worth was in the toilet, but at least I owned it. And Bre was an attractive woman. She didn't look like the Stephs and Mackenzies of the world, but she didn't need to. She had her own beauty that was being overshadowed by the fake tan and pillow face caused by too many fillers.

"I assume Jenny's not coming," Bre said while she scrolled.

"No, she had to cancel at the last minute," Steph said.

"Didn't her cat die?" Mackenzie asked, sitting back and eyeballing her nail polish under the side lamp. "I could have sworn she said something about Pearl's passing."

Steph's eyebrow shot upward. "Pearl wasn't a cat. She was a hamster. And no, she cancelled because her mom is sick."

"I've been feeling off for a while. Wonder if there's something going around?" Bre asked.

"What about Leah?" I chimed in.

"She doesn't need to be here. She trusts us to lead our meetings, and she has, like, a million people in her downline that need more coaching. But that's not why we're here," Steph said. "We need to talk about the conference. This is going to be a big one for our team, and we need to make sure we shine."

"Shine, shine, shine!" Bre exclaimed.

Mackenzie wrinkled her nose as Steph continued. "I'm going to resend everyone the itinerary. We need to be at every event, especially the welcome dinner on night one, so make sure you don't miss your flights. Drew, you're flying out with me, so we should be good. But Bre and Mackenzie, you have separate flights, so set your alarms. Get to the airport three hours early at least. Especially you, Mackenzie. No sleeping in. We don't want a repeat of last year."

Mackenzie put down her wineglass. "I'll go to bed early, I swear. I'll make it a true crime and cuddles night. Chase has been asking for a chill date night for a while."

"You too, Bre." Steph arched a brow toward Bre. "I know you've been sick lately, which is why you've been missing hot yoga."

"Are you serious? I couldn't be more exited. And it's just a cold. Or allergies."

Satisfied, Steph opened her laptop. "I'm also sending everyone this month's early sales reports. There's still time to make monthly quotas, and just because we're at the conference doesn't mean we stop working. In fact, the conference is a great opportunity to boost numbers."

Mackenzie rested her body against the arm of the tufted chair and suppressed another yawn. Lately, she had been less engaged than when I'd first met her. We didn't spend time one-on-one, but she had texted me, late at night, mostly asking about my work as a journalist. Part of me wondered if she was looking to change careers.

Bre, meanwhile, was as excited as a kid the night before going to Disney World. The mere mention of the conference sent her into convulsions. "I can't wait for the welcome dinner. I heard Dixie *herself* is going to be there."

"Who's Dixie?" I asked. The name sounded familiar.

"You don't know Dixie LaVey?" Bre asked, aghast. "She's the founder of LuminUS!"

Dixie LaVey, that's right. The breast cancer survivor whose health struggles inspired her to form LuminUS. The queen mother of the LuminUS ladies. The relationship between her and the downlines wasn't the usual boss-employee relationship—it was laid out in the personal letter she'd written to the women who joined the same month as me. I distinctly remembered the ending to the letter because it was so strange. Dixie had written: "Every LuminUS lady is like my own child. You are all my daughters now."

Steph poured herself a glass of wine. Red. She didn't offer us any. "Dixie and Leah go way back," she said, taking a sip. "Leah was one of the first to join LuminUS. Dixie is her direct upline. I joined after and was lucky enough to become part of Leah's downline before her team got so big she stopped having time for everyone. So you can see how close our team is to Dixie. To the very top of LuminUS."

I hadn't known this, but being so close to the top made me feel better about joining. I already had an advantage.

"Even though she's friends with the founder, Leah isn't less strict with my team. In fact, she expects more from us," Steph added. She glanced out the window as she spoke.

Bre chewed nervously at a finger, and Mackenzie crossed her arms. It was like a cloud had suddenly descended on the room. It suddenly occurred to me—were they *afraid* of Leah? Maybe she was a tougher upline than the warm exterior made her seem.

"What do we do? Now that Jenny is dead in the water?" Bre asked.

"Don't worry about Jenny. I'll deal with her myself," Steph said.

Bre added, "Her posts are garbage anyway. She doesn't know how to photograph herself, and she's always showing her worst angles. Who wants to see the front of her face, full on? With that nose, too."

The other women's silence meant they agreed. I shifted uncomfortably in my chair.

Steph continued. "As for the rest of us, we really need to ramp up our efforts. I'm hosting a Facebook Live party tonight and I'm going to need everyone to tune in and interact. According to my RSVPs," she read from her screen, "three hundred and twenty-four people have already marked themselves as attending. These are big girl numbers, y'all."

"Woo!" Bre cheered. Mackenzie sank further down in her chair.

"Drew, have you been completing your daily checklist?" Steph asked. "I noticed you haven't posted any product videos."

"I'm still working my way through the welcome booklet," I admitted.

Steph let out a disappointed sigh that cut me to the bone.

"I know you're new, so I don't expect your numbers to be on the same level as the other girls," she told me in a soothing but strained voice. "But the only way you're going to do well with LuminUS is if you follow the Success Plan. Directly. Every day, you need to check off each item on the daily checklist, including the weekly goal of three product videos."

"You're right. I'm sorry. I'll do it as soon as I go back to my apartment."

"This is a business, Drew. One where you are your own boss. If your employee wasn't completing their daily tasks, how would you feel as a boss?"

I didn't feel like my own boss. I felt like Steph was very much in charge. "I would encourage them to do better."

"That's right." Steph pulled out her phone. "Here. I'll forward you the checklist again."

Steph spoke to me as though she were a school headmistress and I'd been caught with my skirt three inches above my knees. Where had my movie night Steph gone, I wondered—the one who laughed so hard at our inside jokes that Diet Sprite shot from her nose?

She tapped her screen and my phone buzzed with a new email.

"Why don't you head back to your apartment right now and get started. The ladies and I have more business to discuss, but it's not as important as getting your numbers up. We need to make up for Jenny's shortcomings before the big conference."

I went back to my place with my tail between my legs and opened my laptop. As a journalist, deadlines were a part of my life—tight ones with fast turnarounds. I was familiar with an impatient editor breathing down my neck to submit an article by the end of the day.

This was different. This was somehow much worse. I wanted to impress Steph and to prove to her that I could be a LuminUS lady. I saw how disappointed she was with Jenny, and I didn't want that to be me.

I reread the checklist. It was overwhelming.

Every day we had to message ten family or friends about the opportunity to join LuminUS, reach out to ten unknown people with the same message, add ten new friends on Facebook with the goal to quickly reach at least 5,000, create a motivational post, a product post, a personal life post, a hobby post, a food post, a fitness post, an infographic post, an engagement post asking an open-ended question like "does no one eat pasta anymore?" and three posts each on our business and team pages.

Weekly tasks were even more demanding: film three product videos, write personal messages to everyone who watched our videos, message fifty people about the opportunity to distribute, and host three Live parties where we applied product as we talked about something in our personal lives.

Then there were monthly goals. By the end of the month, we were expected to have sold $3,000 of product, added ten people to our downline, messaged three hundred people about joining, and posted twenty product videos and ten recruitment videos.

The math didn't add up between weekly and monthly goals, but Steph insisted I focus on daily tasks first.

"The number one thing," she stressed multiple times, "is signing women to your downline. That's how you level up. And the higher your level, the more bonuses you get."

Bonuses sounded promising. But convincing other women to spend $1,800 to join LuminUS seemed impossible.

Steph had solutions to that problem as well. "Find women who are single moms or in military families where their husbands are out of the house a lot. That also includes wives of the incarcerated. Honestly, any wife who's unhappy in their marriage. Most of them are dying to have something of their very own, something that they control without the influence of their husbands. If their husbands won't give them the money for the starter fee, you can encourage them to take out another line of credit without anyone knowing. Like you did."

Wasn't that scummy, I wondered? Preying on women who were unhappy?

Steph disagreed. "Having a job where they're in charge and make their own hours is a blessing to them, their husbands, and the children they get to stay home with. They want to be able to support their families. Just like you."

Just like me. It was the phrase Steph used whenever I felt doubtful about my new endeavor. They were just like me: the women down on their luck hoping for an opportunity to better themselves.

If I wanted to better *my*self, the first thing I needed to do was film a product video.

I put on some lip balm and tousled my hair. That made me look more disheveled, so I smoothed it down behind my ears. The unruly waves stuck out while the top flattened, giving me a pyramid look. Whatever. Steph had sent me a link to an app that filtered your face. I hated the idea of using it, but if it added a little mascara and blush and volume to my hair, would that be so bad?

I sat on a chair and aimed the camera at myself. I held up a bottle of the acne cream Steph had given me and recorded a thirty-second video about how well it was working, making sure to say LuminUS at least once every fifteen seconds, as the manual suggested.

I stopped recording and watched the video back. My arms looked stiff and I spoke too quickly, but it would have to do. At least I wasn't lying: My skin *did* look fantastic. I was down to a handful of blemishes, and still no new eruptions.

As I played around with the filter controls, I felt gross. With a single click, I could change the entire shape of my face—not only eye color, makeup level, and hairstyle, but my actual bone structure. I could be anyone. It made sense why so many of the women's photos looked nothing like them in real life, but it upset me that they felt pressure to change themselves so dramatically. It upset me even more that the real me wasn't as pretty as the tuned photo.

Feeling depressed, even with my newly clearing skin, I closed the face changing app and posted the video—zits, wrinkles, dark circles and all.

Then I texted Jenny. The other women had been so harsh when speaking about her. I wanted to make sure she wasn't feeling as shitty about herself as I was.

DREW

Hey. It's Drew. How are you? How's your mom feeling? Want to grab a coffee sometime?

Blinking ellipses appeared. They flashed for a few seconds before disappearing.

Jenny was ignoring me, but another message came through.

STEPH

Let's talk about the video. Have some pointers.

STEPH

Will email flight info for conference. Let's get LuminSANE!

Post from Steph Murphy's Instagram

May 2018

LuminUS sure knows how to spoil us!

This is my 3rd? 4th? (I lost track! 🤚) LuminSANITY Conference. Once a year, I am so blessed to go on an all-expenses paid trip to meet up with my other FABULOUS LuminUS Ladies. This time, in beautiful Utah!

But it's not all butterflies 🦋 and unicorns 🦄. We do a lot of learning too! New coaching styles, team-building exercises, and, my absolute fave, learning about NEW products!

This "work" trip (in quotes because it's too much FUN to be work), is only for top performers like me.

But there are SO many benefits to joining LuminUS! Like:

🤍 FREE products

🤍 FREE friends

🤍 FREE transformation

We don't need to beg you to join. We want you to be ready.

The choice is yours.

#LuminUSLadies #LuminSANITY

Chapter 10

Steph and I didn't talk much during the two-hour car ride to the airport. It was a $400 plane ticket from Philadelphia, which I had to pay for myself. I used my new credit card. Under Steph's instructions, I'd also bought new clothes and makeup, and gotten a proper haircut and blowout, a manicure, and a lash lift and tint. My new haul cost me another $400, which I also charged to my card.

So far, LuminUS had cost me $2,600, and I had little to show for it. A few people had bought products; mostly coworkers and distant relatives I hassled until they bought something just to shut me up. I hadn't signed any people into my downline yet, but I was hoping my forthcoming commission check would begin to put a dent in my debt.

Steph turned on a motivational podcast called *Being Your Own Brand* she said I would find helpful.

"It's about marketing yourself," she explained. "We sell LuminUS, but we're mainly selling *ourselves*. You need to make customers want to *be you*, so when they see you using LuminUS, they'll use it too."

I was distracted by the view of my skin in the car mirror. "Do you think my skin's getting worse?" A pimple had sprouted in the crease of my nose, and I felt a few deep cysts brewing.

"You're probably purging. It means the product's working."

"Purging?"

"Your skin cells are being regenerated at a higher rate. Right now the dead cells are being pushed out by the new, healthy cells. Nothing to worry about. It'll go away soon, and your skin will look the best it ever has."

Seemed scientific enough. And Steph should know—she had aced AP bio.

Steph took her right hand off the steering wheel and began chewing at her nails.

"Everything okay?" I asked. Besides the nail biting, Steph had been uncharacteristically short with me lately.

"Why wouldn't it be?" Steph asked.

"Because you're about to gnaw off your acrylic."

She took her hand from her mouth. "I guess I am a little nervous. Conference jitters."

I reached to the back seat to grab one of the sandwiches Steph had made us for the ride. It was dry and difficult to swallow. Alongside the cottage cheese, I tasted something much sweeter—gritty. LuminUS's SkeleSlim powder in the acai flavor. I tried not to puke.

△ △ △

The flight went smoothly, even with mild turbulence over the Rockies. Steph ate a Xanax and ordered two white wines while in the air, but still stayed wide awake. We still didn't talk.

A black luxury SUV picked us up from the airport. Around five in the afternoon, we arrived at the Grand Temple Hotel. Two uniformed bellhops greeted us and offered to take our luggage. They handed Steph an envelope with our room keys.

"You're going to love the suite!" Steph said. "LuminUS knows how to spoil us!"

This must be how the other half live, I thought, impressed by the world-class treatment Steph was receiving. While Bryan and I dated, I'd had a taste of this lifestyle, but this world belonged to him: fancy restaurants, trendy cocktail bars, and invitations to exclusive events, thanks to his connections and credit card. I wasn't immune to how intoxicating the lifestyle was, but it was never mine. I felt like an imposter that everyone could see through.

Steph strutted through the gold and black marble lobby as if she was accustomed to the high life. How much *was* Steph making with LuminUS?

When we arrived at the suite, it was even nicer than the lobby, with a full kitchen, living room, and two separate bedrooms, each with an en suite bathroom. The decor was deep mahogany wood accented by giant ferns and leather sofas; a mix of rustic ranch and trendy modern. I was willing to bet a single chair cost more than all of my assets combined. My credit card shivered in its slot.

"This room is exquisite," I told Steph, afraid to put my dirty duffel on the rug. "But how much is it costing you?"

"Don't worry. It's on LuminUS."

"My room too?" I asked.

"The entire suite. Now put down your bag and get ready. We don't have much time. Leah is joining us for dinner."

△ △ △

The LuminSANITY welcome reception was hosted in one of the hotel's banquet rooms. Blue lights throbbed to pop music as we took our seats at the designated table. Leah was already seated, dressed in a crisp white pantsuit with crimson lining.

"Have the other girls arrived yet?" Steph asked loudly over the music.

"Mackenzie's at the open bar, but I haven't seen Bre or Jenny yet."

Steph scanned the room. Between the strobe lights and crowds of women who looked like clones of each other, if either of them were in attendance, it would be impossible to tell. Steph slumped on a chair, her phone out, furiously texting. "I knew this would happen," she huffed.

"Did you remind them of how important it is to be seen at this dinner?" Leah threatened with an arched brow.

"I did." Steph's typing frenzied. "I'm so sorry, Leah."

Leah sniffed. "I'm not surprised about Jenny, but I *am* disappointed in Bre."

Mackenzie gave us a curt nod as she took her own seat. She had a champagne flute in each hand.

"I already have a drink," Leah said, holding up her own flute.

"They're both for me," Mackenzie said. After catching Leah's stern eyes, she added, "You know how long those bar lines are. I don't want to wait all over again."

"Where the hell is Bre?" Steph asked her.

"Not sure. I called her before I boarded, but she didn't answer."

"Isn't that unlike her?" I asked. Bre was never off her phone; it was practically superglued to her palm.

Ignoring the others, Leah turned to me. "I have many women in my downline, and they have hundreds more in their downlines. But Steph and Mackenzie are special. That's why I expect so much more from them. I see a potential in them that I don't see with the others. So does Dixie."

She held up a clean knife and used its reflection to reapply her coral lipstick. Chanel. "You have the same potential," she said.

"Doubt it," I said with an awkward laugh. "I can't get comfortable with any of it—the posts, the selfies, the selling . . ."

"You'll get the hang of it. So long as you don't go NATO, you'll be fine."

"The North Atlantic Treaty Association?" I asked. What did international politics have to do with skincare?

"No Action, Talk Only. Those who talk the talk but can't walk the walk. You know what I mean?"

"Not really."

Leah put away her lip gloss and leaned toward me. She smelled like expensive perfume. "A lot of excuses, but no results. Like Jenny Fitzsimmons, unfortunately. She follows the guides, she posts her required photos and messages, but she doesn't go the extra mile. She doesn't make any sales or get new recruits. She does have excuses, though. Plenty of them. Talk, talk, talk, but no action. It's not like it's hard, either. I always say that if you find the right targets, it's like selling ice to an Eskimo. Get it?"

"Now I do," I said, shifting in my seat and wondering if anyone else heard Leah casually dropping a slur.

Leah leaned in even closer. I pulled back in my chair.

"Your skin's looking great, but have you given any thought to that medspa I linked in the group chat? A little filler *here* and *here*"—she stabbed a finger at each side of my face—"would make those cheeks pop."

"I'm not big on cosmetic injections," I said. I thought of Bre and her ever-expanding lips.

"You don't know what you're missing," Mackenzie said. "I've been getting fillers and Botox for years now. I recently started a laser treatment. Makes my skin look like raw meat for a week, but it's worth it."

"Wait, really? I thought you only used LuminUS," I said.

"Oh, please. You can't get these results on LuminUS alone," Mackenzie said with an eyeroll.

"But don't tell anyone," Steph cut in. "Never ever. We want our clients to think they can achieve perfection if they buy enough LuminUS."

"Isn't that false advertising?" I asked. "Can't we get in trouble?"

Mackenzie pursed her lips. "We're not lying to them. We're just not sharing our entire beauty regimen, which is no one's business. Did Leah publicize her third boob job, or did Bre tell everyone about her liposuction? No. They're medical procedures and those are protected by HIPPO."

"It's HIP*AA*," Steph said, rolling her eyes.

"I was making a joke," Mackenzie snapped back.

Leah stared daggers into Mackenzie. Before she could say anything, the music stopped, and voices began to lower. More women hurried to sit our table—others in Leah's downline—but two seats were noticeably empty: Bre's and Jenny's.

A woman took the stage, holding a microphone. She was wearing a LuminUS-blue bodycon dress. "Before we begin, I have a message that, unfortunately, Dixie will not be in attendance tonight."

The crowd sighed audibly.

"I know, I know," the woman soothed the room, "but she sends her deepest apologies. In fact, she hopes you all will forgive her once you see these fantastic welcome gifts!" The woman clapped as a line of hotel staff members came out with arms full of blue LuminUS bags. At the sight of the freebies, the crowd chattered excitedly to each other, trying to guess what was inside.

Bags were passed around to each table, and I ripped into mine.

"No freakin' way!" I blurted out while holding up my gift. "An actual iPad? This is awesome!"

Steph briefly glanced at hers before putting in on the table. Mackenzie and Leah didn't even open their bags. Maybe to them, this was a small token, but my old iPad had cracked last year and there was no way I could justify buying a new one.

Cameras clicked and flashed as the other women took photos of themselves with the swag. Steph took a few herself.

After a speech officially welcoming us to the weekend "packed with fun, festivities, and invaluable learning opportunities," the woman, who I found out was LuminUS's brand director, wanted to take a moment to identify some exemplary distributors.

"These ladies have shown such high consistency in their sales that they have qualified for LuminUS's car! That's right, let's give a hand to our newest owners of a beautiful, LuminUS-blue Mercedes-Benz GLA 250 SUV!" The crowd applauded as three names were called out, one of which was Mackenzie's.

She tried taking a drink from her flute before standing, but both glasses were empty.

"You can get a free car?" I whispered to Steph.

"Pretty much," Steph answered. "If you maintain a certain level of continuous sales, LuminUS will give you a monthly stipend toward your car lease."

Mackenzie stood up and waved as a spotlight hit her. It felt forced, as though she was a marionette controlled by an untalented puppeteer.

She looked like she was about to sit back down, but Leah shoved her forward, and she stumbled toward the stage, the spotlight following her. The champagne had made her a little unsteady on her feet.

Mackenzie joined the other two women onstage, who were jumping up and down and sobbing hysterically as the display car rotated on the platform. Mackenzie plastered a stiff, closed-mouth smile on her face.

How could she not be thrilled about a new car? Especially a Benz? For *free*! I was overjoyed about the iPad, and couldn't imagine being gifted a car that was made in this decade, even with its tacky paint job and affixed chrome emblem bearing the LuminUS logo.

As blue balloons rained down on our heads and glitter canons exploded, Mackenzie looked like she'd rather be anywhere else.

It wasn't just Steph who was off lately—something was seriously up with Mackenzie.

From the Podcast *Being Your Own Brand*

Episode 11: Wake-Up Call

Imagine this scenario.

You come to someone and tell them, "I have an amazing opportunity that can skyrocket your income to over $100,000 a year or more."

What does that person say?

Do they say "Maybe, but I'll need to look into it"? Or what about a flat-out "no"?

Those answers alone tell me everything I need to know about that person. It tells me that person is scared. And I know from experience.

Listeners, I was once that person. I was presented with opportunities that I continuously rejected. I made excuses: "I'm too busy right now. I need to research it. It sounds too good to be true."

Empty excuses. Each and every one of them.

The truth was that I was scared. Truly successful people don't make these excuses. They don't ask "why." They just do.

If the gravedigger stood around and pondered the hole, the grave would never get dug. Listeners, he doesn't overthink. He picks up the shovel and digs.

Chapter 11

To celebrate Mackenzie's new car, Leah took us out to a trendy sushi restaurant that she claimed the Kardashians had once been spotted at. She put the whole meal—including five carafes of sake—on her bright-blue LuminUS company card. By the time we got back to Mackenzie's room, everyone was beyond buzzed. Her suite was gigantic, larger than Steph's and mine, even without the extra bedroom. I didn't think it was possible. How much did these rooms cost per night?

Mackenzie popped open another bottle of champagne. The cork shot against the wall and clipped the corner of an ornate ceramic elephant plant stand, chipping off the tip of its trunk. No one seemed to care. LuminUS would cover it.

"I cannot tell you ladies about how much I've needed this getaway," Mackenzie said. She overpoured her glass and sucked the cascading foam from the top. "The girls have been driving me absolutely batshit crazy, and Chase hasn't been any help. God forbid he pull himself from ESPN to give me some time to my damn self."

"Tell me about it," Leah said. "It doesn't get any easier once they're grown. Now it's the grandbabies. I'm constantly having to watch them for the afternoon. It's not like their mothers have jobs anyway. And Aaron's been so busy with the ministry—attendance has been up twenty-five percent."

I knew Leah was a grandmother, but she didn't look it. She must have had her children in her late teens, like Steph.

Steph nodded along while chewing on her nails. I, being purposefully child-free, had nothing to add.

"Let's put on some music!" Mackenzie exclaimed. Being drunk had pulled her out of her angsty mood. She whipped out her phone and began playing Ariana Grande's new single and plopped the phone into a glass to amplify the sound.

"Can we listen to something more relaxed? My head's starting to hurt, and I can't stand that girl's wailing," Leah asked. She sat on the deep purple velvet sofa with her legs crossed, showing off her red-bottomed high heel.

Mackenzie danced her way over to Leah. "That means you need another drink!" She handed the champagne to Leah, who topped off her flute before passing the half-empty bottle to the rest of us.

I waved it away.

"Come on, Drew! You're so tense. Live a little," Mackenzie encouraged as she massaged my shoulders. I was past buzzed and into drunk territory. Any more champagne and I'd be spending the rest of the night in the toilet.

"I'll take it," Steph said. She grabbed the bottle and drank directly out of it.

Mackenzie cheered. "That's the spirit! Let's get crazy!"

Steph let out a forced "Woot!"

"Can we not scream, please?" Leah asked sharply. She closed her eyes and rubbed her temple. "Steph, your voice can break glass."

Steph rolled her eyes and continued drinking. Mackenzie danced near the bar area. Another song came on from the same artist, and Steph said, "Turn it up!"

Mackenzie cranked up the volume.

"Steph!" Leah snapped.

As the oldest women in the bunch, it made her the elder—the group mother—a role she proudly lived up to. And her children were misbehaving—though most of her ire was directed at Mackenzie. For what reason, I had no idea.

"Chill out. It's not that loud. And it's only ten o'clock. Besides, aren't we celebrating Mackenzie's car perk?" Steph said.

"Can we not talk about that?" Mackenzie groaned.

"If you don't want the Benz, I'll gladly take it," I half joked.

Mackenzie shuffled over to me and sat on the arm of my sofa. "It's not really a free car." She was trying to whisper, but was too drunk to keep quiet. "It's a $450 monthly stipend toward your car lease. Steph and Leah have it too."

I glanced at Steph. She was sitting next to me on a plush armchair. She had started browsing her phone with furrowed brows. I kicked her shin, gently, to get her attention. When she looked up, I mouthed, "Is everything okay?"

She mouthed back, "Yup," and gave me a weak thumbs-up.

Leah took out a palm-size gold box and put a green pill under her tongue.

"Want one?" she offered, after catching me staring.

I waved it away but asked, "What is it?"

"An herbal supplement. Ginseng, matcha, guarana, and sage. Keeps me focused." She clicked the box closed. "Mackenzie, do you want one?"

Mackenzie was mid–booty shake. "Ew, no," she said firmly. "The

LuminUS supplements are all I use. I don't even like taking aspirin."

"Aren't those LuminUS?" I asked, eyeing the pill case that Leah slid back into her purse.

"These?" she asked. "No. These are a custom blend that I special order from a chemist in the city."

"Leah refuses to take LuminUS," Steph interjected, her tone judgmental.

"It's not that I *refuse*," Leah corrected, "it's that I have many allergies and have to be extra careful."

"Sure," Steph said.

I didn't say anything, but privately, I was shocked. The queen of the Pinecrest LuminUS ladies herself, Leah Monroe, didn't even use the supplements?

As if eager to change the subject, Leah began to share the latest gossip from her husband's congregation.

Vanessa Gibbons was had been spotted in Atlantic City with a mysterious blue-eyed man who wasn't her husband. Florence Franconi's daughter needed to take a semester off from college not because of a bout of mono, but to deal with her cocaine addiction. And Sandra Baker owed the IRS $90,000 in back taxes and rented out rooms in her five-bedroom house despite telling everyone her husband's insurance company was making loads of money.

I didn't know any of these people, but Leah was a natural storyteller. It felt like watching a trashy reality show that I secretly loved.

"Isn't there, like, minister confidentiality?" I asked.

"That's for Catholics and their confessions. We're Lutherans," she corrected. "Besides, I hear everything from Lia, my hairstylist, who's a Methodist, so I'm pretty sure she can say whatever she wants."

"What about you, Drew?" Mackenzie asked. "What type of Christian are you?"

I hesitated, thinking about the diamond-crusted crucifix necklace Mackenzie wore and the inspirational Bible verses Leah always posted. Even Steph, who never mentioned church or God or Jesus, posted the occasional motivational Bible verse, although less frequently than the others.

"I'm not very religious. But my mom was Roman Catholic," I said, hoping that would soften the blow. She was a lapsed Catholic, only going to church once a year on Christmas Eve. After she died, I became an atheist, because what sort of God would let the person you loved the most suffer excruciating pain until they withered and died? After college, my cynicism softened a little, and I became a pessimistic agnostic.

I braced for a lecture, but Mackenzie shrugged, and Leah adjusted her marble-size pearl earring. "You might want to consider adding a few posts about thanking God for the opportunity to sell LuminUS," she said. "If clients feel they're being called to LuminUS by a higher power, they're much more likely to join. You don't need to mean it."

Mackenzie gripped her necklace. "I mean it whenever I post," she said directly to Leah.

"I know you do, and so do I, of course," Leah said placatingly. "But not everyone has to." She turned her attention to Steph. "You've noticed an uptick in interest when you throw in a psalm or two, don't you?"

"It's true. Our audience is big into religion," Steph said.

"It gives them comfort knowing there's a higher power supporting them. How can you fail when God's on your side?" Leah said.

"What's the one about God's tribe?" Mackenzie asked. "That's my favorite."

Leah puffed her chest, shut her eyes, and recited: "The smallest family among you will become a tribe. The smallest tribe will become a mighty nation. When the time is right, I the Lord will make it happen."

"That's the one!" Mackenzie yelped. "You girls are all my tribe." She walked over and hugged each one of us individually.

There was no more talk of God or Jesus or religion for the rest of the night. But I privately resolved that I wasn't about to stoop to pretending to be a believer to gain customers.

While Mackenzie and Leah discussed how unruly Bre's eyebrows were becoming since she had gone to a discount microblader, I turned to Steph.

"Since when did you become religious?" I asked.

"I'm not. But you heard what Leah said. It boosts sales."

The night continued, the music growing louder. Mackenzie had a playlist on shuffle, and at the start of each song, she'd yell, "This is my jam!"

Maybe it was just the champagne, but I got wrapped up in the excitement. I never knew what it was like to be in a close friend group of other women. Leah was stern and serious, Mackenzie was loud and bubbly, but they welcomed me into their "boss bitch tribe," as Steph called it, with open arms. Despite not being on the same level financially or aesthetically, it didn't matter. I felt like one of them.

△ △ △

I awoke in the middle of the night, draped over the velvet sofa and using a bath towel as a blanket. Mackenzie's dress lay on the floor beside me. She had ripped it off during a spirited rendition of "Dirty" by Christina Aguilera. Leah had tried to slap her hands away from her zipper, and eventually threw the bath towel at her so she could cover herself up.

My bladder was ready to burst. The hangover was coming on like a bullet train to my brain. The room was dark as was the sky outside. It could have been anytime between two and five, since I vaguely remembered reading my phone's clock at one thirty before my battery died. After that, both my phone and memory went blank.

I closed my eyes again. Everything spun. My full bladder was replaced by nausea. I had to get up, to go to the bathroom to pee or puke or both.

Get up, get up, get up, I urged myself.

I hadn't been this drunk since college. My elation at having new girlfriends, my old friend back, and access to free champagne resulted in a night of overindulgence.

As I stumbled to the bathroom, stopping a few times to get the spiraling room under control, I heard voices coming from the bedroom. The door was closed, so I couldn't hear what was being said, but I could tell they were angry.

I glanced around the living room, squinting to see better in the dark. Someone was on the armchair, curled up in the fetal position. She was hidden beneath an oversized camel mohair sweater with LOEWE in embroidered letters on the breast pocket. *Must be Leah*, I thought. She'd bragged to me about the price of the sweater earlier that evening—$1,300. I couldn't see her face, but a tuft of blond hair peeked out.

That meant it was Steph and Mackenzie arguing.

I tiptoed to the door, careful not to make any noise. Not that it mattered. I could have been a charging rhino, and still would have been undetected. The commotion from the bedroom was growing louder and louder.

Both women were shouting now, the only words I could catch being obscenities. Mackenzie screamed. Not a scream like she was in danger or hurt, but one of sheer, guttural frustration.

Crash!

Something heavy fell onto the floor. Or was it thrown?

The room grew quiet. Steph said something in a hushed tone.

Mackenzie screamed again.

I heard feet stomping—getting closer to me.

I ran over to the couch and laid down, closing my eyes and rolling toward the back so my face wouldn't be seen.

The bedroom door opened and the stomping continued past me, out the suite door, and into the hallway.

Leah hadn't woken. I waited a few minutes, until the pressure from my bladder turned into a stabbing pain, and finally made it to the bathroom.

On my way back to the sofa, I stopped in front of the bedroom door. I almost raised my hand to tap on it, to ask Mackenzie if she was okay, but at the last second I decided not to. She was probably already asleep.

The bedroom was silent.

Chapter 12

When I awoke for the second time, the sun was up. My hangover was getting worse and the bright light wasn't helping. Also, I needed to pee. Again.

Leah was gone. She'd left her sweater behind on the chair. No one else was in the room. That's right; Steph had stormed out last night after their fight and Mackenzie was likely still conked out in the bedroom.

Not wanting to stay in a room that wasn't mine, I took my phone and key card—that were in the bar sink, for whatever reason—and made it to the hallway.

A pair of men in suits eyed me as I got onto the elevator, no doubt thinking I was a cheap prostitute or else on a regular walk of shame. I hadn't washed off my makeup from the night before. My eyes were smudged with bronze eyeliner, and my foundation had worn off, revealing my flaking acne. I could smell myself stinking up the cramped elevator—I reeked of night sweats, body odor, and a little bit of puke. Nothing was going to feel better than wiggling my way out of my dress and jumping under the covers in my un-slept-in bed.

When I returned to our suite, I saw Steph outside on the balcony. She was facing the glorious view of the sun rising over the mountains. Her feet were bare.

I opened the sliding glass door and was hit with the smell of cigarettes. Steph held one with one hand while her other arm was crossed over her stomach.

"Since when do you smoke?" I asked. Steph and I tried smoking once, out back of the high school cafeteria. We'd bummed a couple cigarettes from the acting club, who spent their time between rehearsals chain-smoking and singing showtunes. After a single drag, and hacking up half my lung, I vowed never to smoke again. Steph did the same.

She turned to face me. Her eye makeup looked worse than mine—it had bled down her cheeks and around her mouth. She had clearly been crying.

In the cold morning light, I saw the old Steph, the vulnerable Steph. The Steph behind the makeup and the hair extensions and the plastered grin.

I hugged her. She fell into my embrace, shaking with more tears.

"Why are you crying?" I asked. "Is this about you fighting with Mackenzie?"

"No." She pulled away and took a drag of her cigarette—no hacking or coughing this time. She must have taken up the habit at some point. Some point when we weren't friends.

Steph shook her head and turned away from me. I couldn't stand her cold shoulder.

"I know you're upset about something," I began, "and I want you to know you can tell me. Whatever it is. I won't judge."

"I . . . I can't," she said.

"If you think I'm going to leave you, I won't. Not again."

"You say that now, but you have no idea." Her voice was raspy and full of phlegm.

"Remember what you told me? Never hide the pain," I said, hoping the words would remind her of how close we had been. I tried reaching out to her to give her another hug, but she pulled away. She squished the cigarette into the metal railing and flicked it from the balcony onto the grassy area below. Then she moved past me and into her bedroom, closing the door behind her.

Everyone was in such an awful mood. If Steph wasn't going to talk to me, she and Mackenzie were going to have to work out their issues by themselves. I decided it was best to stay out of whatever drama was stirring. I couldn't even be sure of what I'd heard last night, anyway. Hell, I could have dreamt the entire thing. The more time that had elapsed, the fuzzier my recollection. I took a shower, chugged a bottle of water, and crawled into bed.

Not a minute later, Steph knocked on my door. She had changed her clothes and fixed her hair and makeup, all immaculate, as though she had never been distressed in the first place.

"Get up. The opening seminar with Dixie is in half an hour. My presentation is after that," she said. "I'm being honored as a top consultant."

She was back already—the picture-perfect, #bossbitch Steph. Where had my friend on the balcony gone?

△ △ △

After chugging two black coffees and downing three aspirin, I managed to rally enough to follow Steph into the large conference auditorium. We'd stopped at Mackenzie's suite on the way down, but she didn't answer our knock. "She must be there already," Steph said.

We took our seats just as the lights were dimmed. I welcomed the darkness and let my eyes close. Seconds later, techno music blasted over the speakers and multicolored lights flashed, jolting me from my momentary respite.

"Are you all ready to dance?! Everybody, get up and out of your seats, and let's get this party started!" an overly enthusiastic presenter screamed into his headset as he clapped his hands to the beat of the song that blared from the speakers.

My head throbbed. Shots of lightning pain burst in my skull. The speakers blasted sound directly into my eardrums. One more beat of the bass and my brain would melt out of my eyes.

"I don't feel well. I think I need to go back to our room," I told Steph. She clapped along and let out a "Woohoo!" when the emcee asked us to give a standing "Luminvation" to the next guest.

"You can't leave now. Look! Dixie's onstage."

Dixie waved at the crowd. Her wrists were stacked with pearl bracelets. She wore a long-sleeved blue dress that perfectly matched the stage lights. Her raspberry-colored lips were pulled back in a toothy smile.

"She looks like a clown," I whispered.

Steph put a finger to her lips.

Dixie walked from one side of the stage to the other as she spoke into her headset microphone. She retold her cancer story, pausing at certain moments to hold back tears.

"I'm at this company for a reason," she told the rapt crowd. "It wasn't chance. It was fate. I know every one of you are here for the same reason. Not by accident, but through God's will. You LuminUS ladies wanted to better yourselves through the power of LuminUS, and look at you now! You are my army of women!"

She threw her arms in the air and cheered as the techno music returned. The crowd roared as Dixie walked to the middle of the stage and sat in a stuffed black armchair across from the emcee, who was also seated, although his chair was smaller and lower to the ground. He drank from a LuminUS mug as he interviewed her.

The questions were bland, Dixie's answers rehearsed. Dixie emphasized LuminUS's record-breaking growth and how the company went from $100,000 in sales per month to $1 million in sales per month. The audience hooted and cheered at those numbers.

"We're the fastest growing direct sales company on the northeastern seaboard!" she said. More applause.

"Tell us, Dixie. What's on the horizon for the future of LuminUS?" the host asked.

"I'm glad you asked!" Dixie turned to face the crowd. "There's an electricity in this room. Can you all feel it?" She scanned the room and paused for effect.

The crowd erupted. Cell phones came out and flashed as photos and videos recorded. Bodies jumped up and down, shaking the floors. I heard someone behind me holler, "I feel it, Dixie! I feel it in my bones!"

"I asked, can you feel it?!" she cried.

The crowd cheered even louder. The woman who felt it in her bones let out a screech that would make a banshee faint. I felt something, but it wasn't electricity. It was nausea and a sore throat from burping stomach acid.

Dixie rose from her chair. She spread out her arms and proclaimed, "I'm thrilled to announce that LuminUS is launching a brand-new, all-natural, organic, GMO-free makeup line. As the first product in the line, I present the twenty-four-hour all-day-stay Hashtag No Filter foundation!"

A video played on the screen behind her. Soothing music served as the soundtrack to vials of foundation pouring the liquid onto soft, white flower petals. My stomach turned as the oily fluids oozed across the screen.

"LuminUS has been the number-one leading direct sales company in skincare and beauty supplements," the video's narrator said. "Now, we will become the leader in makeup. Beautify yourself inside and out. Long live LuminUS!" The screen turned black.

The room full of women, including Steph, responded with a chant: "Long live LuminUS! Long live LuminUS!"

From the side of the stage, someone pushed out a metal cart topped with a black cloth and rows of products. Dixie took one of the bottles of foundation and held it up to show the audience. "You are so fortunate to be the first to get a peek at these products! In the upcoming week, we'll be sending information packets to your emails, so keep your peepers peeled!"

The foundations ranged from chalk white to orangey but still white. So much for a shade range. No one minded. Cameras flashed and people applauded, loudly whispering to each other about what a thrilling opportunity it was and how blessed they felt.

"The fun doesn't stop here!" Dixie said, placing the bottle on the tray and prompting the crew member to wheel it off the stage. "I want to move on to our next segment, and, girls, it's one of my favorites. We call this portion 'Because of LuminUS.'" The lights dimmed except for the spotlight over Dixie.

"We're going to invite actual consultants onstage to speak about how LuminUS has impacted their lives. These are real stories, y'all. I get chills." She rubbed her arms and shivered. "Let's not waste any time and welcome our first speaker! She's Platinum level and has been with LuminUS for over two years. Her team sales have averaged $50,000 per month. Ladies, please welcome Steph Murphy!"

Steph shot up from her seat and began waving at the crowd as though she were a pageant queen riding a parade float. She walked past me, stepping on my foot, and joined Dixie onstage. They air kissed. Dixie mouthed something and Steph threw her head back in laughter. A microphone was handed to Steph, and she turned to face the audience. She thanked everyone, with a special shoutout to Dixie for allowing her the opportunity to share her story. After a brief re-hash of her background—two kids (#boymom), a husband, Platinum level, sales numbers—she began telling her story.

"I want to share something personal. Before I found LuminUS, I was lost. My husband's landscaping company was barely hanging on by a string. I wasn't sure how I was going to pay the bills or, much worse, feed my children."

I'd heard this story before. She shared it when I was hesitant about joining LuminUS.

"The energy in my home was tense. I was angry at the world for putting me in this position, and I took that anger out on my husband. He was angry that he couldn't be the man of the house and provide for his family. Ladies"—she paused to take a tremulous breath and give the crowd a slow scan—"we were this close to getting a divorce." Steph held her thumb and pointer finger together. Women hummed in sympathy. "My husband slept downstairs. We barely spoke, and when we did, we argued. I even set up a consultation with a divorce lawyer."

Dixie put her hand on her chest and motioned for the crew member to hand her a tissue box. I heard sniffles around me.

"But then, a miracle happened," Steph continued. "A good friend of mine, Leah Monroe, introduced me to a new skincare company called LuminUS. At first, I was scared to join. My family couldn't afford the start-up fee. What if I failed? How would I make it up to them? Leah assured me that whatever I put into the company I would get back tenfold. As you ladies know, the harder we work, the better our results."

I glanced around the auditorium, looking for Leah. It was too crowded and dark to tell if she was in the audience. I couldn't find Mackenzie either, although I spotted Bre near the back row. She saw me and waved. I waved back, wondering when she had arrived.

"I bit the bullet and said yes. And let me tell you all, it was the best decision of my life! In less than two months, I made enough to pay off, in full, both of my credit cards that I had maxed out. Two years later, I'm standing before you as a Platinum with a team of so many amazing women! Because I said yes. Because of LuminUS. And because of Dixie!"

Steph turned to give Dixie direct applause. The crowd joined in. Dixie took a bow from her seat and mouthed the words "Oh, stop" as she waved her hand.

What a spectacle, I thought. Any more bootlicking, and Dixie's head would puff to the size of a hot-air balloon.

Steph and I had lost touch, but I still knew her well enough to see behind the mask. Her expression was one of joy, but it was forced. If you listened hard enough, you could hear the shakiness in her voice. Not from nerves, but from trying too hard to sound believable.

And her marriage hadn't improved after LuminUS. It was worse than ever. Rob was still sleeping in the basement and spending late nights in the garage.

I knew that salesmanship was showy by nature, but this felt a step beyond—this felt dishonest. And the Steph I knew had always been honest to a fault.

△ △ △

Around noon, lunch was served in another conference room.

Steph didn't want to attend.

"None of the executives or top sellers go to the lunch. It's mostly a meet and greet for lower levels who had to pay for their ticket. They got catering from Panera, so we're not missing out on much," she said.

"I like Panera," I said. "They put avocado on their mac and cheese." My stomach was empty. I hadn't eaten breakfast because of how sick I felt, but my hangover was subsiding, and I was famished. My head still pounded. Even after the three aspirin.

"I brought more cottage cheese sandwiches," she said. "They're in our room fridge."

I wrinkled my nose and stuck out my tongue in disgust. Steph didn't notice.

"Are you having a good time?" she asked.

I wasn't.

"I think I'm going to go home early," I told her. LuminSANITY wasn't teaching me anything, and Steph was waffling between stand-offish and overly cheery, which I couldn't stand.

"What's wrong with you?" she asked, grabbing me by the shoulder and spinning me around.

"What's wrong with *you*?" I asked back. "One minute, you're crying in my arms, and the next, you're prancing around onstage kissing Dixie LaVey's ass."

Steph pulled me into a quiet corner in the lobby of the arena. "Keep your voice down," she whispered sharply. "Somebody might hear you."

"I don't care who hears me."

"Drew!" Steph scoffed, offended. "Don't you realize how important this conference is? The amount of content we can make from it alone is worth it."

"I'm not posting anything. Steph, to be honest, I don't know how comfortable I am with the whole selling thing." The more I listened to the speakers, the more ick I felt. I also wasn't sure how much I believed in the products. My face had backslid, looking worse than before I started using the supplements, and the moisturizer had given me a rash.

"That's another problem," Steph began, this time not pretending to be offended. "You're not engaging online. You've only posted one thing today and it was a repost of the photo I took. We're at Lumin-SANITY 2018! You should be taking pictures of everything. Don't you realize how many consultants would die to be here?"

Steph's eyes bulged from her head like a crazed frog. She gripped my shoulders tightly, her acrylic nails on the verge of cracking. "I can't lose my Platinum status," she said. "I *can't*."

"Isn't Leah your friend? And doesn't she have ties to Dixie? They wouldn't demote you. They said your team makes $50,000 a month."

"Leah and Dixie demand the absolute best from everyone. Besides, it's a numbers game. Even if they didn't want me to drop a level, if my team's sales numbers fall, so will I."

My resolve was softening, and she sensed it. Steph was legitimately worried. The levels didn't mean much to me, but they were important to her. "I don't understand why it's so important to you, but I'm on your side."

Steph let go and sighed. "I know you are, Drew. I know. You always have been." She frowned at the carpet, seemingly considering something. Finally, she lifted her head. "You know what, let's blow this conference off for a bit. Remember what we used to do when we were hungover?"

"We'd treat ourselves to a s'mores pie from Wawa."

"True. But instead of pie, let's make it bottomless mimosas. And instead of Wawa, let's walk to that cute restaurant across the street."

"Deal!"

Stephen put on her Celine sunglasses as we walked out of the hotel. I'd left mine behind, a twenty-dollar pair I had bought at Duane Reade, and had to use my hand to shield my eyes from the sun.

"I need to tell you something, Drew," Steph said quietly. "And I should have—"

She stopped midsentence as we were confronted with the scene on the hotel lawn. A group of police paced behind an area roped off with yellow ACTIVE CRIME SCENE: DO NOT CROSS tape.

"Active crime scene?" I asked. "What do you think happened?"

The police were joined by investigators clad head-to-toe in white jumpsuits, holding plastic evidence bags. A forensic photographer circled a patch of grass, taking flash photos despite the overhead sun.

"Drew," Steph said slowly and pointed upward. I followed her finger to a balcony. The doors were open, the curtains billowing out like sails of a ship. I knew that balcony. Only last night, I had been on that balcony, knocking back flutes of champagne, many of which were still propped against the railing, along with a blue LuminUS tumbler half full of Diet Coke.

Two officers stood on the balcony, conferring quietly, while another investigator took notes.

"Hold up, ladies," an officer bellowed, puffing out his bony chest as Steph and I approached the tape line. "This is an active crime scene. Please return to your rooms."

"Our friend is staying right up there," Steph protested, pointing at the balcony directly overhead. "Mackenzie Russo. Did something happen?"

The cop kept out his hand, but used his other to click on his shoulder speaker. "We have two women here who say they know the victim."

Crime scene? *Victim?* What was going on?

I crossed my arms tightly and tucked my hands under my elbows to keep from shaking.

"Wait right here," he told us.

Steph and I shared worried glances.

I craned my neck and stood on the tips of my toes to try to see over the sea of police. A camera clicked. Sounds of police radios mixed with low, serious mumblings.

Victim. Even thinking the word made the blood freeze in my veins. Maybe it was something mild. An injury. Something that could be solved with a quick hospital stay and plenty of rest and fluids.

Then why were there so many officers? And why were so many of them wearing purple rubber gloves?

I couldn't wait a moment longer. I pushed past the cop. "I'm press!" I called over my shoulder at his protests.

That's when I saw her: Blond hair soaked in blood and clinging to the sides of her face in wet crimson clumps. Her thin arms and legs twisted in impossible angles, bones breaking through her soft, tanned skin.

One eye stared at me—one blue eye that used to twinkle, its brightness dulled by the cloud of death.

Mackenzie.

Chapter 13

Mackenzie was gone. Poof. Now you see her, now you don't.

Just hours ago I had danced with her hip-to-hip, using a remote control as a microphone. Now she was dead.

I wasn't a stranger to death, but I had never experienced such a sudden loss. I had thought the three months it took for my mom to pass were cruel, but in a way, this was harsher. I was able to say good-bye to my mom. I didn't remember the last thing I said to Mackenzie, but I'm sure it was drunken nonsense. All I could think about were her husband and kids at home—Chase no doubt counting down the hours until she returned while he struggled to wrangle their three little girls on his own. He didn't know yet that those hours had just become an eternity.

After our cursory interview with the police, Leah joined Steph and me in our suite as we waited for the cops to finish wrapping up at the scene. I felt their investigation was barely a once-over, much less an episode of *CSI*. I tried questioning one of the detectives, asking about the details of the scene, but was met with resistance.

"Off the record, Ms. Cooper, this isn't a murder investigation," the detective said. "The cause of Ms. Russo's death was likely accidental. We see it all the time: A bunch of women on vacation get overexcited and drink too much. Then accidents happen. Toxicology will show she had enough alcohol in her to put down a Clydesdale. She probably went outside for a smoke and tumbled off her eleventh-floor balcony. You're not the first group of 'direct sales' women"—he made air quotes—"to go a little wild during their annual conference."

A freak accident had killed Mackenzie.

Or had it? Something about the scene gnawed at me, the conclusion sitting about as well as the black coffee and aspirin I'd had on an empty stomach that morning.

One technique I'd learned in my crime reporting class in grad school was to visualize the incident from beginning to end. The method was to find extra questions to ask, to find gaps that needed filling.

I imagined Mackenzie, wobbly from too many drinks, going out to the balcony for . . . for what? Why was she out there? She didn't smoke. It could have been to get some fresh air, but it got freezing cold in the Utah desert at night, and Mackenzie was so skinny she was always cold.

Gap number one.

If it was an accident, she would have had to get close enough to the banister to fall over it. But the banister was at least four feet high. Mackenzie was five three without heels. She was barefoot the entire night, as was her twisted body when I saw her. Even if she had put on her shoes on at some point—and they flew off during her long plunge—that would leave about a foot and a half of clearance. Hardly enough to fall off with ease, although I supposed it was possible.

Gap number two.

Was it a suicide? I thought of her disengagement in our Lumin-US meetings, her blasé attitude the previous night toward winning a brand-new car, her snippiness with Steph. She certainly could have been depressed. It would explain the fall, wrap up the incident with a neat bow—but I couldn't quite bring myself to believe it. She was a mother of three young girls, whom she doted on with endless amounts of love. Wouldn't she at least have left behind a note?

Gap three.

As the three of us sat around, lost in our individual thoughts, Leah broke the silence with about as much finesse as a meat cleaver.

"Would anyone like to pray?" She reached out, palms upward, but neither Steph nor I moved.

"I'm going to lie down," Steph sniffled. She threw off the pillow she was hugging and went to her bedroom, slamming the door behind her.

Leah's palms flopped to her sides.

I decided to take pity on her. She knew Mackenzie much better than I had. "I'm not a believer, but I can listen along if you'd like to say a few words."

Leah seized my hand. She held on like a vise, her skin clammy. She bowed her head and said, "Lord Jesus, peace I leave with you; my peace I give you. I do not give to you as the world gives. Do not let our hearts be troubled and let us not be afraid. Grant me peace and serenity to calm my troubled heart. And welcome Mackenzie into your kingdom. Amen." She gave my hand a final squeeze before letting out a sigh of relief and saying, "Thank you. I needed that."

Someone knocked on the door and I heard Bre's voice ask, "Steph? Drew? Anyone inside?" I let her in. Her eyes were red and puffy and startlingly small without her false eyelashes, like tiny blue beads. Bre rushed past me and clung to Leah like a lifeline, breaking down as Leah rubbed her back.

To my surprise, Jenny was standing behind Bre. "Can I come in too?" she asked, waiting at the open door. She looked pale, her eyes glassy, but she hadn't been crying.

"You're here," I said.

"Came in last night."

"What happened?"

"I slept in and missed my alarm. Guess I had too much wine and not enough Lean Cuisine." She rubbed the skin between her brows.

"Shit," I said. "Why didn't you join us at the party?"

"It was past midnight, and my motel is twenty minutes away."

"You're not staying here?"

"Are you writing a book?" Jenny snapped back.

"Sorry," I muttered, standing back to let her in. For a moment, I'd allowed the journalist in me to take control, forgetting that these were real people—mothers, sisters, daughters—and not an assignment I was working on.

Jenny joined us, but hung back from Leah and Bre, who was now lying down and crying into a pillow. She kept apologizing for missing her plane and repeating the line, "If I hadn't ended up in the ER, she might still be alive!"

Through her broken murmurings, I gathered that she had passed out at the gym the previous morning and missed her flight out—she had been dehydrated and needed to be hooked up to IV fluids for a few hours.

I bustled around, awkwardly offering water and snacks that no one touched. We didn't have long to console ourselves. Within minutes, the police arrived to take Bre and Jenny for their interviews, and Leah insisted she tag along.

When everyone had left, I went to Steph's door. It had been eerily quiet from her side of the suite.

I knocked gently. "Steph. It's me. Can I come in?"

She didn't respond, but I heard her blow her nose. Steph stayed in her room until the police showed up to tell us the interviews were concluded, and we were allowed to go home.

When Steph finally came out, her eyes were swollen and raw from crying.

All she said was, "I changed our flights for tonight. It's a red-eye. You can Venmo me the money later."

It cost $250 to pay for the difference in fares, plus a $75 change fee. Another hit to my credit card. No matter. I was anxious to get home and away from the hotel of death.

Steph remained silent on the car ride to the airport, the flight, and the drive to her house. I didn't press her, but I kept sneaking glances at her face—red and raw and covered in tear tracks.

A thought kept creeping into my mind—an awful, unwelcome thought. But I couldn't let it go. There was one more gap in the story:

What had Steph and Mackenzie fought about the night before her death?

GoFundMe Posted by Chase Russo

May 2018

Hi, my name is Chase Russo, Mackenzie's husband. On the morning of May 6, Mackenzie suffered a tragic accident. She left behind our three young daughters, Brynlee (6), Kinslee (5), and Hadlee (4). Our family is asking for any help and support you're able to provide to cover the costs of Mackenzie's funeral and some of our living expenses. We have a long journey of healing ahead of us.

Thank you all in advance for giving what you can.

$75 raised out of $10,000 goal

Post from Bre Santos's Instagram

May 2018

Hey, Girls!

My beautiful friend Mackenzie Russo became an angel this morning.

She was proud of her LuminUS business and her team of LuminUS Ladies. She leaves behind her husband Chase and 3 children: Brynlee, Hadlee, and Kinslee.

In her memory, I will be offering 20% off LuminUS's YouDewYou hydrating facial oil. Add radiance to dull skin with a few drops of YouDewYou featuring a mix of essential oils, vitamin E, and snail mucin.

Use coupon code GOODBUY at checkout or DM me for more information.

"They will soar on wings like eagles; they will run and not grow weary; they will walk and not be faint." Isaiah 40:31

#SheWillSoar #LuminUSLife

Chapter 14

Call it journalistic instinct. Call it an intuitive nature. Call it being nosy.

Whatever you call it, when we returned to Pinecrest, I was left with a nagging feeling about LuminUS. The police had been too quick to rule Mackenzie's death as an accident, never stopping to deeply investigate the scene. Had they, it would have been clear that Mackenzie didn't take an oopsie fall over the banister that was practically her height. If she had been pushed over the edge—as I was privately beginning to believe—the conference hotel full of LuminUS ladies were all suspects.

Plus, our team's sales numbers were off. I'd had questions about them before Mackenzie's death, but as soon as I got home to my little garage apartment, I started doing the math. Before the conference, Steph had forwarded everyone's sales numbers for that month so we could check how close we were to making our monthly quotas. Jenny and I were tied at the bottom, with my one sale pushing me out in front by a hair. My bonus gift had arrived while I was in Utah: a tube of LuminUS-branded SPF 15 lip balm with a note encouraging me to post about how "LuminUS sure knows how to spoil us." The tube was half melted. I tossed it in the trash.

Bre's numbers were as expected despite her constant hustling: enough to keep her an Emerald, but not enough for an upgrade. Leah's numbers weren't included, nor were any others in Steph's upline. Mackenzie's *were* included, but I couldn't figure out why. In fact, why had Mackenzie attended our meetings at all? She was Leah's direct downline, as was Steph. Mackenzie had her own downlines to lead, but wherever Steph went, Mackenzie followed. Was their friendship that close? Or did they have other common interests?

Likewise, it was Steph's and Mackenzie's sales that didn't make sense. The bulk of their earnings came from signing others to their downline. The rest came from the sales those women made, while personal sales accounted for hardly anything. The commission I'd earned from my one sale was a whopping $8.76. To make real money in LuminUS, you needed to sign on new distributors. But Steph and Mackenzie weren't pulling big enough numbers to warrant their lavish lifestyles. Steph had only signed two downlines in the past six months, and Mackenzie three. No matter which way I looked at it, I couldn't figure out how Steph made so much money or how Mackenzie had earned her car perk.

My phone pinged: a new post from Mackenzie Russo. My breath caught in my throat until I opened the app and saw that it had been posted by Chase to her account. He'd set up a GoFundMe page to raise money for the family.

Weren't the Russos supposed to be flush with LuminUS money? Why was Chase so desperate for $10,000?

I had to find out. I sent Chase a private message asking if he would meet with me to talk about Mackenzie. I didn't expect a reply. He had just lost his wife—tons of concerned friends and family were likely pushing themselves on him. The same had happened when my mom died: suddenly, every second and third cousin twice removed felt the need to drop by our house, deli platters in hand, even though my dad and I just wanted to be left alone. By the sixth salami and pickle tray, we'd started locking the door and pretending no one was home.

Chase felt differently. He messaged me back immediately.

CHASE

Come over tomorrow.

△ △ △

My mother taught me never to arrive at someone's home without a gift. I had been lax about this rule in the past, but felt I should bring *something* to the Russo household. My bank account wouldn't allow for anything extravagant. I thought flowers would be pointless, so I settled for a bag of Double Stuf Oreos and two cups of coffee.

Chase thanked me for the cookies, but immediately tossed them onto a side table next to a tower of mail. He did accept the large coffee and brought it outside to the porch.

"Do you mind if we sit outside?" he asked. "I've been trying to be out in the sun as much as possible."

It *was* a lovely morning. The clouds were wispy but shielded the sun enough to keep it from being scalding. In an hour, the humidity would spike, and the mosquitos would awake and begin their hunt, but at that moment, all was peaceful.

The last time I saw Chase was at Steph's party. Since then, he'd let his five o'clock shadow turn into a patchy beard. His fingernails were dirty, and he had black grease stains on his cargo shorts. I remembered Chase had worked as a mechanic in the Walmart auto department, although I thought he'd quit once Mackenzie joined LuminUS. She'd boasted about retiring her husband, allowing him more time at home with the kids.

"Your yard is beautiful," I said. The Russos' front yard was expertly landscaped. Plush hydrangea bushes in violets and blues outlined the porch, and an illuminated stone path snaked from the front of the home to the back pool area. "Did you use Rob's company?"

"I did. Mackenzie insisted. The grass is getting overgrown. I haven't had the time to mow the lawn."

"You do it yourself?" I asked. "Doesn't Rob's company come out once a week to maintain the area?"

What the hell were we talking about? I didn't want to talk about landscaping, I wanted to jump into the real reason I was there—the GoFundMe. But I also felt like a vulture for grilling this poor man in his moment of grief. I didn't know how to bring it up organically.

"He does," Chase admitted. "But I had to cancel the service. It was way too expensive, even with the family and friends discount," he said.

Jackpot.

"I saw your GoFundMe page," I said. "How is the fundraising going?" I knew it wasn't going well. He was only at $150 of the $10,000 goal.

"It's not going well," he said. "I don't blame anyone for not giving. If I saw a family like ours begging for money, I wouldn't give either."

"Why *do* you need the money?" I asked. "No offense, but I would kill to have what you have. I'm living in my friend's garage, and I'm not sure how I'm going to pay my phone bill this month."

"You're in LuminUS, right?" He turned his head toward me, slowly. Somewhere a dog barked, warning us of danger.

"I haven't been a distributor for long. But, yes. I am," I said.

He laughed. The sort of laugh that said, *Oh, you stupid, sweet summer child.*

What he actually said was, "You should quit. Right away. It's not good."

It was a thought I myself had been having lately. But I wanted to hear what he had to say.

"Why?" I asked.

Chase let out a deep sigh. He look a long swig of his coffee, as if for courage. "Mackenzie was such a positive person," he finally said. "When she told me about LuminUS, she was so excited. It's not cheap raising three kids on a mechanic's salary. Mackenzie wasn't working except for the dance lessons she taught part-time at the rec center. She had her degrees, but she'd left social work a few months earlier. She'd burned out. The long hours and low pay weren't worth all the time she missed out on with the kids. We were struggling."

Uh-oh, I thought. *Here it comes again.* I was beginning to see a pattern—the LuminUS family archetype: A suburban household with one working parent, typically the father, in a blue-collar, pennies-over-minimum-wage position. The wife—stay-at-home or part-time somewhere low-paying—is raising their plus or minus two children while worrying each day about how to pay the bills. How will she support her family, she wonders? How will she feed her kids? How did she get here?

Then LuminUS shows up like a magical beacon from the heavens promising a road to milk and honey and riches. All she must do is pay the one-time-only start-up fee, and then sit back and watch her account grow. The products are so good, they sell themselves! Only it didn't work out that way. Anything *that* good had to be too good to be true. I kicked myself for ever allowing myself to forget that.

As if reading my thoughts, Chase said, "I didn't think it was a great idea, but Mackenzie was insistent. At first, she wasn't making any money. It was supposed to be part-time work, but it turned into full-time, then nights and weekends. She was always on her computer or phone, doing those Live parties, or filling in spreadsheets. None of it made sense to me. I come from the school of 'you get paid for the work you put in.' Mackenzie would come back and tell me that she would be rewarded in the end. She promised if it got too much, she would quit."

"But she never quit," I said.

"She didn't." Chase took a sip of his coffee. A neighbor yelled at the barking dog. "Things got really bad. It must have been two or three months into her *business*." He said the word as if it were a curse. "I saw our finances. Mackenzie was always in charge of all that, but something told me I should log in to our accounts. She had drained them. We never had much to begin with, but we always paid off our cards and kept a low amount of debt. Not anymore."

"Let me guess," I cut in. "She had maxed out the cards."

"Yep. Each expense was LuminUS. Row after row of charges for LuminUS. Combined with her student loan debts, we were in hot water. Boiling."

"But it turned around for her, right? She moved up a level last month and earned the car perk. Last time we spoke about her progress, she said she had one of her best months yet."

"It turned around," Chase agreed. "When I found the credit card bills, I told her she had to quit. She refused. We made a deal. She would attend an upcoming sales conference, which cost a grand we didn't have, and if she came back and still wasn't making money, she would quit. No questions asked."

Chase looked out over his perfectly manicured lawn, a faraway look in his eyes. "She came back from Utah and was suddenly making sale after sale. It was wild. It was like we finally found the pot of gold at the end of the rainbow. Her commission checks were huge. At least

I thought they were."

A prickle ran up my arms. "What do you mean you *thought* they were?" I asked.

Chase ran his hand through his thick, wavy hair. Flakes of dandruff cascaded down. He clearly hadn't showered in a while—not that I blamed him. "What was I supposed to think? She told me we were flush, and I trusted her. She bought a new car, a bunch of designer bags, this house. I never saw the accounts myself. She'd changed the passwords and begged me to trust her to manage things responsibly from then on. It wasn't until after she died I found out the house is rented and the car's leased. We're deep in debt. I was a fool not to realize sooner."

Chase hung his head. He rubbed his hands together and cracked his knuckles. "It's what we fought about constantly," he said. "I wanted her to spend more time with me, the kids, but she was obsessed with LuminUS. The last time we spoke was a fight. I'd found box after box of unused products in her 'she shed.' Must be tens of thousands of dollars' worth of useless LuminUS crap. I told her she needed to start focusing on our family or else I would take the girls and move back to Virginia with my parents. Can you believe that? My last words to her were a threat that I was going to leave."

He put his head in his hands. I said nothing. I allowed him the time to feel what he needed to feel without any clichéd comforting lines like "She's up there listening. She knows how you feel about her."

"After all that, I'm on the hook for her funeral, too," he said. "That's another reason I started the fundraiser."

"It's awful how expensive funerals can be," I offered.

We sat in silence for a while, watching dusk fall over the lawn, fireflies sparking to life. Eventually he lifted his head, pointing his tired eyes toward the street. "I don't think she fell."

"Do you think she . . ." Killed herself? Was murdered? I didn't know what to say. I felt it wasn't an accident either, but I didn't want to put words in Chase's mouth.

"I don't know what I think." He paused for a moment, then stood abruptly. "I need to go shower and get ready for work. You really need to leave LuminUS. Something's wrong with that company. I can't explain it, but I know they killed her. One way or another."

Post from Bre Santos's Instagram

May 2018

I can't stop crying.

Everything reminds me of you.

The only way to calm these sore, puffy eyes is by using LuminUS's 24karat Gold Under Eye Patches. Use code MACKENZIE4EVER to save %15!

Also, forgot to post my outfit for my best friend's funeral.

Dress ☞ "Miranda" long-sleeved peasant dress, size XS

Jewelry ☞ Paula's Pearls, spring collection

Nails ☞ ColorCore polish in "Always Love Me"

Wanted to honor my best friend, Mackenzie. I'll always love you, boo!

#WishYouWereHere #Bummer #SadSelfie

Chapter 15

"I've been an absolute mess," Steph told me as we got in her car. The sky outside was blindingly blue, without a cloud to be seen. Birds flew by in groups, squawking at each other and spinning in the air, throwing their carefree nature in our faces. Such cheerful weather for such a depressing event.

"I can't imagine how you're feeling," I told her. Steph had been holed up in her room since the incident at the hotel. Since Mackenzie's death.

"I don't know how I'm going to get through today," she said as we pulled out of her driveway. "Seeing everyone is going to be . . ." She didn't finish.

I squeezed her shoulder as we drove to the cemetery. Mackenzie's family opted not to have a public church funeral, just a service at the burial site. Not that an open casket would have been an option. Getting her body from Utah to New Jersey was an ordeal. Utah was slow with the release paperwork, New Jersey was slow with the intake paperwork, and by the time her body arrived, it was in worse shape than ever. Cremation wasn't an option. Mackenzie had been opposed.

I hadn't been to a funeral or cemetery since my mom died. I didn't visit her plot. Maybe to onlookers, it made me a bad daughter, but I believed that if her spirit had lived on, it wasn't locked in a two-by-eight-foot plot at the Clearfield Community Cemetery.

Seeing the huddled mass of saddened faces surrounding a mound of pink lilies—Mackenzie's favorite—atop a raised casket sent my heart rate into overdrive. I wanted to run as far from the cemetery and the grieving people as possible. But I needed to be strong for Steph.

Family and friends read from the Bible as the priest prayed over Mackenzie's casket. No one read Mackenzie's favorite psalm about becoming a tribe. The closed coffin shone brilliantly under the noonday sun, and I couldn't stop myself from wondering what Mackenzie looked like beneath the mahogany lid.

My mom's funeral had been closed casket as well. No one wanted to see a hollow-cheeked skeletal body with cakey funeral makeup and a cheap wig. Just like no one wanted to see the pulpy remains of someone they needed to scrape off the cement. We wanted to remember our loved ones as they were when they were alive.

I held Steph's hand as she shivered with tears, but my eyes were fixed on Mackenzie's daughters. They wore matching black dresses with tulle around the sleeves and hems. The younger girls looked confused and bored. They didn't know what was happening—that their mother would never come home again. The older one stood stony-faced and rigid. She knew. As did I.

I knew too well what it was like to lose a mother. You lose a part of your soul. At least I got to have sixteen years with mine. Mackenzie's oldest daughter only had six.

Her tiny heart was broken, and now she was alone.

△△△

After the service, everyone piled back into their cars and drove in a procession to Leah's house. She'd offered to host the reception. I was a little surprised Chase had taken her up on it, considering his feelings about LuminUS, but I figured it was one less thing on his plate.

Steph immediately left me to go hit the bar. I milled about the main floor, which was crowded with people, mostly women Mackenzie's age. I recognized a few of them—LuminUS women I'd met at a party or the conference.

I spotted Jenny, leaning against an oak side table with a scowl on her face. We met eyes. I lifted my hand in a wave. She nodded perfunctorily and walked away. I followed her through the crowd. Another gap that needed to be filled was Jenny's late arrival at the conference—and whether she'd had time to sneak into Mackenzie's room without being noticed.

"How have you been?" I asked, cornering her beside a glass curio cabinet full of German porcelain figures. "I texted you a few times to see if you needed to talk. I tried finding you after you left our hotel room that morning."

"I packed up and left," Jenny said. "My mom called and said she was having another gout flare-up, so I went home. They told her to stop eating sugar, and that the bill would be in the mail."

"Why didn't you tell us? We could have flown back with you."

"Us?" Jenny said, her tone loaded with distaste. "You've been a part of the team for five seconds, and suddenly it's us versus me?"

"That's not what I meant," I said, trying to soothe. "We're on the same team here."

Jenny rolled up the sleeves of her dress, revealing her black tattoos and not caring who saw. "Aren't teammates supposed to support you? Where was my support when my hamster died? Or when my mom was hooked up to an IV bag for the second time this month? The only thing I got from my 'tribe' was an email from corporate about plans to expand into the Midwest. Yee-fucking-haw."

I bit my lip. I hadn't reached out either. Not as I should have.

Jenny wasn't finished. She was unloading her frustration, and I was the closest target. "I'm disappointed in you, Drew. I thought you were better than this white feminism bullshit."

"Whoa," I said. Jenny was hitting hard, and I wasn't prepared.

"Listen." She leaned in, whispering loud enough that I could hear. "I owe you one from when you stopped Mr. O'Brian from kicking me off the newspaper. So let me warn you. Be careful who you trust around here. Some of them are snakes. They're out to get you."

I was too stunned to respond. Jenny slid past the curio cabinet, bumping it with her hip and toppling a little boy dressed in lederhosen, and disappeared into the crowd.

Before I could gather my thoughts, Bre came up beside me and pulled me into her arms.

"I still can't believe it," she hiccupped. "I simply cannot believe it."

When she pulled away, I noticed her face and nearly gasped. "You, um, have some blood on your chin. Do you want a tissue?" I searched for a cocktail napkin as I checked my shoulder for bloodstains.

"Oh, this." She motioned to her face. "It's nothing. I just used a LuminUS chemical peel this morning. I'm trying to get rid of these dark spots from the tanning bed."

Bre's face was covered in red sores, some of which were oozing. She pulled a tissue out of her large tote bag and dabbed her forehead. "I'm still goopy. The peel also helps boost collagen production. Did you know we stop producing our own collagen when we turn twenty-five?"

"Aren't you twenty-six?" I asked.

"Don't remind me!" Bre said, putting the tissue back in her bag. "A whole year without producing my own collagen."

She was in surprisingly high spirits for a funeral reception. One for a supposed friend.

"You and Mackenzie were close, right?" I asked.

"We were like sisters," Bre said. "I don't know what I'm going to do without her."

I didn't want to doubt Bre's grief, but I couldn't help it. Instead of returning home on the first flight, like the rest of us did, Bre had stayed for the remainder of the conference. She also hadn't stopped posting online. Everyone else had taken a social media break, even Leah. Not Bre. Sure, her posts were more solemn than usual, at least the ones dedicated to Mackenzie. And she'd shared old photos of her and Mackenzie with the hashtag #HeavenHasANewAngle. But she found a way to shill LuminUS in every one of her posts.

Before I could ask any follow-up questions, Bre and I had to shuffle back as two women squeezed past us, their arms hooked together and heads hung low.

Bre leaned in to whisper into my ear. "See those two?" she asked, pointing at the pair as they wended their way through the crowd.

"What about them?"

"That's Linda Wagner and Taylor Bosly. Both Rubies. They were Platinums until Nicola Dale died. She was their team leader. I'm surprised they're here. Mackenzie used to talk shit about them because she introduced them to LuminUS, but they signed with Nicola. Nicola was always being shady like that. Swooping in on other people's leads."

"How did she die?" I asked.

Bre leaned in even closer. She was delighted to have gossip to share. "The obituary didn't say much, but *I* heard it was a drug overdose. And I bet she got Linda and Taylor hooked too. Look at them.

Twitching. If they're not on something, I'll eat my hat."

The two women stopped at the bar to refill their wineglasses. They were skeletal, their collarbones jutting from the low necks of their black dresses. I could see blue veins bulging from their shriveled hands. They moved with the speed and grace of someone walking through molasses. It certainly was possible they had addiction issues, but I thought it was just as likely they had eating disorders. Many of the women at the reception looked and moved the same: zombies with beachy waves.

"Are you sure they're on something?" I asked.

"For sure. This town has a huge drug problem. It started in Clearfield, and it's spreading to Pinecrest. Especially with the women. I guess drinking a bottle of wine each night stops being enough, so they turn to the harder stuff. There's an OD death nearly once a month."

Once a *month*? In a town of ten thousand at the most? I had become familiar with the Clearfield drug epidemic—and the national opioid problem—but this seemed excessive.

"You don't think . . ." I began.

Bre finished the thought for me. "That Mackenzie was high when she died? I do," Bre said. "It pains me to say it, and I don't have any proof, but I wouldn't be surprised. The last few months, she was acting weird."

"Weird how?"

"Losing a bunch of weight—more than usual—and exercising less. Every other night, she'd binge on drive-through burgers and was still dropping the pounds. And don't get me started on the mood swings. One day, she'd be bouncing off the walls and the next, she'd be in bed, unable to move."

"Sounds like mental illness. Combined with an eating disorder," I said.

"I thought that too. But to change so much in such a short period of time? And she was having money problems. She hid it well, but her cards were constantly being declined. Where was all that money going if not to a dealer?"

I considered this. It would certainly align with Chase's account of their financial problems. But something didn't add up. "At the party, the night we arrived at the conference, Leah offered Mackenzie an herbal supplement and she didn't take it," I said. "She said she didn't take anything but LuminUS. Not even aspirin if she could help it." If Mackenzie was an addict, why would she be so put off by a harmless herbal supplement?

Bre pursed her lips. "I'm still so bummed I missed that party. I should have never gotten in that ambulance. I only blacked out for, like, a second. The people at the gym overreacted big time."

I wanted to ask her about her fainting spell, but Bre waved at someone across the room. The woman saw Bre's bloody face and recoiled, but quickly recovered. "That's Debbie McBride. A Platinum. I need to say hi."

Bre left me, a lowly Silver, to speak with Debbie the Platinum. I didn't try to follow her. I needed to ask Leah a few questions.

As I searched the first floor for Leah, I wondered what I was doing—interrogating grieving women who lost a friend to a freak accident? But no—I corrected myself—I didn't believe it was an accident. Even if the rumors were true, and Mackenzie was using drugs, I didn't think she'd fallen off the balcony. And I couldn't help but feel like I wasn't getting the whole truth about LuminUS—not from Jenny, not from Bre, and not even from Steph.

Leah was in the kitchen, talking to a waiter. "I don't care if they're not eating any of this stuff, you still have to circulate instead of taking twenty-minute smoke breaks out back." She held out a tray full of puff pastries that she handed back to the waiter.

"Crab puff?" she asked as I came in. I nodded and took two. "I love organizing parties, but these are my least favorite."

"Have there been many funerals lately?" I asked through a mouthful of flaky pastry.

"Isn't one funeral one too many?" she asked with a sigh, briefly hunching her shoulders, and allowing herself to show how exhausted she really was. Catching herself, she straightened up and asked, "How's Steph? She hasn't answered my calls or messages, and I'm beginning to worry about her."

"Mackenzie's death is hitting her hard. She's shut off from everyone. I wouldn't take it personally."

Leah considered my words as she rearranged chocolate-covered strawberries. "I'm worried about her. Avoidance breeds contempt. Jenny did the same and now look at her. Sour-faced. Full of anger. That sort of negativity has no place here. It's bad for sales."

"What's going to happen to Mackenzie's customers? And her downline?" I couldn't believe Leah was worried about sales at a funeral reception, but I had to wonder if they were a potential motive—had someone killed Mackenzie for her downlines?

"You're forgetting her inventory," a man's voice interjected. Aaron stood next to his wife and put a hand on her lower back. "We've decided to buy it all, full price. Hopefully it will take some of the load off the family."

"Financially?" I asked.

"Nothing like that," Leah said with an awkward laugh. "Just want to save Chase the trouble." She nodded toward a staff member who was trying to get her attention. "If you'd excuse me, there's an antsy event planner who I must soothe. Feel free to take anything home," she offered.

I laughed along politely. I was searching the counter for a spare bag to stuff with uneaten hors d'oeuvres, wondering why Leah was so eager to skate over the Russos' financial troubles, when I noticed Aaron hadn't left with his wife. He took off his glasses and rubbed the lenses with a handkerchief he pulled from his back pocket. It matched the emerald silk of his tie.

"I've always thought it was a shame LuminUS is only for women," he said, blowing hot air onto his lenses. "With my years of business experience, I think I'd make an excellent independent consultant."

"Maybe you can call yourself a LuminUS lad," I joked. To my surprise, Aaron let out a deep laugh.

"You're funny," he said, "and you seem intelligent." Aaron crossed one ankle over the other and leaned against the counter. He wasn't tall, but he was trim, with a cyclist's build. His handsomeness was slightly offset by his large, froglike mouth. "Leah and I have been developing another business venture. One I'm sure you'd be interested in."

Another sales pitch. This time I was prepared, and it wasn't coming from a friend like Steph. I crossed my arms, my face turning stony.

Aaron sensed my tension. "Sorry, I didn't mean to come on so heavy." He chuckled. "Let me explain. We're not leaving LuminUS. We would never. It has provided us with too many blessings to count, and Dixie has become a close personal friend. Our newest venture is a personal passion project of mine. Wipr is an innovative company focused on natural cleaning products for the home. Plus, it incorporates tech with the iWipr app that sends you cleaning tips and reminds you to order refills for your Wipr products."

He could not have chosen a worse tree to bark up. The last household chore I'd done was vacuuming tuna salad hoagie crumbs off the floor because I found an ant. "Mr. Monroe—"

"Aaron. Please call me Aaron."

"*Aaron*, I appreciate the opportunity, but I can't start anything new right now. I've only been with LuminUS for a short time." And I was sucking at it. The only lead I had for signing someone into my downline, a distant cousin, had backed out. She had sent a one a.m. text telling me she couldn't join after all—"Sorry, need to bow out, bearded dragon got sick and vet bill's crazy expensive, but thx anyway"—before unfriending me on Facebook. She didn't have a bearded dragon.

"I completely understand," Aaron said. If he was dejected, he didn't show it. He reached into his front pocket and handed me a card. "I'll tell you what. I'll send you a free Wipr starter kit, valued at over $99. If you don't like the products, you don't have to join, but you get to keep the kit. I know that a strong, smart young woman like yourself would do exceptionally well at Wipr. And Leah would be your direct mentor. There's no one better at taking someone green and making them a boss. Look how well she did with Steph."

"Was Steph a bad seller at first?" I asked. Steph had mentioned Leah being the source of her success, but she'd never told me about any selling struggles. All I knew was that she became a top earner nearly out of the gate.

"She wasn't bad, necessarily. I would say she lacked confidence. She was unsure of her abilities. Much like you are now. She didn't see her potential."

"Can we go?" Steph appeared from behind me to tug on my dress, wiping her eye like a sleepy toddler. I could tell she'd had too many drinks too fast. She was having trouble balancing on her wedge heels. I let her lean against me so she wouldn't snap her ankles.

Aaron noticed her inebriation and said, "You have your hands full, so let's make a plan to discuss this later. How about this Tuesday? I'm free at either one or two. Your choice."

"Uh, two?"

Aaron patted me on the shoulder. Steph and I said our farewells and searched for her lost purse, which we found in one of the guest bathrooms. I was pouring Steph into the passenger seat when she asked, "Did Aaron try to sell you on that ass-wipe stuff?"

"Did you get the same song and dance?"

"Sure did. Free cleaner kit and caboodle." Steph was slurring her words. "God, Leah can be so annoying with her holier-than-thou attitude. I don't know how Aaron puts up with it. I have half a mind to tell Dixie about that Wipr business. If she knew Leah was dividing her time with another company, she'd be mega pissed."

"Don't do that until they've bought out Mackenzie's stock."

Steph reclined her seat and turned toward me, fighting with the seat belt. "I can't believe they're bragging about that. Did they mention they're absorbing her downline?"

"Why didn't they go to you?" I asked. Steph and Mackenzie were both in Leah's downline, but surely she could have a chance to take some of Mackenzie's clients.

"Because she offered them incentives. She's going to buy up Mackenzie's stock and give it to them for free." Steph gave up the fight with the belt and flopped her head toward the window.

"Then you should sweep in and buy the stock instead," I offered as I buckled her in.

Steph scoffed. "I can't. How am I supposed to compete with stupid Leah, our supreme leader?"

"I thought you loved Leah," I said. Steph had never uttered a single negative word about her before—the woman who, according to Aaron, was singlehandedly responsible for turning Steph into a Platinum.

Steph muttered a few incoherent words before pressing her face against the window and falling asleep. I drove the rest of the way home with one thought in mind:

I wasn't going to get straight answers out of anyone involved with LuminUS. I needed to widen the net.

Team Leah Monroe Group Chat

January 2018

Bre_Santos_♡

Hiya girls! I'm having some issues with a (hopefully ☝) new distributor. I was soooooooooo close to signing her onboard, but she's freaking out about the cost. ☹.

Leah_Monroe_💎

Have you told her about the savings? Tell her that even if she doesn't sell the product, she can use it herself. Buying a $1800 starter kit gets her $3000 worth of LuminUS. By joining, she's already saved $1200!

Krista_Lowry_🤍

Not to mention the distributor discount. 15% off, BABY!

Bre_Santos_♡

I said all that, but she's not budging 😕

Lilly_Farber_🖤

Anyone having issues with the under eye cream? Is it supposed to peel and burn this much?

Heather_Kelly_♡

Ask her how much she would be willing to pay for a business degree. Way more than $1800, right? LuminUS gives you all the tools and training that an MBA would. That's how Mackenzie got me to join.

Mackenzie_Russo_🤍

And I'm so THRILLED you did! 💕

Heather_Kelly_♡

Me too! Love ya! 😘

Lilly_Farber_🖤

Okay, but seriously, what about the scabs?

Mackenzie_Russo_🤍

Love ya, back! 😘

Chapter 16

The shower water scalded my skin, turning it pink as I scrubbed my face with bar soap. Beside me was a nearly full bottle of LuminUS's low pH daily cleanser, but it somehow made me drier than the soap. As I washed, I thought about what I'd learned at the funeral. Bre had mentioned an overdose a month, but an overdose death per month in a small town was odd. It wasn't just odd, it was worth investigating.

I rinsed and wrapped a towel around me, too eager to get on the computer to waste time putting on my pajamas. After Bre had ditched me to talk with Debbie the Platinum, I'd written the names she mentioned in my phone notepad app so I wouldn't forget: Nicola Dale, Linda Wagner, and Taylor Bosly. I would start with Nicola, the dead one.

As Bre had said, Nicola's obituary didn't mention an overdose, but did say that she "finally succumbed to a lifelong illness." A possible euphemism for a drug addiction, but lifelong? Unlikely, unless she was a toddler who enjoyed juice boxes, playing peek-a-boo, and railing lines of coke.

I checked Linda's and Taylor's profiles. Both were LuminUS distributors with carbon copy pages: edited photos, forced poses, and lengthy captions touting how #blessed and #grateful they were to be a part of the LuminUS family. Taylor had less engagement, so I focused on Linda. I scrolled to the date of Nicola's death. Like Bre had for Mackenzie, Linda had posted a collage of photos of her and Nicola together on trips, lunch dates, and girls' nights out. Unlike Bre and Mackenzie, Linda and Nicola's friendship went back to when they were girls—their bond seemed more genuine. Despite their closeness, Linda didn't hesitate to use the tragedy to sell more LuminUS, in nearly the same verbiage as Bre had used after Mackenzie's death.

I pulled up Bre's profile to compare her #grieving posts with Linda's. They weren't just similar—they were *identical*. Only the names of the deceased were different. A chill went down my spine.

When I returned home from Utah, I'd been bombarded with emails from LuminUS's corporate office. They had been notified of the accident and sent sympathy letters encouraging us to stay strong during this difficult time. After the fiftieth inspirational message paired with a fresh Bible quote ("If we live, we live for the Lord; and if we die, we die for the Lord," Romans 14:8), I trashed the emails. But the identical posts from Linda and Bre reminded me of one I'd deleted. I searched my trash folder and found it: "Your LuminUS Guide to Grieving."

The guide began with typical tips on how to deal with the loss of a loved one—seek out the comfort of family and friends, realize that emotions will come and go, understand that everyone has a unique journey through the grieving process, and so on. It was as generic as any of the lists I used to write for BuzzFeed, until the second part of the guide: "Coping the LuminUS Way." Apparently, the way to cope was to use the opportunity to sell, sell, sell! "As difficult as it may be, it's what your gone—but never forgotten—LuminUS Lady would have wanted." Then there was the script—the one we were supposed to post after the death of a fallen LuminUS lady, and the one that Linda and Bre had used, word for word:

Hey, Girls!

My beautiful friend [insert name of loved one here] became an angel this [morning, afternoon, or night] on [insert date of passing].

She was proud of her LuminUS business and her team of LuminUS Ladies. She leaves behind her [husband if married, pets if not], and [insert number] children: [insert names of children].

In her memory, I will be offering 20 percent off LuminUS's YouDewYou hydrating facial oil. Add radiance to dull skin with a few drops of YouDewYou featuring a mix of essential oils, vitamin E, and snail mucin.

Use coupon code GOODBUY at checkout or DM me for more information.

"They will soar on wings like eagles; they will run and not grow weary; they will walk and not be faint." Isaiah 40:31

#SheWillSoar #LuminUSLife

Besides the crassness, what bothered me was why the guide needed to be written in the first place. How many LuminUS ladies had to have died to warrant hiring a writer to draft the script and a graphic designer to lay out the guide, full of stock photos of expertly styled women with winged eyeliner glancing longingly out of rain-beaten windows? Wait. How many women had died?

I did a quick search of drug overdose deaths in Clearfield and Pinecrest. It yielded several articles about the uptick in drug usage in the areas, but those were about teenagers getting hooked on heroin. Tragic, yes, but not what I was searching for. Although it did prove that Bre's statistic of a death per month was slightly exaggerated, but not entirely incorrect. According to a report from the Department of Health and Safety, there had been 2,853 confirmed overdose deaths in New Jersey in the last year. One hundred fifty-five of these were in Clearfield County—nearly the same amount as in Bergen County, home of Hackensack and Rutherford, whose combined populations were eight times that of Clearfield County.

Why so many deaths in Clearfield? Those numbers were astronomical for such a small area. Why wasn't anyone reporting about this? This flew past epidemic and into crisis territory. I was about to close my tabs and finally get dressed when a comment on Linda's post caught my eye. Someone named JB Jankowski had posted a link to a Facebook group called "The Truth." The same JB Jankowski had posted links to Bre's and Taylor's pages as well. The group was private, so I couldn't see the posts, but the description read: "Exposing the dangers of the 'silver lotus company.' If you know, you know, but do you want to know the Truth?" It seemed like tinfoil hat material, but I hit JOIN after answering a screening question: "Would you recommend the 'silver lotus' supplements to a friend?"

I typed: "Nope."

Not two seconds later, my membership was approved.

Photo after photo of dead LuminUS ladies flooded my screen, each of whom was rumored to have died of an overdose. Between Clearfield and Pinecrest, there were at least a dozen of them. I plugged each name into my search bar. Unlike Nicola's, many of their obituaries and articles were open about the fact that the women had died of an accidental overdose. Even the ones that didn't failed to mention a single car accident or choking incident or any other freak event that had nothing to do with drugs. Clearfield wasn't the healthiest town on earth, but this was extreme.

Members of the Truth group agreed. They claimed the deaths were due to LuminUS products, which they continuously referred to as the "silver lotus company" to avoid a lawsuit. Their pinned post, next to a clip art photo of a red stop sign, read:

> We are a group of women focused on warning the public of the dangers of the silver lotus.
> If your health has been impacted by this company in some way, we offer a safe space to share your story! If you're still using these products, STOP NOW! It may not be too late. SILVER LOTUS KILLS!

The most recent post was an invite to a group meeting at the Wild Flour Café just outside of Clearfield. I RSVP'ed "Going" and texted my dad that I would be late to dinner at his new apartment.

I had to make a quick stop at the Wild Flour Café.

△ △ △

The Truth group met in a cozy room in the back of the café. A sign advertised poetry readings on Friday nights. Three people were in attendance, sitting on mismatched stuffed chairs. One of them stood in front of the group, holding a five-inch-thick purple binder with sticky notes and loose pages bursting from its sides. As I scanned the room, I noticed the women were dressed down and casual. These weren't current LuminUS distributors, and I wondered what had driven them to join the group.

Everyone eyed me as I sat in the back, no doubt wondering if I was an ally or a foe. According to their page, the group was frequently bombarded with threatening messages from LuminUS distributors claiming they were going to sue for defamation, so it made sense they were cautious around a new member.

One by one, the suspicious-eyed women looked away, as if having determined I wasn't a threat—probably because I didn't look like a LuminUS lady. I refused to bleach my hair or get the recommended extensions that cost almost a thousand dollars, and I wasn't wearing any makeup or designer clothes. My face had calmed down a bit from my latest eruption, but was still a far cry from the signature LuminUS glow.

"Thank you all for coming tonight," the woman in the front said. "For our new members"—she stared at me—"I'm JB Jankowski, the founder of the Truth group."

JB Jankowski was in her thirties, wore cat-eye glasses, and had a wild head of purple hair with black roots. She wore jeans and a loose-fitting green sweater that matched the green clover tattoo under her ear. I liked her immediately.

"Before we get on to new business, I'd like to share my story for anyone who isn't familiar." JB again focused on me. "Two years ago, I joined the 'silver lotus' after learning about the opportunity from someone I thought was an old friend. She reached out to me on social media after I posted about restarting my gym membership to lose the rest of my pregnancy weight. Six months later, I became seriously ill. I had lost my pregnancy weight, plus another fifteen pounds and chunks of my hair. My teeth became brittle and one of my molars cracked when I was eating a blueberry muffin. I knew something was wrong, but no doctor could tell me what it was. My friend encouraged me to keep taking more silver lotus products to deal with my issues, but the more I took, the worse I felt." The two women in the audience nodded along, as if they'd heard this story many times before but still found it captivating.

"When I ended up in the hospital, hooked up to a monitor and an IV, I knew I had to stop taking silver lotus. I weighed ninety pounds, was practically bald, and didn't have the energy to be awake more than half an hour. A week after I stopped taking the supplements, I immediately felt better. I've had a long road to recovery, but each day I'm not taking the vitamins is another day I feel like I'm getting back to my old self."

One of the women raised her hand. "Go ahead, Marjorie," JB said with a slight sigh.

Marjorie cleared her throat and sat up straight. "I read this article this morning about Lady Gaga drinking the blood of children to stay young. They call it adrenochrome harvesting. I'll bet you dollars to donuts that Dixie LaVey is doing the same thing and putting adrenal gland secretions into her serums!"

Marjorie's cheeks turned apple red as she spoke. She looked as though she was about to stand when JB chimed in firmly, "Thank you for sharing, Marjorie. I got that article you forwarded to me, and all the others, and will take them under consideration."

I recognized a brush-off when I saw it, but Marjorie gave a satisfied nod.

The other woman in the audience spoke up. She had a sandy blond bob and tortoiseshell eyeglasses. "There was a distributor death last week. Do you think it could be connected?"

I sat up straight. She was talking about Mackenzie. How did she know? They must have been keeping track of local distributors. Marjorie looked the type to spend evenings in front of a bulletin board with photographs connected by red string.

"Possibly. Although from what I heard, her death was an accident,"

JB said.

"She fell off a balcony," I interjected. Everyone paused and turned to look at me, somehow even more fascinated by the new girl than before.

"Did you know her?" JB asked.

"Kind of. She was on my team." I wasn't sure how much to divulge. So far, the Truthies hadn't shared anything of interest. I believed JB was sick, but there was nothing pointing to LuminUS except for anecdotal evidence.

"I'm sorry for your loss. I'm also sorry that I have to ask this, but did she look or act off before the accident?" JB asked.

I thought about what Bre had told me about Mackenzie's rapid weight loss, mood swings, and binge eating. She'd made no mention of hair loss or cracked teeth, but Mackenzie had a head full of extensions and veneers. There was no telling what was under those nylon blond strands.

"Not that I witnessed firsthand. Like I mentioned, I wasn't friends with her for very long," I said.

"Did they cremate the body? I'll bet you dollars to dumplings that Dixie took it to harvest her adrenal glands," Marjorie added.

I ignored her. So did JB. "Was she taking any silver lotus supplements?" JB asked. "BeautyBoost or SkeleSlim?"

"Probably. I saw her posting about them. And we're encouraged to buy and use our own products. Many of the women join because they're fans of LuminUS—"

"Silver lotus!" JB interrupted. "Sorry, they've threatened to sue for slander, so we have to be extra careful."

"They're fans of *silver lotus*," I corrected, "and want the distributor discount." I paused before adding, "Wait a second. What's wrong with BeautyBoost? I take those myself."

"You need to stop!" Marjorie shouted. I flinched.

JB sighed. "Marjorie is . . . *excited* . . . but she's correct. You should stop taking them right away," she said.

I wasn't convinced, and I was growing frustrated by the lack of cold hard facts—of real data. And Marjorie was clearly a nutbar. I needed to be sure that JB wasn't more of the same. "No offense, but you haven't given me any proof that they're harmful," I said, sitting back in my chair and crossing my arms.

"Tell me," JB began, "have you experienced any side effects? Weight loss, hair loss, bouts of mania?"

"No, no, and no," I said. I ran my tongue across my teeth to test their hardness.

"What about headaches?"

"I . . ." I thought about my throbbing head that had been getting worse since, well, since I started taking the supplements. I had chalked it up to drinking too much with Steph and being old enough that hangovers lasted more than one day, but I was up to six aspirin a day—extra strength. Every morning, I had to take two with my coffee.

My hesitation answered JB's question. "That's how it started for me too," JB said. "A nagging ache behind my eyeballs. Sometimes I'd wake up seeing spots that flashed with each throb. Eventually it spread to the back of my head and down my neck. I thought it was a sinus infection. Or allergies. But now I know it was the supplements. Once I stopped taking them, the pain disappeared."

Shit. JB had described my symptoms exactly, down to the achy eyeballs. I wasn't to the point of having pain in the back of my head, but that morning, I had woken seeing spots that flashed with the beat of my throbs like strobe lights at a nightclub.

Maybe there *was* truth in what she was saying.

"If you don't believe me," JB added, "take a closer look at the victims. Sixteen women dead since 2017. All from the area, all silver lotus distributors who openly took the supplements, and all ruled as overdoses. Except none of the women had a history of drug use. Not a single one."

"But would they have openly been using?" I asked. "Isn't drug addiction typically a secretive act?" I wasn't on JB's team, not completely, but I was getting close.

"True," JB agreed. "But you know that friend I mentioned? The one who got me into silver lotus in the first place? She was my best friend since childhood. She was staunchly sober. Not because she was in recovery, but because her father had died from cirrhosis of the liver from drinking, and she vowed never to touch the stuff, much less any drugs. The hardest thing I'd ever seen her take was a chewable daily vitamin."

I fought the urge to take notes on my phone. Information was coming at me at a rapid pace, and I needed to remember all of it.

JB continued. "After I was released from the hospital and began feeling better, I begged my friend to stop taking the supplements. She refused. No matter how much I pleaded with her, she wouldn't listen. A few weeks later, she died. Her heart burst while she was in the bathtub. Coroner ruled it an overdose. I knew it was bullshit. Laney didn't use drugs. Ever. She didn't OD. She was poisoned."

Marjorie nodded so hard, I thought her veiny neck would snap. She opened her mouth to say something, but JB cut her off before she could speak. "I know you're still on the fence. So here, take this." She handed me a sheet of paper with a list of names, dates, and causes of death. At the top, the title read VICTIMS. Mackenzie's name hadn't been added yet. "Take a look into the cases. We can't post every detail on the Facebook group because of liabilities."

I scanned the paper, reading name after name. "There are way more than sixteen women on here."

JB nodded knowingly. "Not everyone we're investigating was a distributor. Some were active product users. I have a feeling you'll be on our side soon enough."

After the meeting, I got into my car. The list beside me beckoned like a siren. *Read me read me read me!* I texted my dad that I had a mild fever and couldn't make it to dinner. Instead, I went home and busted open my laptop.

An hour into researching the first five victims, I stood up from the stool, took my bottle of supplements, and flushed them down the toilet.

Chapter 17

"Do you mind driving?" Steph asked me that morning, giving me her Mercedes keys. "I'm super tired and can't focus. Barely slept more than an hour."

I agreed and tried to make sense of the dashboard. Between the glowing blue lights and row after row of buttons, I felt like I was at the helm of a spaceship: the starship *Overpriced*.

I hadn't slept either, not for a few nights. After convincing myself there was something dangerous in the LuminUS supplements, and that I was about to have a brain aneurysm at any moment, I bought an online blood test kit. For $330, I could send in my sample and get results in less than a week. Since I didn't know specifically what I was testing for, I opted for the deluxe kit that included tests for heavy metals and toxins, and a full panel of drug tests.

Before pricking my finger with the lancet, I wondered if I should use someone else's blood—someone like Steph or Bre, whose bodies were saturated with years of LuminUS use. But both gave a resounding no, even after I framed it as an overall wellness check and not a toxicology survey. Bre claimed needles made her pass out, despite getting them stabbed into her actual face at her monthly microneedling sessions, and Steph ignored the text. Not wanting to wait any longer, I used my own sample, hoping the supplements had penetrated my system enough to show up on labs—but not enough to cause permanent damage.

"I'm tired too," I said in the middle of a yawn. We were on our way to Leah's house for a charity dinner. Seemed strange to have a party so soon after the funeral, but I supposed it was for charity, after all.

"Did you get that job at the *Boston Globe*?" she asked.

"The what? Oh, yeah that. No, I still haven't emailed them back. And it's the *Brooklyn Globe Online*." After the conference, I had received an interview request from an online newspaper. It was only an HR screening to make sure I wasn't a total weirdo, but weeks ago, I would have been elated. Now, as I sat in Steph's car, chewing the inside of my mouth, all I could think about was LuminUS.

Steph tucked a loose hair behind her ear. She had tried to dress up, but her usually effortless beauty seemed forced. Her hair was curled, but only in a few random places, as though she had given up halfway through. She smelled not of perfume but Febreze, and I wondered about the last time she showered. Mackenzie's death was crushing her, and she wasn't coping well. It wasn't the best time to talk to her about the Truth group and what I'd found in my searches, but I had to warn her against the supplements. I didn't want her to end up like JB's best friend.

"Are you still taking the BeautyBoost pills? Or the SkeleSlim powders?" I asked.

"Huh? Yeah, why wouldn't I?" Steph went to chew on a nail, but the tip was already chipped off. She chewed on her cuticle instead.

"I would stop taking them for a while. I was having these bad headaches until I stopped taking the BeautyBoost. Now they're gone." I was beginning to sound like JB, but it was true. The morning after flushing my pills, I awoke without a headache for the first time since I started taking them.

"Weird," Steph said. "Maybe you're allergic."

"Or maybe there's something in them that's unhealthy?" I chose my words carefully, not wanting to get her defenses up. But Steph just shrugged. It seemed she had totally lost interest in LuminUS lately. I didn't blame her.

As I drove us to Leah's house, I turned over everything I had learned the previous night in my mind. The list JB gave me had included the sixteen deceased LuminUS ladies as well as over twenty more women who were frequent buyers, specifically of BeautyBoost and SkeleSlim, LuminUS's top-selling products. Previous party streams and public posts were easy to find. Each of the users consistently spammed the distributors' posts: "Gimme gimme gimme!" They never missed a month to re-up their supply.

What hit me the hardest were the final posts on their pages, the ones shared by their husbands, letting the world know their wife had passed and would be missed by her family. These were raw sentiments, not sugar coated with a script or an airbrushed photo alongside a LuminUS product. Many posts included photos of the ones left behind: the children (mostly young), the pets, the parents, the sisters, the brothers. Now all alone.

I reached out to as many husbands I could find. Most had stopped using social media. Some were unwilling to engage, telling me in so many colorful words or by blocking me outright. One, Kurt Dale, husband of Nicola Dale, responded to my message with: "are you a reporter?"

I wasn't sure how to respond. I wasn't technically a reporter, but I was a journalist at heart. I also didn't want to scare him off. Figuring the truth would be best, I told him, "No. Just a concerned user of LuminUS."

He replied shortly after: "too bad. i want to get nicola's story out there. all they do is lie. nicola wasn't on drugs. it wasn't an OD."

I wasn't sure who "they" were. LuminUS? The police? But I knew I had to find out. I crafted my response more carefully than I ever did with any of the LuminUS scripts: "I'm not working for any media outlet now. But I've started to investigate Nicola's old company, and I believe there's something there. Any of your personal insights would help me immensely."

He didn't respond.

I called him. Not a single ring. He had blocked my number.

Fill in the gaps, I reminded myself.

The biggest gap was how the women had died. Obituaries and news articles weren't detailed enough. Linking the times and dates of death to the public police blotter netted numerous claims of "suspected overdose" and comments complaining about Clearfield's drug problem. If I was going to get real answers, I needed to contact the source.

I sent an email to the Clearfield coroner's office. Three minutes later, I received a canned reply: "We're sorry, sir or madam, but we cannot divulge protected information." I called and left a voicemail. This time, I didn't mention the story I was unofficially working on, just requested a call back. Might as well pull from the LuminUS handbook: "Get them on the line! Face-to-face is the best, but a phone call is better than a text. Hook them with the bait of unlimited potential and watch as you reel in catch after catch! You never know when you're going to pull in a whale!"

What stood out after an entire night of research was how much the dead women had changed after using the products. It was harder to tell with the distributors, underneath their loads of makeup and filters, but small changes became noticeable as I scrolled through months' worth of photos. Weight loss was openly flaunted. The minute a new bone became visible, a photo of it went online, along with a caption touting how well LuminUS was working.

With the users, the differences were alarming. They didn't have the same slew of editing tools, so when they showed off their "results," their gray tinge, yellowing eyes, and hanging skin were on full display.

I didn't have the details, but now I was sure something was wrong with these products. How—and *if*—it was connected to Mackenzie's death was still a giant question mark.

It took everything in me not to drive back to Steph's house and throw out all her pills and powders. But to convince her they were dangerous, I needed solid evidence.

△ △ △

Leah's charity dinner was held in her backyard, which had a pool along with a hot tub, pool house, and outdoor kitchen (complete with a gas oven and flat-screen television). Much like Steph's party, this one had bow-tie-clad caterers and tall standing tables, but this time draped in green tablecloths. I wondered if they used the same event planner. Unlike Steph's party, there was a live band, two open bars with bartenders, and a giant white screen playing a slideshow of photos from the Bread of Christ, the Monroes' charity. In the photos, Leah and Aaron smiled toothily as they posed with skinny brown children.

The vibe was livelier than Mackenzie's remembrance gathering, which made sense, and the budget—judging by the top-shelf alcohol and piles of food—was twice as high.

"Let's hit the bar," Steph said. She ordered a vodka martini—dry, no olives—and downed it on the spot so she could order another.

"Are you sure you don't want some food?" I suggested. "They have these flatbread wedges going around that look amazing. I think they're covered with onions and goat cheese."

"Gross," Steph said. She downed the other drink. "I hate goat cheese. But I love martinis. Let's get another."

I was still nursing my club soda and lime. "I don't think that's a good idea. You've already had two, and we just got here."

"That's rich coming from you," she said under her breath.

"I'm not judging you," I said, keeping my voice neutral. "I want to help."

Finally, Steph turned to face me. Her eyes filled with unshed tears. "I know you are. You've been there for me this whole time after Mackenzie. You're a good friend." Her words were shaky. She chewed her lower lip and frantically tapped the empty martini glass with her thumbnail. "Drew, I want to tell you something . . ."

We were interrupted by the band's playing coming to a halt. Leah spoke into a microphone. "Can y'all hear me?" she asked, standing in front of the screen, a spotlight shining upon her. "I would like to thank everyone for attending tonight's event, and I hope y'all brought your checkbooks! Especially you, Russell—I know you recently sold a condo building in Hackensack worth millions!"

The audience laughed. Russell waved to the crowd and mimed signing a big check.

"For those of you unaware of the Bread of Christ, we are a faith-based charity focused on feeding children in impoverished villages in Mexico."

Behind Leah, the screen showed photos of children grouped to-gether in dusty streets. Leah and Aaron stood among them, handing out metal plates full of rice and colorful vegetables. The houses were made of stones and chipping plaster. Chickens and skinny dogs ran in the streets. Pandering at its best. Each image was purposely staged for maximum effect. In the ones without the Monroes in the frame, the children had saddened faces with sunken eyes, tattered clothes, and bare feet. Once the Monroes entered the scene, the children's faces brightened into smiles, and magically, their clothes became newer, cleaner, and covered in embroidered flowers or sports emblems.

"My husband, the wonderful Reverend Aaron Monroe, and I *personally* visit these poor, *poor* villages at least twice per year to feed the hungry children, give them new clothing and toys, and spread the word of our lord and savior, Jesus Christ," Leah said. "As you all know, Aaron and I have recently founded Wipr, an exciting new business venture that will revolutionize the way women clean their houses! Tonight, not only will we be asking for donations, but you can also bid on a silent auction featuring Wipr gift sets curated by yours truly. Please take a moment to browse the items. Likewise, products are available directly for purchase!"

The spotlight turned to an area next to the pool house. Wide tables were placed side-by-side, covered in mint-green Wipr products. A single small, blue LuminUS basket filled with lotions and serums sat among the rest. The pool was filled with lotus-shaped candle holders that floated around and bumped into each other.

"Now let's get those donations flowing, y'all! And don't forget, we also take Visa, Mastercard, PayPal, and Venmo payments!" Leah clapped her hands in the air to applaud her own speech. The band returned to playing a jazzy cover of Hall and Oates and the crowd reluctantly shuffled toward the Wipr display.

"This is so fucking tacky," Steph said suddenly. "Mackenzie just died, and Leah's acting like a carnival barker." It was the second time

I'd heard her bash the queen bee.

"Are you going to tell Dixie about Leah's new business venture?" I asked.

"Why bother? If Leah's going to be people's direct mentor, the company's going to take off with or without my tattling. Say what you will about her tackiness, but the woman knows how to sell."

We both watched as Leah approached Aaron and the man he was speaking with. Aaron was about to pull out a Wipr business card when Leah firmly hooked her arm into his and motioned for a caterer to bring crostinis. As the man decided which crostini to choose, Leah whispered into her husband's ear. Aaron's smile quivered at the edges.

"Everything's about business with her," Steph said. "She's been riding me so hard to make my quotas and I can't deal with it right now. Not with everyone wanting to jump ship."

Was this directed at me? I had texted Steph about getting my money back if I left LuminUS. There was nothing about termination in any of the paperwork or on the website. People had to quit, right? Or was dying the only way out?

"When I asked about the return policy, I didn't mean I wanted out." I *eventually* wanted out, but for now I needed to stay in the mix to gather as much information as I could. But Steph didn't need to know that yet.

"No, not you," Steph said. "I know you're struggling with sales, and I haven't been a good mentor. I know you're not a natural salesperson. It's everyone else. My downline is shrinking. People are quitting and moving to different companies, and I'm sure to drop a level. Meanwhile, Leah won't shut up about buying more makeup starter kits, even as she's planning her own exit with Wipr."

I was about to press for details when I heard, "Ladies! Aren't you going to check out the silent auction?" Leah had found us.

"Sure thing. After I've had another martini," Steph said. She tapped on her empty glass.

"Feel free to bid on anything you like or, if you buy directly, my entire commission from the sales go to the Bread of Christ," Leah told us.

"Is it only Wipr stuff?" I asked.

"Of course! What else would it be? There is one package that's different, though. You might like it. It's a vacation."

"Oh?" A vacation sounded nice, although I hardly had the money to pay my phone bill, much less bid on a trip.

"A one-week opportunity to join Aaron and I on one of our mission trips to Mexico. All expenses paid except for airfare and meals," Leah told me. She noticed my disappointment. "If you don't win this trip, maybe you can join us another time. Dixie organizes a yearly pilgrimage to Cabo for a select group of ladies. I'm sure Steph can tell you more about it."

Steph wasn't paying attention. She ordered another drink, this time a glass of red wine. I was pleased she was moving away from the harder stuff until I watched her down a giant gulp and then throw back a shot of something amber.

Leah didn't notice. She flitted to another pair of women who, judging by their Birkin bags, were wealthier than Steph and I combined.

"Can you believe that shit?" Steph asked once Leah was out of earshot.

"What? The auction?" I asked.

"No, the 'pilgrimage to Cabo,'" she sarcastically mimicked Leah. "You know what that is, don't you?"

I didn't. "An excuse to lie around on the beach and pig out on all-inclusive buffets?"

"It's a cosmetic surgery trip." She hiccupped as she spoke. "They get cheap lipo over the border and spend the week drinking fruit juices and shitting themselves in their adult diapers. That's what all this is." She waved at the party, but threw herself off balance and nearly fell over. "It's a sham. A dirty diaper. Leah calls them mission trips, but it's a cover-up for getting work done. Why else does she always come back with lifted brows or a skinnier nose? It sure as hell isn't from doing God's word feeding the hungry 'bambinos,' as she calls them."

I held her upright. Steph was going off on a drunken, angry tangent. I wasn't thrilled that she was drinking enough to put down an elephant, but I was thrilled she was finally unloading. Steph had been a knotted ball of tension—she needed to let it out or else it would fester like a rotting wound. I needed to get her home and into bed. I planned to sit with her, make her drink water, and talk. Her house was a safe space for her to vent. A fancy dinner party filled with Pinecrest's finest was not.

As I pried her half-full glass of wine away from her, I heard a crash. Glass broke somewhere near the silent auction. I thought a server had accidentally dropped a tray of champagne flutes—until I heard the screaming.

"This is all your fault!" a high-pitched voice hollered. Then the sound of more glass breaking. The crowd fanned outward from the auction tables. "I hope you burn in hell, you evil bitch!"

I moved closer to the auction area and squeezed myself in between two suited men until I could see clearly.

I recognized the angry shouter. It was Jenny.

She looked crazed. Her hair was cropped short, showing patches of scalp between black tufts of hair, while her clothes—pajamas by the looks of it—were stained with smears of bright orange cheese dust. The right side of her face drooped downward like melted wax. I hoped she wasn't having a stroke.

Jenny tore through the auction table, sending bottle after bottle crashing to the ground with wide swings of her arms.

"Calm down!" Leah shouted, hurrying over to the scene. "Stop it this instant, Jenny! Security!"

"You bitch! I hate you!" screamed Jenny. From the gift basket of LuminUS she grabbed a bottle of YouDewYou daily moisturizer, full sized, and hurled it at Leah, who held up her arms to protect her face. It hit her wrist and bounced off before exploding into a white, gooey mess on the patio. Then Jenny picked up the YouDewYou morning facial serum and pelted it at Leah. It hit her directly in the forehead, making a sickening thud against her skull. The bottle didn't shatter this time, but clattered to the ground and rolled into the pool.

"Stop! Where the hell is security?!" Leah screamed, pressing both hands to her injured forehead.

A tall man wearing black grabbed Jenny from behind as she wound up to throw another bottle at Leah. She wriggled and kicked, trying to fight her way out of his grip, but he was three times her size. There was no way she was getting free.

Realizing she was outmatched, Jenny went limp and continued screaming while he dragged her away from the crowd. "This is all your fault!" she told Leah, only one side of her mouth moving. The other side drooled spit. "You did this to me! You ruined me!"

Once Jenny was removed, Leah was tended to by a group of guests who were suddenly brave enough to approach now that the threat was neutralized. She was visibly shaken, but tried to laugh it off to save the party. A golf-ball-size welt sprouted from her forehead.

"I guess the auction wasn't so silent, after all," she joked.

Steph watched, her mouth hanging open in an O, struggling to stay balanced on her heels and clearly trying to make sense of what just happened. I was sober and still couldn't imagine what had driven Jenny into such a frenzy. She wasn't angry, she was enraged—I had never seen someone that furious. Without intervention, how far would she have gone to hurt Leah?

I led a wobbly Steph inside the house where I put her on a Victorian fainting couch and handed her a glass of water.

"Drink this whole thing," I ordered her. "And stay the hell away from the bar."

I found Jenny in the formal dining room. She sat on a chair, arms crossed, while the giant security guard pointed a finger at her. "Get your stuff and go. You're lucky the Monroes don't want to press charges."

"You know what? Fuck you too!" Jenny said.

He moved back as Jenny stood to leave, but not without a final word. "If Mrs. Monroe wants you charged, I'll find you!"

"Find this!" Jenny said while giving him the finger. She walked out the front door, and I hurried to follow her. She strode down the sidewalk, seemingly without a destination in mind.

When I caught up to her, I cut to the chase. "Okay, spill. What was that about?" I panted.

"Leah deserved it. She ruined my life."

"I heard you say that to her. But *how* did she ruin your life? Is it about your face? Or your hair? Do you need to go to the hospital or something?"

"This?" Jenny gestured to the limp side of her face. "This is just the icing on the crap cake. It's Botox from the medspa Leah shoved on everybody. They hit the wrong nerves and now I have to wait three months for this toxin to wear off."

"That sounds terrible," I said.

"It is, but that's not why I hate Leah. Well, it's not the only reason."

Jenny stopped to inspect her reflection in the window of a car parked on the street. "Jesus, I look awful." She touched one of the bare spots on her scalp. "My hair's fried from bleaching. It's been falling off in clumps. I've been wearing wigs, but my doctor said it's suffocating my scalp and causing more to fall out."

Jenny's hair didn't look like a casualty of too much peroxide to me—there were no sores or red spots, only quarter-size patches of porcelain-white scalp. "What else did Leah do?" I asked.

Jenny abruptly sank down onto the curb, putting her head in her hands. "She's why I'm broke. I lost everything. My bank accounts are empty and what little I had in savings is gone. My credit cards are maxed, and I had to put a second mortgage on my house and now I can't begin to pay it off. My husband found out, and he's leaving me."

"I didn't know you were married," I said. None of Jenny's social media posts mentioned a husband.

"I don't post about him. He likes his privacy. Plus we've been fighting nonstop since I joined LuminUS."

As gently as I could, I said, "I still don't understand how this is Leah's fault."

"Don't you get it, Drew?" Jenny spat. "LuminUS is a scam and Leah's the ringleader—she's the one who recruited me and handed me off to Steph to pad her downline numbers. Leah promised me I would make so much money. I'm sure you noticed that Clearfield isn't exactly rife with jobs. I didn't go to college. Leah promised LuminUS would change my life and that we could afford to pay off the house and go on a vacation. She promised it was guaranteed. It sounded so nice. For once, I wanted to walk into a grocery store and shop without finding the lowest cost per unit price on every item, ya know?"

"Trust me. I know," I said.

"Leah didn't care that I wasn't making money. She didn't care about the debt I was drowning under. She kept pushing me to buy and sell more and more. When I wasn't selling, she wanted me to buy. 'You need inventory,' she said. 'Clients want to see that you have every product available and then some.'"

"I thought we weren't supposed to have a bunch of stock," I said, remembering a training video Steph sent me. The presenter recommended we keep our inventory digital since most of our clients purchased online, framing it as another one of the perks of joining LuminUS.

"Sure, that's what they tell you to get you in. 'It's a one-time fee, you don't need to buy your own products, all selling is done through social media,' yada yada. Lies upon lies. Once they know you're struggling, they want to bring in money even if it means the consultants are buying thousands' worth of junk they'll never use. Leah got a commission each time I bought anything."

"How much have you spent?" I asked, thinking about my own ballooning credit card bill.

"Besides the outrageous start-up fee?" Jenny said. "Tens of thousands."

Tens of thousands! My knees went weak. I sat down beside her with a thump. Jenny was a smart woman. She would have graduated with honors if not for those pesky dress code violations. And she had common sense. She could sniff out a bullshitter a mile away.

How did she end up here? And as I studied the profile of her drooping, drooling face, I couldn't help but wonder—was she angry enough to kill?

From "At the Bottom of the Pyramid: Stories from Ex-LuminUS Distributors"

First published in *New York* magazine

"What I hate most about having been a part of LuminUS is that people think I'm dumb. I'm not dumb. I have a law degree. I passed the New Jersey bar on my first try. I trusted the woman who recruited me. I believed everything she said. Wouldn't *you* trust your own sister?

"If you think you're too clever to be conned by a MLM, you're not. This was me and this very well could have been you."

—Anonymous, active in LuminUS 2016–2018, Gold level

"I want people to recognize the warning signs that are so obvious in hindsight. Everyone wants to hear that they'll get rich quick, but LuminUS never told us how we would go about doing it. They would say vague stuff like 'this is a once-in-a-lifetime opportunity, and if you sleep on it, someone else will get the chance.' They wanted you to feel pressured to say yes. As though you were winning something big and important.

"I quit within two months. My friends weren't as lucky."

—Emma Goodman, active in LuminUS 2018, Silver level

Chapter 18

Steph was too drunk to put herself to bed. Her bedroom was nearly as disorganized as mine. Heaps of dirty laundry were scattered in piles along the floor, and her side table was filled with half-empty diet soda cans.

She didn't remember much from the dinner party. I tried talking with her as I wrestled her out of her party dress and into her PJs, but she was fading in and out of consciousness. Each time I tried to mention the incident at the party or what I'd learned from Jenny, she groaned and writhed under the comforter. Eventually I gave up, planning to entice her the next morning with strong black coffee and a box of chocolate croissants.

"I'll see you tomorrow," I told her as I shut off the lights.

"Mackenzie?" she asked in a dreamy voice.

"No, it's Drew."

"Mackenzie? I'm so sorry. Please forgive me," she whimpered.

A chill went down my spine. "Sorry for what?" I asked, holding my breath for the answer.

"I'm so . . ." She began snoring.

I poked her, but she didn't wake. My finger hit a rib bone. She was getting so thin; I'd hardly seen Steph eat anything since Mackenzie's death. Her calories came from cabernet sauvignon and the occasional tumbler of straight whiskey. I eyed a bottle of BeautyBoost on her bedside table. The supplements couldn't be helping. I quietly stuffed the bottle in my pocket to throw out later.

I walked up the stairs to my apartment, eyeing the blacked-out garage windows on my way. There had been more loud crashes the other night. *Typical man*, I thought angrily—Rob would be rather be tinkering with his precious car than spending time with his depressed wife. He and Steph seemed more distant than ever.

I sat down on the couch to browse the binder JB from the Truth group had given me. Even though I'd pored over it twice, there was always another tidbit to discover; another question that didn't have answers. Questions like: What was in LuminUS's proprietary blends and why didn't they list each ingredient? JB had emailed each executive, asking them to send her an itemized list of ingredients, but received more canned responses: "LuminUS reserves the right to not disclose all ingredients for its products. According to the Fair Packaging and Labeling Act of 1996, no labels shall be deemed to require that any trade secret be divulged (FPLA, section 1454(c)(3))."

I was searching for the Fair Packaging and Labeling Act online when a notification popped up on my screen. The Russos' GoFundMe was ending soon, and they were far from their goal. Chase had sent out another plea:

"Please know that every dollar counts and will contribute greatly to covering Mackenzie's funeral expenses and to helping our family at this difficult time."

Out of the $10,000 goal, Chase had raised $1,150. I doubted he would reach his goal. Who would want to give money to a family who rode around in Benzes and flaunted the condo they rented on the Sea Isle City beach? No one knew about the debt Mackenzie left behind.

Through the open window, I heard Rob muttering angrily to himself as he hunched over the open hood of a riding mower. Fueled by frustration, I marched outside, ready to confront him about his midnight mechanic sessions when he raised his head with a hangdog expression. No matter how heated I was, I was weak to that expression; as if the weight of the entire world was crushing him and only getting heavier by the day. Chase had the same look. So did my dad.

"Broken mower?" I asked. "Can it be salvaged?" I leaned to look under the hood, mostly for solidarity with Rob, since I couldn't tell a valve from a sprocket.

"It better be, because I sure as hell can't afford a new one."

"Must be hard now that Steph isn't devoting as much time to LuminUS," I probed. Steph had missed all of her scheduled Facebook Live parties.

Rob pulled a grease-stained rag from his back pocket and wiped his hands. "I guess you could say that," he said with a sour expression.

"Have you seen her today?"

"I check in on her every hour. She barely wants to talk. I need to force her to eat and drink. She refuses to let me sleep in bed with her. I'm really worried about her, Drew. Has she said anything to you?" Rob looked at me with pleading eyes.

I had nothing. "No. I was hoping you'd know more."

Rob groaned and shut the hood of his mower. It slammed harder than he expected, and we both jumped at the sound before laughing at our reactions. "Remember that haunted house we went to?" he asked.

"You mean Eastern State Penitentiary? How could I forget?" Our senior year, the three of us made a trip to attend the haunted attraction hosted at a historical prison despite Steph's numerous attempts to turn the car around.

"Steph was so scared she didn't open her eyes from the ticket booth until we were back at the parking lot." Rob chuckled. "Someone shook a can full of pennies near her ear and she grabbed me so hard, I had puncture wounds from her nails."

"Do you remember how we tormented her on the car ride home?"

Rob laughed. "You mean when I kept pretending the car was stalling on its own?"

"And how I kept saying I thought I saw a woman dressed in all white floating between the trees?"

When our shared laughter died down, Rob heaved a deep sigh and said, "We had some good times, didn't we?"

"We did." Thinking back, when it was the three of us, there *were* good times. Rob had been a perfect boyfriend to Steph. My issue with him began after the proposal, and I could see how Steph's misery was affecting him. Despite their problems, I could tell he loved her as much as I did. "Rob," I began, "I think I misjudged you and the situation years ago."

He put up a blackened hand. "Stop. No need. We should focus on Steph. If the two of us work together, I think we can help her."

"I didn't realize how close she was to Mackenzie. Her death has wrecked her."

"They were close enough, but I wouldn't call them best friends."

I thought about the times they snuck off together for whispered exchanges and how Bre seethed with jealousy each time she wasn't included. "They spoke everyday," I said.

"Only about LuminUS." Rob kicked the mower's tire as if he was imagining Dixie's face on it.

"Not a fan?"

"Of that cult? No, I'm not," he said, wiping the bottom of his boot on the grass.

"Chase isn't either. He told me to quit."

"You're still in LuminUS? Why haven't you left?"

My mouth opened and closed like a trout out of water. "I . . . uh," I stumbled. The reason I hadn't quit was to keep myself connected to the company so I could keep tabs. I'd learned what happened to distributors who'd left thanks to reading the chat boards going back years. If you left LuminUS, no matter the reason, you were blacklisted: deleted from groups, socials, message boards. Others still on the team were warned not to interact with the deserter. I needed to maintain the illusion of loyalty, or my investigation was dead in the water.

"Doesn't matter," Rob said. "I'm trying to get Steph out as soon as possible, and I suggest you do the same. Steph's not honest with me. I don't know the full extent of it, but I know she's in trouble. *We're* in trouble." We both stared at our feet until Rob muttered to himself, "If only she hadn't gone to that damn conference."

"Then she wouldn't have seen Mackenzie die."

"No, that's not it. The other one. The first conference." He inhaled deeply, held it for a moment, then said, "Leah signed her up for the event shortly after Steph started. She told her it would be a life-changing opportunity that couldn't be missed despite the thousands it would cost. When Steph came back, she was different."

"How so?"

"That's when the money started flowing in," Rob said bitterly. "I should have been happy. Steph *seemed* happy, but she was—almost manic. More stressed out than ever, and spending more and more time with LuminUS and less with our family. It's changed her, the success. I don't think it's worth it. We'd have to downgrade our lifestyle if she quit, but the landscaping business has ticked up enough that we could make ends meet. But every time I suggest it, she goes into hysterics. Our priorities are just . . . different now. I miss the old Steph."

I nodded in silent agreement.

Rob looked up and gave me a forced smile, his eyes pinched. "Sorry to dump all this on you. I'm gonna go check on her." He tossed his rag onto the pavement before heading back into the house.

Rob's story was eerily similar to the one Chase had told me about Mackenzie: struggling with sales, being lured by Leah to an out-of-state conference, and then coming back changed like the transformation scene in *The Stepford Wives*.

It made me wonder: *What exactly happened at that conference?*

△ △ △

My apartment was as messy as Steph's room. I felt awkward using Steph's washer and drier, so I hand-washed my dirty clothes and hung them to dry over doors and curtain rods. I had planned to roll right into bed, but Rob's warnings twirled in my mind. They reminded me of what Chase had told me.

You really need to leave LuminUS.

I know they killed her.

There *was* something wrong with LuminUS. Something sinister. I knew it from the start, but didn't follow my gut. The glamorous women with glass skin and promises of riches swept me away despite my better judgment. I was ashamed. Embarrassed. Twelve years living in New York City, and I couldn't tell snake oil from essential oil.

No. I couldn't be hard on myself. Not now. I needed to find out exactly what LuminUS was doing. Between the Truth group's claims, the dead women, and both Chase and Jenny claiming they were broke, there was too much to unpack to make clear sense of it all.

One thing was definite: I needed to let Steph know. I couldn't wait for her to feel better to spill the beans. She could hide in bed all she wanted, but it was time I got both myself and her out of LuminUS. Before it was too late. Before she became another name in the Truth group's list of victims.

I walked down the apartment stairs as my brain whirled with thoughts.

Wait a minute, I thought, stopping on the last step.

Something else Chase had said just hit me: "*I'd found box after box of unused products in her 'she shed.'*" Thousands of dollars' worth.

My gaze travelled to the red riding mower in the driveway, a giant red flag that I hadn't noticed waving until just now. I was such an idiot. Rob was working on the mower outside because the garage was full—and not with a classic car.

He had gone inside to check on Steph. The boys were asleep at this hour. I was alone, but I had to act fast.

There was no way I was strong enough to pry open the garage door, and I didn't know where they kept the door remote. The small windows above it were sealed shut, but I climbed onto a planter and gave one a hard push to see if it would budge. It didn't.

Going back upstairs, I grabbed a butter knife, then ran down to shove it into the space between the window frame and the sill. I tried prying it open, using my weight to push the knife down. That didn't work either. I tossed the bent knife into the grass and looked around. A pile of garden stones were stacked against the bottom of the steps like a makeshift cairn—leftovers from one of Rob's recent jobs.

Screw this, I thought. It was too late to play nice. I grabbed the biggest stone I could find, the size of an oblong softball, and smashed it through the window. The sound of shattering glass broke the silence of the summer evening, and I whipped my head around to see if anyone was stirring in the main home.

I waited a minute. There wasn't a peep from the Murphy household, so I turned my attention to the shattered window. Remnants of glass jutted from the frame, sticking out like angry teeth that would cut right through my tender skin. I was wearing a tank top that liked to ride up—it would be a massacre. I used another rock to break away the shards, careful to leave no piece behind.

Satisfied that I'd cleared all of the broken glass away, I lifted my arms in a diving pose and stuffed my body through. The window was narrow. My hips got stuck in the frame and I hung there, half in and half out, worrying that Rob would find me stuck like Winnie the Pooh in Rabbit's house. But with a final wiggle, I slipped through, falling elbow-first onto what felt like a bed of cardboard boxes. I breathed a sigh of relief that I hadn't been deposited directly onto the concrete floor.

I tried to stand, but lost purchase on the uneven surface and fell backward, slamming my elbow into something hard. "Ouch!" I hissed, rubbing my sore bone. I flexed my arm a few times to make sure nothing was broken before getting back on my feet.

The room was dark. Even with the outside floodlight coming in through the newly broken window, I could only see clouds of dust. But before I took out my phone, before I turned on my flashlight, I knew I wouldn't find a car.

When I finally lit up the space, I was face-to-face with towers of blue boxes. The walls were lined with boxes by the hundreds—no, thousands—a colosseum devoted to LuminUS. They were even tucked into the ceiling rafters. I couldn't see the floor at all—any empty space had been stuffed with a blue LuminUS box.

For a moment, I told myself they were empty. Maybe Steph saved the boxes, and these were all leftover storage from sold products. Maybe this was all a misunderstanding, and I was jumping to conclusions.

Maybe the moon was made of green cheese and Leah Monroe was a natural blond.

I reached for the closest box. It was too heavy to move, so I opened the top instead. As I feared, it was packed with LuminUS's CleanMe foaming, pore-purging cleanser. It was $37 per bottle, $33 using our distributor discount.

I didn't need to search the other boxes. I knew they were filled with the same LuminUS crap, as Chase had put it.

What had Steph gotten herself into?

What had she gotten *me* into?

Many of the boxes had been there for months, if not years, judging by the layers of dust. Steph must have known what a sham LuminUS was before she recruited me.

I was so frustrated, I nearly screamed.

Best friend or not, I was going to kill Steph Murphy.

Chapter 19

I found the garage door switch in between two seven-foot-tall columns of boxes and opened it, no longer caring if I was caught snooping.

Marching into the main house, I barged past Rob, who wore a shocked face in the kitchen, and into Steph's bedroom. I shook her awake.

"Get up!" I ordered the lump under the covers.

"Arghhh . . ." Steph groaned.

"Get up! Right now!"

I threw off the covers. Steph shut her eyes and pressed a pillow over her eyes. "What time is it?" she groaned.

"It's time to explain yourself."

Steph rubbed her eyes and the crusty drool from her face and propped herself up. "What's gotten into you?" she said. "You sound like a crazy person."

I cut straight to the point. "I found the boxes in the garage."

Steph's face dropped. She'd been caught. But she recovered quickly. "How did you get in there?" she accused. "I told you the garage was off-limits. It was the *one* rule you needed to follow!"

I wasn't going to let her turn this back on me. "You also told me it was occupied by Rob's classic car," I said. "Now tell me what's really going on. I know about Mackenzie and Jenny going bankrupt. And now I know about your secret stash. Why do you have *that* much unsold product?"

I could see the wheels turning in Steph's head as she tried to figure out a way out of the conversation. Her legs shuffled under the covers. She picked lint balls from her sleep shirt. She craned her neck left and right. I just stood there, waiting patiently. I deserved answers, and I wasn't leaving until I got them.

Finally, she said, "Can I at least get some coffee?"

"No. You need to tell me everything."

Steph told me everything.

△ △ △

Not *everything* Steph had told me was a lie. For one, it was true that she started selling LuminUS after Rob's landscaping business took a sharp downturn. They really had been struggling to make ends meet and were weeks away from filing Chapter 11.

"I had a part-time job at the grocery store. I worked in the bakery department, frosting cakes for eight dollars an hour," Steph explained. "Unless I was offered full time, which I had begged my manager for and was refused each time, I didn't know how I was going to pay our rent. Or where we could go if I couldn't."

When Steph first told me this story, and retold it at LuminUS events, she said she was a bagger because it made her situation seem even more desperate. The real story was desperate enough. Her parents had cut her off. Apparently, I wasn't the only one who disapproved of her marrying Rob at eighteen. She asked them to help, either with a small loan or by allowing her family to stay with them in Florida—after all, they had a two-bedroom condo on a golf course.

But they told her they had too many guests to give her the spare bedroom. "Besides," they said, "how will you learn to make your own way if we bail you out? Isn't a husband's role to support his wife?" Steph knew this was code for "if you leave Rob, we'll help you," but she refused. She loved Rob, always had, and would do whatever it took to make their family work.

One day, by some miracle, when Steph was at her lowest, she met Leah. "She wanted a custom cake for a youth group event at her husband's parish: a yellow and white two-tier vanilla cake with a scattering of Peppa Pigs in pink fondant."

Steph tried explaining that the scope of the design was too complicated for the untrained decorators of the Pinecrest ShopRite, and that she wouldn't be able to complete Leah's order. "I thought Leah would cause a scene. Demand to see my manager. You know, pull a Karen and make sure she got her Peppa Pig cake no matter what."

Instead, Leah asked, in a caring voice, "Are you happy here, honey?"

Steph had felt seen. Leah asked if she was happy there at the Pinecrest ShopRite, but Steph took it as her asking if she was happy in life.

"I wasn't," Steph said. "And I told her as much. Leah has a pull with people. She tricks you into believing she's a safe space."

She unloaded on Leah, sharing that she had been denied a full-time position because the company would need to pay benefits and that Rob was contacting bankruptcy lawyers who operated on a sliding scale. Leah listened intently the whole way through. She then invited Steph to have a coffee next door, her treat, at Starbucks. Steph agreed, told her boss she was taking an early lunch break, and Leah spent half an hour telling her about LuminUS.

It's a one-time fee with no other hidden costs.

You'll be supported by a team of women who won't let you fail.

Your husband doesn't have to know. He'll be thanking you later once those bonus checks roll in.

"So I went back to the bakery, threw my apron on the floor of the break room, and never came back."

"What did Rob say about it?" I asked.

"I told him about becoming an independent consultant but didn't tell him about the cost. I'm so ashamed now, but, to cover the fee, I sold some of his landscaping equipment behind his back. The business was going under anyway. What use did Rob have for some electric hedge trimmers and a few wheelbarrows? It felt dirty, no matter how much I tried to convince myself it wasn't, but I kept reminding myself it was an investment." Steph explained that Leah had guaranteed she would be able to pay back the $1,800 and have money left over. Guaranteed! Then she could buy Rob a brand-new hedge clipper and all the wheelbarrows he wanted.

Months went by. Steph wasn't making sales. She wasn't used to online marketing and expected customers to come to her. When they didn't, she started buying her own product to reach quotas. Even with the discount, it was expensive. Her expenses skyrocketed along with the balance on her credit cards.

Rob had scored a client, a golf course, that kept them barely afloat. When that job was done, they'd be back to square zero, except now Steph didn't even have the bakery job to fall back on.

How did I get myself into this mess? she wondered.

One day, after a particularly disastrous Facebook Live, Steph gave in and told Leah she needed out. Leah invited her to come to a training conference under the condition that if it didn't help, she could quit. No questions asked.

At the training conference, Leah introduced Steph to Dixie, who offered Steph a once-in-a-lifetime opportunity.

"Stick with us, keep selling LuminUS, and we'll cover your living expenses," she promised her.

LuminUS would cover the rent on a new house, the lease on a new car, and a monthly wardrobe and wellness stipend that included hair appointments, Botox injections, eyebrow shaping, lip fillers, and manicures.

I didn't understand. "What was LuminUS getting from this deal?" I asked.

"I was skeptical at first too," Steph admitted. "Those payments and treatments cost them thousands of dollars a month. Why would they spend so much on some college dropout from Central Jersey who hadn't signed a single downline?" Steph waited for me to agree, to join in on her self-deprecation, but I didn't. "They wanted an ambassador. Someone to show off how life-changing LuminUS can be if you sign on. I was the perfect plant. A young mom and wife, pretty and thin, and in an area where LuminUS was experiencing rapid growth. They figured if they dolled me up and plastered photos of me and my splashy lifestyle all over the place, other women would want to join by the hundreds. I knew it was scummy. By that point I'd realized that actual success with LuminUS was impossible, unless you got in on the ground floor like Leah. But when they offered to cover the boys' tuition at a private school, I couldn't say no."

Steph signed on. There wasn't a sprawling papyrus contract that needed her signature in blood, but it felt like it. She told Dixie she would be part of LuminUS and would live the public persona the company wanted her to.

Dixie told her there was one condition: reach and remain Platinum, or the deal was off. LuminUS would front her lifestyle, but it wouldn't supply her with sales or products. They didn't want her slacking off, and they didn't want the disparity between her numbers and flashy lifestyle to be obvious enough that anyone on her team would catch on.

"Don't worry," Dixie assured Steph. "Leah and I will be holding your hand every step of the way. Every gal in my direct downline has hit Platinum. Are you a hard worker?"

"The hardest!" Steph answered assuredly. No one was a harder worker than Steph. Her shift didn't end at four like Rob's. She didn't have the luxury of coming home, grabbing a hot plate of that night's dinner, and plopping herself on the couch until ten o'clock. Steph was the one cooking that dinner—and making the breakfasts and packing the kids' lunches. Her shift started at six a.m. when she had to wake and dress the boys. And it didn't end until well into the night, when everyone was washed and asleep, and the house was cleaned.

"Then you'll have no problem," Leah said. "One of the best perks of LuminUS is that you get out as much as you put in!"

"I asked myself, 'how hard could this be?'" Steph told me. "Once I started posting about my new fancy life—'thanks to LuminUS!'—the sales poured in. Women couldn't wait to become part of my downline." Her old coworkers, other moms from her boys' school, wives of Rob's employees, and every soft target who witnessed how rapidly Steph was able to turn around her circumstances were eager to join.

I thought of the spreadsheet showing everyone's earnings, and Steph's low numbers from last month. "When did it slow down?" I asked.

"When I ran out of people to recruit. The more distributors in a small town, the more the market becomes oversaturated, until there's hardly anyone left who hasn't joined already. I panicked. If I lost my

Platinum status, I would lose it all. Then Leah gave me advice: 'Buy your own product.' The levels are based on total sales. They don't care where they come from."

Steph told herself it was a slow month, and if she self-funded the amount needed to stay Platinum, it wouldn't be a big deal. "What's one month? What's an extra $2,000 bill when LuminUS is paying for so much?" she asked.

"Only if you're able to bounce back," I added.

"One month turned into many more months which turned into that catastrophic mess in my garage." Steph shoved her face into a pillow. "Now you know how fucked I am. I mean, look at me. I can't function. And look at this." She wove her fingers into the base of her hair and pulled out a blond wad. "My hair's falling out in clumps."

"How much have you spent?" I asked, watching the wad of blond hair cascade onto her white comforter.

"I don't know. I lost track. Ten thousand. Fifteen thousand. Who knows?"

"Get rid of it! Tell Dixie and Leah you don't care about the deal, and you're getting out. Rob's business has been getting better. You won't have the big house, but so what?"

"I can't," she says. "It's not that simple. The rental agreement and the leases are in my name. If I stop paying, the debt is my responsibility. Every. Last. Cent."

"You can't be serious," I said. LuminUS was even scummier than I imagined—offering to cover Steph's expenses while making sure none of the debt would be their problem if they pulled out.

"Trust me, I wish I was joking." Steph put her head back and rested it on her upholstered headboard. She stared at the ceiling. "It's ruined everything. Rob's about to leave me. My credit score is so weak, I don't know how anyone will ever give me a loan. You need credit for everything. I won't have a car or be able to rent an apartment. And the boys. They're going to have to leave their school and their friends. I don't know what I'm going to do."

"Steph . . ." I began.

Steph crossed her arms. "If you're going to tell me I'm a moron, you can save your breath. Nothing you can call me will be any different than the names I've called myself."

"I don't think you're a moron," I said. If she was a moron, then so was I. Hadn't I fallen for the same lies? And who knows how far I would have gone if the same opportunity were given to me. She'd been cornered at a conference in a moment of vulnerability, outnumbered and away from her family. *Come to the training*, Leah had told Steph and Mackenzie. *If you don't leave with a new perspective, you can quit. No questions asked.*

"Wait," I said. "Were they going to give me the same offer at the conference? LuminUS would pay for everything as long as I acted as their puppet?" I asked.

"No," she said. "As far as I know, they stopped those arrangements. Or maybe they thought you were too smart and wouldn't fall for it. Not like me—a washed-up townie." Steph's shoulders convulsed and she began to cry.

As upset as I was, I couldn't stand seeing her cry. I sat next to her on the bed. "Why didn't you tell me before?" I asked. Steph had been dealing with the guilt and shame and anxiety all on her own. This was the reason she'd bitten her fingertips to bloodied stumps; this was why she'd been so distant.

"I almost broke down and told you the truth so many times. But I signed an NDA. If anyone else found out, I would owe LuminUS millions. On top of the tens of thousands I already owe. Who has that kind of money?"

I sure didn't. "What do you mean by anyone *else?*"

"Mackenzie," Steph said. "She came over one night. It was spring-time and she needed help planning the dance for her kid's school. They call it the Bunny Hop. It's actually pretty cute." Steph almost let out a smile, but then the memory turned from warm to sour, and the smile was gone.

"Anyway, we had too much wine and began talking. I don't remember who said it first. Maybe I let out a hint or maybe she did, I dunno. Either way, Mackenzie broke down and admitted everything. She was a plant too. She'd been offered the same deal by Dixie and Leah. Then I broke down too and told her we were in the same sinking ship. No, it's not even a ship—it's a raft made of Popsicle sticks and held together by bubble gum."

"What happened after? Did you ever talk about it again?" I asked.

"We did. All the time. It's all we could talk about. We came up with a million different plans to leave, but none of them held water. Finally, we planned to break our NDAs and go to the press, hoping the story was so juicy it would be picked up by major news outlets."

It *was* a juicy story. If I was being honest, that thought fueled me to keep following the story almost as much as my own self-interest did. It had the makings of a hit: beautiful young blonds being duped by a corporation worth millions—their flashy lifestyles nothing more than smoke screens—glitz, glamour, and greed. People wanted women like Steph to fail. They wanted to see the shiny elite pushed off their thrones.

I didn't. She was my friend and she was in pain.

I shuffled closer to her until our arms were touching. She leaned her head on my shoulder. "Weren't you worried they would sue?" I asked.

"I knew they were going to sue," Steph said. "LuminUS loves being litigious. They have dozens of intellectual property lawsuits as we speak. And they can afford the best legal team. Mackenzie and I knew we didn't stand a chance unless we could raise enough money to fight back—book deals, exclusive interviews, crowdsourcing . . . The story blowing up was the only chance we had."

"I could see that," I said. "It's risky, but it might work."

"Too risky. It wasn't worth the gamble. I told Mackenzie I couldn't do it. She was furious. She called me a coward, a flaky bitch, and threatened to go public with my name anyway."

I was about to ask what happened next, but I already knew. Mackenzie died.

Then, like a poisonous vine, a vicious thought crept into my mind.

How *did* Mackenzie die? Her husband didn't think it was an accident, and neither did I. Was Steph somehow involved?

I tried remembering the fight I heard that first night at the conference. It was late and dark and the world was spinning from too much alcohol. I had heard voices arguing while Leah slept beside me.

I imagined the scene unfolding: They took the argument to the bedroom for privacy, not wanting me to hear. Mackenzie threatened to go public. Steph barked that she wouldn't let her. After a night of drinking and fighting, her stress level at eleven and her emotions magnified, Steph acted on impulse—

She pushed Mackenzie from the balcony to keep her quiet, to keep their devil's deal with LuminUS a secret.

I slid across the mattress, away from Steph, my heart suddenly pounding a million miles an hour.

"Steph," I began. "That night at the conference. You and Mackenzie . . ."

Steph knew where I was going with that. She whipped her head toward me. "Are you serious?" she snarled. "What is wrong with you?

I finally get the courage to tell you what's been going on, you watch me break down, and your response is to accuse me of murdering my best friend?" Her tone was sharp, cutting me to the marrow.

Ouch. *Best* friend? What the hell was I, then?

"What am I supposed to think?" I snapped back, my anger taking over. "You *used* me! You knew I couldn't afford to join LuminUS, you *knew* it was a scam, and you still pushed it on me. I don't know what you're capable of. I don't know you anymore."

"Whose fault is that?" Steph shrieked. "You were the one who ditched me all those years ago! You always thought you were so much better than everyone. Drew the Ivy League graduate who lived in a big city, looking down on me and my pathetic little life. Big deal. Look at you now! Do you know why they didn't choose you to be the next face of LuminUS? Because you're not pretty enough and you're too stubborn to do anything about it!"

"Fuck you!" I spat.

"Fuck you too!" She threw a pillow at my head. It hit the wall and knocked over a painted canvas of a serene beach scene. "Get out of my room! Get out of my house! And get out of my life!"

I stormed out.

Steph didn't need to throw me out, I was going to leave on my own. I'd been right about Clearfield the first time. It was a black hole full of nothing but heartache.

For the third time that year, I shoved my things into trash bags and boxes, leaving behind anything I couldn't stuff into the Uber. Let Steph clean it up. She already had enough junk in that garage, what was another pile of dirty clothes?

I left the apartment determined to leave Clearfield, Steph, and LuminUS behind once and for all.

I was going back to New York.

Chapter 20

I never made it to New York. Not even close.

After renting a car with money I didn't have, I shoved my things into the trunk and drove off. I didn't even stop to say goodbye to my dad. He would be happy I was finally getting out, I told myself. On the way to the Turnpike, a red light stopped me near Main. It was a corner I wanted to avoid.

The Feldman Funeral Home was where my mother's services had been held. I remembered the worn floral carpet and nauseating perfume of too many lilies, and staring at the glossy casket, picturing how my mother looked inside.

As unluck would have it, there was a funeral happening that morning. It was letting out as I turned on the radio to keep me occupied. The coffin was being loaded into the hearse as a man in his thirties walked out, holding the small hand of his young son who wore a suit too big for his frame. I could see by their pallid skin and slumped shoulders that they were the ones left behind.

He was so young to have lost a mother. Had another Clearfield woman died? Would they blame it on an overdose, leaving the husband and son to wonder if the ache in their hearts would ever dull?

"No," I said out loud. "No, no. No." I wasn't going to let LuminUS get away with this. I didn't know if this funeral was for another one of their victims, but what did it matter? LuminUS had a bunch of them already—dozens, if JB and her Truth group were to be believed. It was only a matter of time before another woman paid the ultimate price.

I couldn't let LuminUS or Mackenzie's murderer get away with their crimes. And there was only one way I could stop them: telling my story.

Hitting my blinker, I made a U-turn and headed back into town.

△△△

The only hotel I could afford was the Thunderbird Inn off Route 9, which was as glamorous as it sounded. Paneled walls, a dusty multi-colored glass lamp that reminded me of something you'd find in an old pizza place, and a mattress that was hard as a rock on one side and soft on the other. Its only upside was it cost $49 a night and had a color television.

I ordered a large calzone and a side of cheese fries, also large, from Santucci's and opened my laptop. One of the better aspects of my time with LuminUS was that it distracted me from my compulsion of applying to jobs and checking my phone. Then again, it was replaced with the equally crippling compulsion of meeting my daily quotas of posting and commenting. It also meant I didn't have any new job prospects. I may have decided to stay in Clearfield and pursue the story, but I still needed a job and a place to stay.

I'd already missed my phone screening with the *Brooklyn Globe Online*, but I sent them a frantic email saying I was battling a nasty case of strep throat. They responded with a generic "Thanks for applying, but you suck and we don't want you here" form.

The online job boards I checked had no new openings in my field and a scattering outside of it. I applied to a few, then opened a tab for apartment listings. There was a 200-square-foot studio in someone's attic. It cost $1,000 per month. I expanded my search to Pinecrest, but the cheapest there was right next to the highway, and also cost $1,000 per month.

Finding a shared apartment wasn't any easier. The rents were basically the same because now they had to cover a two-bedroom. One ad listed an 800-square-foot shared unit with hardwood floors and floor-to-ceiling windows in the Pinecrest area for $403, but the description mentioned the poster was specifically looking for a "female between the ages of 18-25 who is clean and no taller than 5'5". Unfortunately, I was too old and too tall, which was a bummer because I was getting so desperate I nearly considered the offer.

Frustrated with the lack of housing options, I returned to searching for jobs. As I munched on Italian food that was getting cold, the cheese congealing, I toggled between refreshing my job feed and refreshing my apartment feed. It was no use, I realized. My heart wasn't in the search, anyway. I couldn't get my mind off Steph.

Did I want to believe Steph killed Mackenzie? Of course not. But no matter how many holes I tried poking in the story, or how hard I tried to remember the fight I heard in Utah, it was the only scenario that made sense: Steph was worried Mackenzie was going to blab about being a plant for LuminUS, so she pushed her off the balcony, assuring Mackenzie would be silenced forever.

It was a twisted thought. But how well *did* I know Steph? I knew the Steph from twelve years ago, but people changed. Hadn't I heard similar stories? There were entire movies and true crime television series devoted to the topic: *My Husband the Killer, The Evil Neighbor I Thought Was a Good Guy But Ended Up a Killer, I Never Thought the Guy Who Ran the Annual Bunny Hop Was a Killer.* I could star in my own: *My Best Friend Who Brought Me Aleve and Caramel Chunk Ice Cream Every Time I Had My Period Turned Out to Be a Killer.*

Still, I couldn't fully believe it. My heart wouldn't let me.

I knew Leah was in on the details of the arrangement the women had with Dixie and LuminUS. But I wondered, did she have the same setup? Was LuminUS also bankrolling her lifestyle? Further, did she or any of her downlines know about the dangers of the products?

I thought of Steph pulling out a clump of her hair. If she knew the products were toxic, she wouldn't be taking them—would she? Bre had fainted at the gym and burned half her face off with a topical. Jenny was half bald. Mackenzie had suffered rapid weight loss before her death, according to Bre. Was it all connected to the products? The only distributor I knew who didn't take the supplements was Leah. What did *she* know?

What about my own health? My headaches were gone, and my hair was still attached to my scalp, so I didn't think I had done any permanent damage. My skin was back to its normal, awful self: peppered with tiny whiteheads, with the occasional cystic acne for that extra dose of pizzazz. I missed the few weeks of clear skin I'd enjoyed, but if the pills were killing people, it wasn't worth it.

I checked on the patient portal for the lab I sent my blood sample to, only to be met with the same RESULTS IN PROGRESS update. I tried to reassure myself that I had only taken the supplements for a short time. My system should flush out whatever was left, but what about the other women? Who knew how much was inside a daily user like Steph.

Steph, I thought. I was furious with her and half convinced she was a killer, but I still didn't want her to die. I texted her: "Stop taking anything LuminUS. Can't get into details right now, but I think they're toxic."

Wondering if any others had discovered new information about the supplements, I opened the Truth group page and browsed. I had exhausted JB's write-up and wanted new information. There was a new post:

Another silver lotus distributor has died. The Clearfield Police blotter reads:

On 06/14 at 7:49 PM, officers were dispatched to 15 Primrose Avenue for a possible overdose. Victim was unconscious at time of arrival. Officers administered emergency Narcan. Victim did not regain consciousness and was pronounced deceased at 7:56 PM.

Victim is identified as Marcela Owens, 27.

Marcela Owens was a Gold level distributor who began selling silver lotus eight months ago. Attached are photos of her drinking SkeleSlim shakes twice per day. Mint chocolate flavor. More photos can be found on her socials @MOwens_LuminUS_NJ

Marcela was a young woman who fit the LuminUS mold. She had round hazel eyes, apple cheeks, and thinner lips she overlined to look bigger. There were dozens of photos of Marcela holding up her blue LuminUS shaker bottle filled to the top with a brown liquid that resembled chunky swamp water. I searched her social pages. She frequently discussed wanting to lose twenty pounds and invited everyone to follow along with her weight loss journey.

Some days she drank what she called "double trouble shakes," which included two packets of SkeleSlim. "You can mix and match!" she wrote. "Here are some of my favorite combos: Mint chocolate and pomegranate, ginger peach and watermelon, and winter mint and cola for that extra jolt of caffeine." I shuddered as I remembered the gritty texture and overpowering sweetness of the SkeleSlim in Steph's cottage cheese sandwiches.

Marcela had lost the twenty-five pounds but continued drinking the shakes to maintain her progress. By her final post, she was down forty-five pounds and drinking shakes for breakfast, lunch, and dessert. Her one real meal was dinner, which was a raw salad, no dressing, with iceberg lettuce and shaved carrots.

Scrolling through the feed felt like I was flipping a flipbook of someone wasting away. Marcela started off as a healthy young woman and, within eight months, had ended up a gaunt skeleton who was too exhausted to walk to the mailbox.

Like the other cases, I could see how people assumed it was an overdose. The rapid weight loss, sudden signs of aging, thinning hair, sagging skin, and inability to keep her eyes open for long periods of time were all signs of addiction.

I knew better. She was decaying slowly, being poisoned by LuminUS.

Marcela had one young son, Bryson, and a husband, Greg. In a group portrait, the happy family of three stared back at me. Sure enough, the husband and son were the men I'd seen outside of the Feldman Funeral Home. Greg worked in the same Walmart auto department as Chase, which was probably how Marcela got involved with LuminUS. Local LuminUS ladies could all be traced back to one another. It was a spider's web, connecting one woman to another through their husbands, children's schools, or churches, with Leah as the black widow in the center, luring them into her den.

I felt sure LuminUS had killed Marcela, but I couldn't jump to conclusions. My journalism training taught me you could never assume. I needed facts. I needed autopsy reports.

I reopened the email to the Clearfield medical examiner's office and thought of ways to convince them to release that confidential information. JB had attempted to reach out, yet was given the same line about protected information each time. What could I say that would get them to budge?

I wasn't anyone special: just an unemployed clickbait writer who was holed up in a seedy motel eating cold soggy fries and sitting on a comforter that was undoubtedly going to give me an STD. But I did have my press pass. According to the 2018 printed on the front, it was valid for the entire year, and there was no way of telling I didn't work at BuzzFeed anymore. It was worth a shot. I could also hear Leah saying, *Get them face to face! It's so much harder to say no to a friendly, smiling face.*

Pulling up the staff directory, I was shocked when I saw a familiar face: a woman in her late twenties with a sandy bob, a scattering of freckles, and tortoiseshell glasses—the third woman at the Truth group meeting. The one who knew about Mackenzie's death. According to the website, she was Hanna Cole, the office's assistant medical examiner. If anyone were to know what caused the women's deaths, it would be her.

I searched the group for her name. She appeared on the list of members, but her profile photo was a black box. Her page was private. Her history revealed she'd never liked or commented on a single post. Hanna was a silent observer, but the connection between the group and her career was too strong.

She knew something.

And I needed to find out what it was.

△ △ △

Hanna knew my face. There was no sense in pretending I was some-one else. JB had singled me out during the Truth meeting, and the group was small enough as it was.

I entered the medical examiner's office and asked to see Hanna Cole. The woman at the front desk looked over her red-framed glass-es and told me, "Hanna's unavailable," before going back to typing on her computer.

"Can I ask when she will be available?"

"I'm sorry, but Hanna won't be available all day." This time the woman didn't take her eyes off her screen.

I was wondering why she was being such a pain in the ass when I realized I had my press pass clipped to my belt loop. No wonder Han-na would never be available. The receptionist thought I was a nosy reporter trying to get access to confidential files. In a sense, I was.

Pretending to be official had backfired. I thanked her for her time, not meaning a single word, and walked to the diner across the street. I asked to be seated in the booth by the window and ordered a black coffee, the only item I could afford.

My eyes didn't leave the window. It was almost lunchtime. Unless Hanna took her break in the office, I expected she was like the rest of the burned-out and mistreated employees of Clearfield who couldn't wait to step away, if only for an hour. As I watched the front door of the government building, I felt a rush. This was what I was meant for, I realized. Following the lead. Letting the story take me where it needed to go. Not shilling crappy skincare on Facebook.

I also felt like a creep, especially when the waitress asked me if I was okay for the third time. She was annoyed I'd only ordered coffee and kept asking for refill after refill. But it wasn't as though the place was crowded—and I was a good tipper.

As I waited, I thought about Clearfield and what it had become. A once-booming suburbia with businesses lining Main Street had turned into graffitied brick buildings and boarded windows. Both the upper and lower middle classes had fled to Pinecrest, leaving behind the stragglers who wanted to work but couldn't. Lost and broken souls clinging onto anything that would give them comfort and allow them to forget their shitty circumstances, whether it was alcohol or drugs or selling LuminUS.

I scanned the diner. In one booth, two teens in gray hoodies picked at a plate of French fries. One of them, a girl with scabs covering her face, took breaks to rest her head on the table and nod off. At the counter sat an older man with an unkempt, bushy beard. He nursed his own cup of coffee, holding it in both hands with dirt-caked nails.

Before I could continue my train of thought, the glass door to the medical examiner's office flung open. Out stepped a short woman wearing teal scrubs that I immediately recognized as Hanna.

I threw a crumpled five-dollar bill on the table and rushed out of the diner, trying to beat Hanna to her car.

"Hanna Cole?" I asked.

Being bombarded by a crazed lady in a parking lot made her jump. She was about to aim the pepper spray attached to her car keys when she realized she recognized me.

"Jesus!" Hanna said as she put her hand on her chest to catch her breath. "You scared the crap out of me."

"Sorry. Not sure if you remember me, but I was at the Truth group meeting the other night."

"I remember you. Lou, right?" she asked.

"Drew. Drew Cooper."

"Right. Well, Drew Cooper, I can't talk right now. I gotta go." She made for the driver's side door, but I stepped in front of her.

"I need to talk to you about LuminUS," I said authoritatively.

"I have nothing to say about it. Now, if you wouldn't mind, can you please move?"

I stood my ground. Reaching into my back jeans pocket, I pulled out the press pass I'd hid after my encounter with the woman at the front desk. It hadn't worked on her, but it was my only play with Hanna. If she was in the Truth group, she wanted to see LuminUS fall. "I'm with the press. We're doing a story about LuminUS and its possible connection with the string of deaths."

She glanced at the pass and read that I was from BuzzFeed.

Crap. I'd hoped she wouldn't look too closely.

"Aren't you that site with the quizzes? What's your interest with LuminUS?"

"We write harder hitting pieces as well," I said. "We have an entire news website with its own investigative section." This was true. I had applied countless times for a transfer. The department wasn't as well funded as the main site. The articles weren't shared as much as pieces like "These Dad Tweets Will Make Your Sides Literally Explode from Laughing", but the stories they covered had meat. From the Me Too Movement to calling out the president's lies, the news department wasn't afraid to find the scoop.

"I have nothing to say," Hanna said, walking around me to her door.

"Anything you tell me can be off the record. I have reason to believe the supplements are toxic. My best friend is still wrapped up in LuminUS. If this stuff's killing people, I need to know."

Hanna sagged, her keys poised at the lock. Finally she sighed, relenting, and turned toward me. "We can't talk here," she said. "There's a Greek place on Filmore. No one from the office goes there anymore after Matt got food poisoning from a bad batch of tzatziki, so we'll be safe."

I followed Hanna to the Greek restaurant. We both ordered coffees. Hanna ordered a side of pita bread and kalamata olives. "It's my lunch break, and I'm starving," she said. "Plain pita and olives seem like the only things on the menu that can't possibly make me sick."

"Speaking of," I said, "tell me what's in LuminUS?" I needed to work on my segues.

"I don't know what's in the stuff. I'm not a chemist," she said. "Besides, didn't *you* say you thought they were toxic?"

"Yes, and I can tell you agree with me that there's a link between LuminUS product and the deaths."

"Before I say anything, you need to promise me this is off the record."

I held up three fingers and placed them against my temple in a Scout's honor gesture.

"And," she added, "I need you to know the only reason I'm here is because I also have someone close to me who's involved with LuminUS."

"A friend?" I asked.

"A sister," she corrected. Her pita and olives arrived, and she stuck an olive in her mouth and chewed around the pit. "She started selling a few months ago. LuminUS sounded like a pyramid scheme to me, so I did some research. It's how I found the Truth group. I saw the women posted on there, the dead ones, and I recognized all of them."

"Did they have autopsies?" I asked.

"It's protocol that if an overdose is suspected, we do a full autopsy of the victim, so yes, they did."

"And you performed them?"

"No, but I assisted. The department's small. It's just me and the actual medical examiner, Dr. Benson, so I've been involved in each case."

"Is your sister using the products?" I asked. "My friend is, even though her hair is falling out. I don't understand the hold these pills have."

"You should tell her to stop. Immediately." Hanna placed her palm on the table. A thin, gold wedding band embedded with a small diamond wrapped around her finger.

"I did. Do you think there are long-term side effects? I took some too. The BeautyBoost pills. Gave me major headaches, but I stopped early on."

"That's good. I don't know what the effects are long term since all my clients come to me past the point of no return."

I took a sip of my coffee. It burned the tip of my tongue and tasted weak. "Has your sister shown any symptoms?"

"Not yet. JB told me what to look out for. I warn my sister nearly every day to never ingest anything from LuminUS. I don't feel safe about her using any of the topicals either. She promises me she hasn't, but I don't believe her. Her team, her 'girl tribe,' as she calls them, pushes her to sell and sell and sell. They're always on her like hungry ticks, and she's a wuss when it comes to peer pressure. Enough people tell her to jump off a bridge and she'll do it."

Steph was the same way. It came from a place of wanting to be accepted. Her parents were never supportive. It was the type of household where you could come home with an A-minus, and they would ask why it wasn't a plus.

"What can you tell me about the autopsies? The toxicology reports?" I asked. Hanna pressed her lips together and tossed a chewed pit into the bowl. "Please, Hanna. I need to know."

I put on my saddest, most beaten puppy dog face. It worked.

Hanna unclenched her jaw and said, "The official cause of death on each report has been 'accidental drug toxicity.' But there's a best practice that if we use that term as the cause, we need to mention the specific kinds of drugs that were in the victim's system. On every other case, we've written things like 'accidental drug toxicity due to opioids, benzodiazepines, and methamphetamines.' The only reports that haven't listed a kind of drug are the ones from anyone selling LuminUS."

"Are you sure?" I asked.

"One thousand percent. It's how I became skeptical in the first place. I found the Truth group and recognized the women because they stood out as the only ones without . . ."

"Details," I finished.

"Not only that, but every 'place of injury' was in their bedroom at home."

"That's not very odd, is it?" I asked. "Don't many addicts OD at home?"

"No, they don't," she corrected with a tone that let me know *she* was the expert. "They're usually in a parking lot or at someone's party or outside in a park. Yes, some die in their beds, especially the older users, but it's uncommon."

"Every one of the sixteen—now seventeen—victims in Clearfield have too many similarities not to be connected." I spoke out loud as I tried to collate the information I'd gathered. "All LuminUS distributors, between the ages of twenty-five and thirty-five, with cause of death as 'suspected overdose' in the same 'place of injury,' but without specifying the actual drugs in their systems."

"That's not the strangest part," Hanna said.

"There's more?"

"When I went to research the toxicology reports, I was told they were sealed. I don't think you realize how bonkers that is. I'm the

assistant medical examiner. My job is literally to go through lab results to help the medical examiner determine the cause of death." She
pointed the tip of a pita wedge at me to prove her point.

"Wait. How were the coroner reports filled out if there were no
toxicology reports?"

"That's not weird," she explained. "If we suspect an OD, we can
complete the form while we wait for the tox reports, minus listing the
drugs like I said. The tox reports never came to me, and Dr. Benson
told me he saw them and finished the reports and not to worry about
it. I only saw they were sealed when I dug into it."

"And you can't get access to them at all? Not even as the assistant
medical examiner?"

"I know, right? Can you believe it? It says they're sealed as per a
request from the police department, whatever that means. As far as I
know, there are no ongoing investigations or legal proceedings related
to the deaths."

The waitress dropped the check on our table. I took it. It was the
least I could do for Hanna telling me what she knew, even if she was
the only one who ate. I planned to take her leftover pita back to my
hotel.

Hanna didn't argue. We walked out to our cars.

"A new woman died," I said. "Marcela Owens. Has she come into
your office yet?"

"I saw that post too. She has. I expect more of the same—one
cover-up after another. I'll let you know if anything changes."

I gave Hanna my cell phone number that I had written on a napkin. I didn't expect her to call. Hanna had pushed herself past her
comfort zone by speaking with me in the first place, and I doubted
it would happen again. If it got out that she was connected with a
curious reporter, it could cost her a job. And those were scarce in

Clearfield.

Before we got into our cars, she gave me another warning. "Don't let your friend take any more of that stuff. Flush it down the toilet or throw it in the trash. Whatever you have to do."

I agreed, but in my mind, it wouldn't be long before Steph had no more access to LuminUS because she was behind bars. My conversation with Hanna only strengthened my suspicion that someone in LuminUS knew about the toxins. Steph told me she was still taking the pills, but had I actually *seen* her pop one since Mackenzie's death? Had Mackenzie known the truth?

If Mackenzie was the one to tell her, Steph made sure she was silenced forever.

Post from Bre Santos's Instagram

May 2018

12 whole hours later . . . and I'm STILL in the hospital. (Good thing I have my LuminUS eucalyptus spray to keep the yucky air clean).

Guess what? I won't let any injury stop me! Especially not this tiny head wound from fainting in the gym.

Too often I hear excuses. I don't have the time. I'm too busy. I don't have the money.

STOP 🔘

I'm strapped to an IV, doctors are saying I'm dehydrated and stressed from my best friend's death, and will need to make sure there's no brain swelling, and I STILL managed to sell $800 of LuminUS during my Live event that I did right from my hospital bed. Nothing will slow me down.

Is it your time?

#Sick #AlwaysTime4LuminUS #BecauseOfLuminUS

Chapter 21

Frothy water spilled from the pot and onto the hot stovetop. No matter how hard I tried, I could never boil pasta without the water overflowing. I tried using a bigger pot, cold water, and putting in less salt, but none of it worked.

"Something's burning," my dad called from the futon.

"Nothing's burning. It's the pasta water." A steam cloud rose from the stovetop as the water drops blackened the metal plate under the flames. On the other burner, a pan of red sauce bubbled. Using both hands, I stirred each pot simultaneously. "Dinner's almost ready," I called. Dad came into the kitchen and began setting the butcher-block island that doubled as a dining table.

My focus couldn't be further from the pasta. I had been glued to my phone all evening, scrolling through Facebook. The Truth group recently got a new member: Jenny.

She had spent the night posting every hour, each diatribe increasingly more unhinged. She explained how she fell on hard times before Leah suckered her into LuminUS, and how she felt manipulated into spending money she didn't have. Jenny blamed everything on

Leah. She posted screenshots of their text exchanges—ones where Jenny made it clear she couldn't afford another Clear Skin bundle even if it meant not reaching her monthly quota.

LEAH
It's the 29th and you're still $700 away from hitting your numbers.

JENNY
not gonna make it this month

JENNY
girls from my volunteer group fell through and are no longer interested

LEAH
And you let them refuse?

LEAH
No doesn't mean no! It only means "maybe later."

Eventually, Jenny began rambling about Leah being "pure evil," going so far as to draw red horns and a black goatee on her headshot. Even unhinged Marjorie commented, "what's wrong with you?" I'd called Jenny that afternoon, increasingly worried about her volatility. She admitted she went overboard thanks to polishing off a bottle of tequila, but regretted nothing.

"I joined the group because I want justice," she told me. "Supposedly they're compiling a case and I want to give them all the information I have."

"That's fair, but I would be careful with how public you are about

Leah. If she finds out you're using her full name and photo and private exchanges, she's going to sue for libel. You know how litigious she and Aaron are," I warned. My research had unearthed lawsuit after lawsuit filed by the Monroes, mostly regarding their ministry and trademark disputes with other organizations using the phrase "Bread of Christ" in their branding.

"I don't care anymore," Jenny spat into the phone. "I want to watch her burn."

My worry for her stuck with me as my dad and I filled our bowls and sat together on the bar seats. In the background, the TV played a rerun of *Star Trek: Enterprise*. Having the noise helped cut the awkwardness between us.

My dad's apartment was smaller than I imagined, and I now knew why I couldn't stay with him. He used the futon as a couch during the day and a bed at night, and it took up most of the shared dining, living, and bedroom space. Spending time with my Dad was pleasant, but seeing the sardine can he called home was miserable. Selling LuminUS was supposed to be a way to escape, for me and him both. Instead, it had cost me my time, my best friend, possibly my health, and $3,766, according to my last tally.

Captain Milton plunked himself on top of the garbage can and watched me slurp pasta with his judging orange eyes. "I thought he was an outside cat," I said.

"The Captain? Not a chance I'm letting him go outside here. That road is busy all hours of the day. He'd be roadkill in no time."

The Captain flicked his tail. He knew he was my dad's favorite child. It wasn't his fault my dad had to sell his house.

"How did the interview go?" Dad asked.

It didn't. The *Brooklyn Globe Online* refused to reschedule the phone screening.

"Fine," I said. "But I don't think they're going to give me the job."

"Of course they will! You're a fabulous writer. They'd be crazy not to," he said.

"I don't know if I want to take it anyway. I might want to hold out for something that gives me more freedom."

"Does that mean your business is going well? With, ah jeez, what was it called?"

"LuminUS?" I nearly choked on the name. "It's going."

Dad knew nothing about Mackenzie, the Clearfield women dropping dead, or my falling-out with Steph. He didn't even know that I was living in a hotel. I didn't want him to worry. And how would I go about it, anyway? "Oh hey, remember Steph, who practically became your other daughter after Mom died? Yeah, she might be a killer. Guess you never know, huh? Anyway, pass the parm."

I was putting our dishes in the sink when a car horn honked. I'd agreed to help Bre with a LuminUS party at her friend's house for no other reason than to get her side of the story. The last thing I wanted to be doing was shilling LuminUS with a big smile on my face, acting like I didn't think the little blue bottles were full of poison, but it was a sacrifice I had to make.

"Gotta go, bye, Dad!" I said, grabbing my sweater and rushing out the door.

I was panting by the time I made it down to the parking lot. Dad lived in a sixth floor walk-up. Bre was waiting in her silver Mercedes Benz coupe with a red leather interior, the back of which was stuffed with blue boxes. Her custom license plate read BO55BABE.

"Get in," she said. "You won't bah-*lieve* the day I've had. Also, does your dad really live here? That's, like, *so* sad."

I didn't know how to respond to that, but Bre quickly moved on, complaining that Steph and Leah were avoiding her despite her multiple texts, calls, and DMs. I knew why Steph was silent, but not Leah.

"They know how important it is to me that I move up to Ruby. I needed their help for this party, and instead I have you—no offense. If I sign two more people, I'm golden. Well, Ruby," she said, busting into a high-pitched giggling fit.

"Should we go check on Leah?" I asked. It was unlike her to be unresponsive, especially when there were downlines on the table.

"Absolutely not. She's probably doing this for attention." Bre looked at herself in the rearview mirror and lifted her eyelashes with a fingertip.

"I wonder how Jenny's doing," I said, fishing.

Bre shot me a judgmental look, her finger still hovering by her lash. "You don't like her?" I asked innocently.

"She's different, that's all. She never fit in with the rest of us. The hair, the tattoos—I thought no one would want to buy from a weirdo, and I was right. Getting her to post was like pulling teeth."

"Do you think she's dangerous? After what happened at Leah's?"

"I wouldn't be surprised, and I would know. I watch a ton of true crime docs. You know, I had a bad feeling about her the moment she wanted to join LuminUS. I can read people, and I could tell she was going to be trouble."

Bre pulled up to the house, a huge three-story with a red tile roof and plaster walls the color of a bad fake tan—Mediterranean, Jersey style. Cars already filled the wide driveway. It was a collection of luxury rides: Audis, BMWs, and one Tesla. One thing was for sure—these people weren't poor. Good thing I wore my best tomato-sauce-stained T-shirt.

Bre opened her trunk and tried picking up a cardboard box of LuminUS. Her arms shook and she put the box down. "Can you help me with these boxes?" she asked.

I grabbed a box. It was light. "Are you feeling okay?"

"I've been a little weak. Feels like a cold I can't shake. This morning, I even had another fainting spell when I was doing my fifteen-minute ab blaster routine." She rubbed sweat off her brow, the exertion of picking up a three-pound box having been too much to handle.

"How much LuminUS are you taking?"

Bre's eyes glazed over as she used her fingers to count. "I'm not sure exactly. I put all my supplements in a daily pill box and then there's the shakes and tinctures."

"You should stop taking them," I said firmly, hoping it would stick. "They might be connected to your health issues."

"You're being silly. I'm fine!" Bre playfully slapped my arm. Her wrist made a cracking sound as it limply hit me. She winced and rubbed it. "Now, come on. We need to get this stuff inside."

I loaded another box on top of mine, and said, "I'm going to go check on Leah later." I needed to figure out what *she* knew. I just didn't know whether to confront her with my knowledge of Steph and Mackenzie being plants or come at her sideways.

Bre huffed. "Don't give her the attention. It'll only make her worse. Trust me. I've known Leah longer than you have. This is her pattern. She enjoys being pursued and worshipped. She has a queen complex."

I still made a mental note to visit after the party. Leah's house wasn't far from here—in fact, only a few streets over.

Bre's argument was flimsy at best. She may have thought Leah was a drama queen, but I knew better. Okay, yes, Leah *did* act like she was the grand dame of Pinecrest, but she was chronically addicted to her phone and even more addicted to LuminUS. There had to be some reason she was ignoring Bre's texts.

Soon enough, we'd moved all of the LuminUS boxes from the car and piled them onto the sidewalk. There was just one thing left in the trunk: a camel-colored sweater.

"Oh, oops!" Bre said, grabbing it and handing it to me. "Can you return this to Leah when you go check on her? Maybe slip it into her closet without her noticing?" Bre put her hands together in a praying gesture. "Steph asked me to return it to her, but I totally forgot. Leah doesn't know Steph took it."

"Steph took it? Why?" I asked, running my finger atop the embroidered LOEWE.

"Steph borrowed it to keep warm that night you guys all crashed in Mackenzie's suite. Then she packed it and freaked out when she got home and realized. Leah paid a fortune for it—she never lets anyone borrow it. Steph asked me to return it because she's terrified of Leah, but I totally blanked! Please don't tell her!"

I held the sweater, my hands shaking, a lump forming in my throat.

The woman asleep next to me on the armchair of the hotel suite that night—the night that Mackenzie died—I hadn't seen her face. I'd only seen her sweater, and a tuft of blond hair. But they were all blond—all the LuminUS ladies except for me were blond. I'd thought it was Leah because it was her sweater, but it wasn't.

It wasn't Leah asleep next to me that night. It was Steph.

Which meant that it was Mackenzie and Leah who were arguing.

"It wasn't Steph," I whispered.

"Huh? I told you, it's Leah's sweater," Bre said.

I couldn't believe how wrong I'd been. Steph had borrowed the sweater, and her long blond hair was tucked into it, an illusion that made it look like Leah's short bob.

I walked down the driveway as if in a trance, the sweater clutched tightly in my hand.

"Where are you going?" Bre called. "What the hell?!"

I ignored her. My feet were taking me to Leah's house, as if on autopilot.

She had questions to answer. One of which was: Why did you kill Mackenzie?

Chapter 22

Tying the tan sweater around my waist, I ran down the sidewalk, holding my phone in front of my face so I could follow the GPS. A left on Dune Drive, immediate right on Orchid Ave, down a tenth of a mile, right on Pacific Ave, and in 0.31 miles, I'd be at Leah's house.

I'd ignored Bre as she shouted down the driveway after me—there was no time to explain, and besides, she would never believe me. I didn't want her with me as I interrogated Leah, fearing it would turn into good cop, butt-kisser cop. Leah would need to be soaked in Mackenzie's blood for Bre to believe she could kill. To her, Leah was an idol. Bre would sell her soul to reach Leah's level of success.

When I arrived, soaked in sweat thanks to the unexpected cardio, I saw flashing lights bouncing against the house's white columns, turning them blue and red and blue again. An ambulance and a handful of police cars were parked haphazardly along Leah's long driveway.

My heart dropped into my stomach. Was I too late? Had she already killed again?

No officials were in the front yard, except for a young cop who was busy corralling the lookie-loos who'd gathered. I pushed my way to the front and asked the frazzled cop, "What happened here?"

"I don't know how many more times I need to ask all of you to back off. This is an active crime scene!" She frowned, as if already regretting admitting that.

"Is Leah okay?" I screamed past the onlookers, catching the cop's attention.

"Did you know her?" she asked. My heart shot out of my chest cavity and into my throat, where it throbbed like a drum. The cop said *did*—past tense.

I thought fast. "I'm her . . . niece."

The cop shrugged and waved me past the imaginary barrier she'd created with her body. I heard her talk into her shoulder radio. "We got a family member coming on back. Get Jackson to contain her in the dining room until the chief can speak with her."

I walked into the house. No one was inside, save for a cop talking on his phone in the dining room. I assumed this was Jackson. Lucky for me, he didn't even look up when I came in. He seemed to be engrossed in a deep conversation with a buddy about getting tickets to the Phillies game.

I slipped past him and into the kitchen. Commotion was coming from outside, by the pool area. The French doors were open, and I saw a group of police and other professionals milling about on the patio. It reminded me of when they'd found Mackenzie: camera flashes, hushed voices, bored faces, and uniformed people walking back and forth, trying to look busy. No one paid attention to me, which, for once, I appreciated. A broad-shouldered officer shielded my view as I stepped through the doors, but when he moved, I saw it—saw *her*.

The swimming pool ran red. Its recessed lights illuminated the colored water, making it radiate like a ruby in the sun. In the middle of the pool was a large object bobbing up and down. For a second, I thought it was a pool float—until I saw the halo of blond hair, stained pink, undulating under the surface.

A cloud of darker crimson framed Leah's head. She was lying face down with her arms spread out to either side, as if she were a religious effigy. I swallowed hard as bile crept up my throat. Déjà vu made my head spin. But this time, there was no question of whether it was an accident—this was murder.

Two officers in waders up to their hips pointed at the body. They stood in the shallow end of the pool and argued about how they were going to get her out without disturbing the scene. By the ornamental bushes, seated on a wicker ottoman, was Aaron. He was being questioned by a detective, but looked too distracted to answer any of his questions. Every few seconds, his head turned to look at the grisly scene behind him, and then turned back with a fresh expression of grief. His glasses lay on the ground beside his foot.

Only days ago, I'd sat in the same spot. Instead of officers, there were party guests, and instead of a corpse, there were floating lotus-shaped candles.

"Who are you?" a steely voice asked. I turned and saw a tall, barrel-chested man hovering over me. He wore a navy-blue hat with gold filigree on the brim and a badge that read CHIEF. "What are you doing here? Who let you in?" His voice grew deeper the more he challenged me. By the way he was puffing out his chest despite being nearly a foot taller than me, I could tell he was the kind of man who enjoyed making women feel small.

"I . . . uh . . ." I caught Aaron's gaze. He looked through me, as if he didn't even recognize me. Suddenly, I felt guilty for intruding on such a private matter. I couldn't stand watching people grieve. It broke my heart.

"I'm her niece," I said.

The chief, whose gold nameplate read M. BRIGGS, stuck out a hairy sausage-size finger and pointed it at my face. "Mrs. Monroe didn't have any nieces. Now you need to leave before I arrest you next."

I put up my hands in surrender and backed away. He tapped on another officer's shoulder, whispered in his ear, and watched me like a hawk as the other officer personally escorted me out the house.

As I waited behind the yellow tape, I saw two officers escorting a handcuffed woman out of the other wing of the house and into the back of a police car. Her head hung low. She stared at her feet as she walked, but she looked familiar. I couldn't place her until I recognized the patchy head of hair and armful of tattoos.

The realization collapsed on me like an avalanche.

"Jenny!" I called out. She spared me a quick glance, frowning, then turned away. The officer pushed her into the back of the cruiser.

My heart was hammering in my chest as the car pulled away, its lights still on. *How could Jenny do this?* I wondered, trying to imagine her breaking into Leah's home, finding her out back, and—what? Cutting her throat? Bashing her head into the paver stones? I couldn't get a read on the cause of death. There was too much watery blood surrounding the body, although judging by where it pooled, the wound was on her head.

It would likely be an open-and-shut case. Hadn't Jenny threatened to get revenge on Leah? Hadn't she caused a major scene at Leah's party just the other day, throwing heavy bottles, trying to purposefully injure her? There were dozens of witnesses who saw it all, myself included. Not to mention the online threats she'd posted in the Truth group. *I want to watch her burn*, she'd told me.

I realized something else: Jenny was at the conference. She'd refused to spend much time with the other women in her group, but she was there. I didn't actually have any way of knowing when she'd really arrived, or what she'd been doing the night Mackenzie died. If she killed Leah, she might have killed Mackenzie too. *But why?* I asked myself. Mackenzie wasn't in her upline—what motivation did she have to kill her?

I had the sudden urge to text Steph. She deserved to know. As angry as she was at Leah, they'd been close at one time. I imagined she was where I left her days ago: in bed, drugged up on a Tylenol PM, NyQuil, and cabernet sauvignon cocktail so she could sleep. She was already so devastated over the loss of Mackenzie, I couldn't imagine how to break the news of another death to her—and we weren't speaking, anyway. I felt another throb of guilt in my chest as I remembered how I'd blamed her for Mackenzie's death. Now I knew it couldn't have been her.

On my way to Leah's house, I'd been convinced *she'd* killed Mackenzie, but now that Leah was dead, I wasn't so sure.

Still, I couldn't square it in my mind—Jenny, the smart, acerbic, funny girl I knew from school—a double murderer?

A sudden murmur spread through the gathered crowd, and I whipped my head up. I watched as Leah's body was rolled through the front door in a stretcher. She was zipped into thick black vinyl that reminded me unpleasantly of a human-size trash bag. Moments later, Aaron was accompanied out by the chief. They chatted in front of Aaron's black Audi S8, both nodding and frowning, before Aaron got into his car and followed the ambulance that held his wife's body. They didn't bother turning the lights or sirens on. She was already dead.

The chief watched Aaron leave and then trudged toward the crowd. "Show's over, folks," he boomed. He spotted me in the group and balled his hands into fists by his side. "Everyone needs to go home, right now! And I mean *everyone*."

The group scattered, pairs of people whispering to each other in concerned tones.

"Was it an accident?"

"I bet she was drunk."

"It was that creepy girl with the tattoos who killed her. She was probably doped up."

Cops began marching back to their vehicles, turning off their flashing lights.

I caught the young officer's attention. "Is that it?" I asked. "They're already leaving?"

She shrugged. "We were told to wrap it up."

"Don't you have anything better to do?" The chief interrupted, pushing aside the young officer with his broad shoulder. "What did you say your name was again?"

"Sorry, I'll be going," I spit out. I rushed away, not eager to give him an excuse to shove me in the back of a cop car like Jenny.

I did have better things to do. One of which was going to see Jenny in jail.

As I stood on the sidewalk, searching Google Maps to see how far I was from the Pinecrest police station, Bre texted the group chat.

BRE

I signed all 3 ladies at the party!

BRE

Ruby here I come! 🖤

BRE

More gals in our Tribe!

Lose one gal, gain three, I thought.

Chapter 23

Overhead, a fluorescent bulb buzzed as I stood in front of the cop who I recognized as the officer guarding the perimeter at Leah's crime scene. Her badge read T. REEVES. It had taken me ages to walk the two miles to the police department, during which time it seemed the crime scene had been packed up and everyone sent back to their stations.

"Ms. Fitzsimmons is not permitted visitors at this time," the young cop behind the desk informed me as though she was reading from a script. Her sandy hair was closely cropped in a pixie cut that fit her fairy-like features. She seemed frazzled. I didn't imagine the Pinecrest department saw very many murders.

"Please, Officer Reeves." I rested my arms atop the desk. "It will only take a second. Jenny's been sick lately, and I need to make sure she has all her medications." I held up and shook a bottle of Lumin-US BeautyBoost pills, my thumb covering the label, then shoved it back in my bag before she could look too closely.

Officer Reeves swiveled her head, checking if anyone else was nearby before lowering her voice and saying, "The chief's pissed at you for breaching the scene. I'm not supposed to let you see her. She's a murder suspect."

"Oh, okay," I said, pulling a pen and paper out of my bag. "Totally understand. Can you just write a little note for Jenny's mom explaining why you have to deny her medical care? I don't want her to think I didn't do my best to get the pills to her daughter—you understand."

This was another trick I'd learned in journalism school. People—especially cops—hated putting things in writing, especially once you planted unsavory phrases like "deny her medical care" in their head.

Officer Reeves shifted on her feet for a moment, clearly weighing her options, then walked around the desk and motioned for me to follow.

I didn't want to make an enemy of her *and* the chief, so I figured it wouldn't hurt to suck up a little. "Thank you *so* much, officer," I gushed. "I completely understand your caution and appreciate any help you can give. I know how difficult it must be to work here. The CCPD has always been such a boys' club."

"You have no idea." Reeves sighed. "Between you and me, the chief plays favorites and I'm never in the mix. I know I'm still a rookie, but so is Hernandez and *he* was invited to Sunday morning golf. He doesn't even play!" Officer Reeves looked around nervously, making sure no one had overheard. She didn't need to worry—the only other person in the station was a dispatcher scrolling through Facebook on her phone.

"Where is everyone?" I asked.

"We're understaffed. Budget cuts. And the chief's interviewing the victim's husband in his office, which is why you need to be quick."

Officer Reeves led me to the holding cells, where I spotted Jenny in the cell on the far right. She was sitting on the floor with her head resting between her knees.

"Don't forget. Be quick," Officer Reeves repeated before leaving me with Jenny.

At the sound of my footsteps, Jenny lifted her head slowly. Her eyes were wide and watery as she stared at me through the bars, making me feel as though I was in a high-kill animal shelter.

"I didn't do it," she said, her words strained. She wore an oversized Henley shirt that was missing a button and had a hole near the elbow.

"What happened?"

"She was dead when I got there!" Jenny exclaimed. She dropped her head back between her knees and began to cry. As she shook, strings of her hair fell off her raw scalp and onto the concrete floor. Jenny used her attitude as armor, and I had never seen her vulnerable. I wanted to reach between the bars to console her, but getting the truth was more important.

"Why were you at Leah's house?" I asked.

"She asked me to come over," Jenny sniffed. "She texted me that she wanted to apologize, face-to-face, and that she wanted to compensate me for my financial losses from LuminUS. But when I got to her house . . ." Jenny didn't finish.

"I need you tell me more. Was anyone else in the house?"

"No. No one except for Aaron. He came out running and screaming that Leah was dead. I panicked. I tried to run, but before I could leave, the cops were already there. And now I'm here." She motioned around the cell. The metal toilet gurgled. It smelled of sewage. "What am I going to do? I can't afford a lawyer. No one's going to believe I didn't kill her. I'm so fucked."

I believed Jenny. The fear consuming her was too raw to fake. But if Jenny didn't kill Leah, then who did?

"Who let you in here?" The booming voice behind me made me swivel. The chief grabbed my arm and led me away from Jenny. "In my office. Now!"

As the chief tried to strong-arm me into his office, Aaron walked out. "Let her go, Mike," he said. "She was Leah's friend too. We're all suffering."

I wrested my arm out of the chief's grip as he reluctantly let go, the muscles on my arm tingling from the grip of his sausage fingers.

Wanting to get the last word in, the chief told Aaron, as if I weren't there, "Escort her out. And I don't want to see her again or else she's going to be my next suspect."

Aaron led me away, much gentler than the chief had, though I didn't enjoy either of them touching me. As we walked through the station, a familiar face on a corkboard in the hall caught my eye. I inspected the photo as we passed: six men in blue polo shirts with a sprawling white clubhouse behind them. In the middle of the group, towering over the others, was Chief Briggs. Beside him, clutching a putter between his hands, was Aaron. The caption read: "Special thanks to Aaron Monroe and the Monroe Ministry for making this year's Putt 4 the Police Golf Classic a raging success!"

When we got outside to the parking lot, I pulled my arm away.

"Don't let his gruffness get to you. Mike has a prickly exterior, but he means well," Aaron told me.

Like Jenny, I thought. "Do you golf with him often? I noticed the photo as we were leaving."

"We go out as much as our wives let us." Aaron forced a laugh before his eyes darkened.

"Leah's going to be missed," I said.

"She was a beacon for many of us," Aaron said, a wobble in his voice. "I'm having a hard time realizing she's gone. That God called home one of his followers. It feels so unfair that the act of one crazy woman could end a life."

"I spoke with Jenny, briefly, but she swears she's innocent."

"I would expect no less. What else would she say? That's it's all her fault? That she murdered my defenseless wife?"

"I only bring it up in case you can think of anyone else who might have done it. Jenny said Leah was dead when she arrived at your house." I knew I was being pushy. Rude, even, considering Aaron had lost his wife only hours before. But I was tired of being in the dark. I needed to get to the bottom of this, before someone else wound up dead—and I didn't trust Chief Briggs to do the job.

Aaron fumbled in his pocket and pulled out his car keys. He pressed the unlock button three times, his Audi beeping close by. "She's a liar. You heard how she spoke to Leah that night at the party. Anyone with half a brain could see she's guilty of shooting my wife."

His answer confirmed my suspicion that the murder weapon was a gun. "Maybe you're right," I said, playing along. "Besides, once they run prints on the gun and trace the serial number, it will prove Jenny did it."

"Yes, right, exactly. Now if you'd excuse me, I need to get going. I have a lot of calls to make."

I watched as Aaron readjusted the glasses that were sliding from the sweaty bridge of his nose and walked across the parking lot to his car.

I'd watched enough true crime documentaries to know that women were most likely to be murdered by an intimate partner. I had no proof, but I couldn't rule Aaron out. He was the only other person confirmed to be on the scene. Jenny had mentioned how quickly the cops arrived, moments after Aaron discovered Leah's body. There were two reasons cops worked that quickly: one, if they were chummy with the caller, like Aaron and the chief, and two, if they were already on their way.

As I imagined ways to prove Jenny's innocence, my phone buzzed: one new message from the testing lab.

My blood results were in.

I opened the patient portal. My hand shook as I clicked on GET MY RESULTS. No drugs, illicit or legal, no tetanus, botulinum toxin, diphtheria, dioxin, or any other neurotoxins, phototoxins, or hemotoxins. No elevated bacterial levels. *Phew*, I thought. That was good. Until my eyes darted to the red warning symbol with the description: "Trace amounts of heavy metals, unspecified, have been detected. Levels too low to determine type."

Heavy metals? In my blood? I scratched at my arms, my skin suddenly feeling itchy all over, and googled symptoms of heavy metals in the body: hair loss, tremors, insomnia, weight loss, impairment of speech and motor skills, and severe damage to the central nervous system that, if untreated, leads to death. The effects were too similar to the ones experienced by the LuminUS women to be a coincidence.

I called Steph as I began walking to her house. If she wasn't going to stop taking the supplements on her own, I would flush them all down the toilet like Hanna Cole suggested. She didn't answer, so I called again. Then three more times, leaving voicemails each time. Finally, I sent her a text: "911 call me back ASAP!"

As I walked down the shoulder of the busy road, heading back toward Cortland Ranch, a Wawa sign appeared before me like a shining beacon. Wherever you went in New Jersey, there was always a Wawa within the general vicinity, which was convenient since my throat felt like cotton from not hydrating all evening. The fluorescent lights blinded me as I walked in. The girl at the counter, an inattentive teenager who smacked her gum loudly and had a piercing above her lip, watched me walk in before going back to reading her magazine.

I knew the layout by heart. Wawa hadn't changed since I lived in the area, except that it now offered cheeseburgers and quesadillas. Grabbing a jug of lemonade iced tea, a family-size bag of Herr's sour cream and onion chips, and a double pack of store-brand soft pretzels, I waited behind a woman holding a toddler. The toddler's lips were stained purple and he held a slobbered-on lollipop that he graciously offered me. A short line had gathered at the register. The girl at the counter gabbed with her first customer in between each scan.

"Did you hear about them knocking down the old library?" she asked, gum clicking between her teeth. "Paper said they're gonna build a park, as if we need another open space. Those meth heads will overrun it. I would love to see them build something I can use. Like a new nail place, ya know?"

This is going to take forever, I thought. My plan was to go to Steph's, show her the results, and make her get rid of the supplements. I would kick down her door, if I had to. While I waited, I pulled my phone from my back pocket and scrolled through my socials. I searched for any news updates on Leah Monroe. There was only a Twitter alert from the Clearfield County Police Department that read:

ALERT: #CCPD is investigating a possible homicide at the Cortland Ranch development. Victim is an adult female, late forties. Suspect has been apprehended. Investigation is ongoing. #ClearfieldCounty

Nothing I didn't know already. The comments were pouring in.

MaggsMomm: Who was the victim?
BeetleBally_69: def drugs involved. when I become mayor im gonna wipe out all the dirty addicks. #BangBang

Todd7625: I live next door. HORRIBLE! Do better, #CCPD!

Jimmy_Jake: Those rich fux deserve it.

BeagleAuntie725: Thoughts and prayers 🙏

Tough crowd. Schadenfreude was in full force. The more Clear-field deteriorated, the less likely locals were to sympathize with some-one driving around in their Audi S8 that had a starting MSRP of $120,000—especially when that someone was a minister spreading the gospel of a Lord who preached about helping the poor.

I checked the LuminUS group chat to see if anyone had heard. Messages were pouring in, but they were all about the new #NoFilter foundation. I guessed the news hadn't reached them yet. I didn't want to be the one to break it.

The teen at the counter was still chatting with the same customer. She was showing her a picture on her phone of the manicure she wanted. "They use this special polish that has metal in it and when you run a magnet over it, it makes this velvet pattern, see?"

Next, I searched for Chief Mike Briggs. If he had any history of botched past cases, I wanted to know. Mike didn't have a social media presence. His history was laid out in different news articles and press releases, none of them particularly interesting. An image search showed rows of professional headshots that all police and government officials take: cloudy blue backdrops with an American flag hanging in the background and Mike Briggs smiling at the camera.

I found the photo I'd seen on the corkboard of Mike and Aaron at the golf tournament. Then I found a few photos of them together at previous years' events. The further back I searched, the more photos I found of Mike and Aaron together. The images came from Mrs. Briggs's profile, which went to show how no one, no matter how hard they try, can truly stay private online.

Mike was at Aaron's church, holding up his grandchild who was getting baptized by Aaron. Mike was smoking cigars and lounging in a chair at a summer backyard barbecue at Aaron's house. Mike was wearing red, white, and blue swim trunks and holding up a Corona on one of the Monroes' Mexican beach vacations. These two were friends. Close friends. It didn't hurt to have a connection with the chief of police, not when your wife was involved in a shady business. Mrs. Briggs was also involved with LuminUS and part of Leah's downline, which came as no surprise to me. She was a Ruby.

There was nothing inherently damning about their connection —it was natural that two pillars of the community would be friends, but it rubbed me the wrong way. I didn't believe in this many coincidences, nor did I trust their relationship was strictly cigars and guy talk.

As I stood in line, cradling my junk food in one arm, the pieces began falling into place. One by one, they locked together, perfectly flush: Aaron was openly involved with LuminUS, so whatever Leah knew, he likely knew as well. Aaron was close with the chief, and if the "overdose" deaths were related to LuminUS products, it would be too easy for Mike to use his power to keep the toxicology reports sealed. He had two motives: his friendship with Aaron and his wife's involvement as a distributor. But if the Monroes did have some kind of deal with Chief Briggs, what went wrong? Why had it ended up with Leah dead? Linking Aaron to Leah's murder wouldn't be easy, especially not with his connections.

"Damnit," I whispered to myself. I couldn't stand here waiting around any longer. I cut in front of the people ahead of me, dropped the chips and pretzels and drink onto the counter, and told the cashier, "Don't want these anymore, sorry!"

She mouthed a curse, but I didn't care. I needed to make a pit stop at Aaron's house on my way to Steph's. What a husband does the night his wife dies is the most telling, or, as I hoped in this case, most damning. The first night without my mom, my dad took two of her painkillers, which wasn't enough to knock him out and keep him from sobbing in bed the entire night.

What would Aaron be doing, when the cops were gone and he was alone in his big house?

Chapter 24

I called Steph three more times, listening to her voicemail recording ("Hiya, it's me, Stephanie Murphy, Platinum LuminUS consultant. Sorry I can't . . .") as I jogged back into Cortland Ranch. I called Rob equally as many times and received the same silence.

It was nearing eleven at night when I approached Aaron's house. I took a moment to catch my breath and wait for the stitch in my side to abate. I was soaked in sweat. I hadn't jogged this much since high school gym class, and I'd skipped most of those, pretending I had my period. I regretted that now. Most of the block was asleep, the only light coming from the replica gas lamps that let off a weak, golden glow. As I suspected, the cops were gone, as was the police tape. That sort of bright yellow reminder that a crime occurred was bad for property values.

Grateful for the cover of darkness, I snuck down the driveway, pressing my body against the hedges and sidestepping landscaping lights. The gate to the backyard was unlocked, so I crept in. Someone was near the pool, leaning over the edge and staring into the empty basin. The water had been drained.

My heart in my throat, I took out my phone to record the scene, hoping to catch Aaron in a nefarious act. As my phone adjusted to the darkness, I zoomed in, which was when the figure turned around and yelled, "Hey you!"

I dropped my phone and was about to run when I realized I recognized that voice. "Rob?"

"Drew?" He squinted. "What are you doing?"

I stood, grabbed my phone, and approached him. "I wanted to check in on Aaron to see how he's doing."

"By creeping around in the dark?"

"I didn't want to barge in on him if he was busy," I said, using my shirt to wipe the dirt from my phone.

Rob didn't bother questioning my obvious lies. He reached down and grabbed one of the green plastic jugs beside his feet. "He's not here. He's at my house. Steph offered to cook him a late dinner since he hasn't eaten."

"He's alone with Steph? What are you doing here, anyway?"

Rob unscrewed the jug's cap, releasing chemical fumes so strong they burned my nose. "Aaron asked me to clean up." He dumped the viscous liquid into the pool. I took a step backward, worried it would splash and eat through my skin. Rob pinched his nose with his free hand. "This stuff's disgusting. I told Aaron we should use bleach, but he wouldn't shut up about how much better Wipr is. I think he wants to dig into his stock. He's got a packed shed. It's almost as bad as our garage."

"How long have you known Aaron?" I asked.

"Only as long as Steph's been involved with Leah."

"I don't trust him," I said outright. "And I don't like him alone with Steph."

Rob paused, letting the empty jug hang loosely from his hand.

"I'm not his biggest fan either. Did you know he had the audacity to try to sell us on Wipr, when Steph's already killing herself trying to stay a Platinum with LuminUS? But he's harmless."

"Do you care if I look around? I won't touch anything."

"Be my guest. You know what? I'm not doing this." Rob let the bottle fall from his hand, the splash of the excess missing his foot by inches. "I don't care how much Aaron is paying me. Cleaning his dead wife's blood is too weird. They have professionals for this. I'm going to head to Fred's Tavern. I need a drink."

"Shouldn't you go home instead? To check on Steph? She's not answering my calls."

"She texted me not that long ago, but I'll call her on the way to the bar. I'm sure she's fine, though. Probably turned off her phone so she can give Aaron her full attention. You know how she gets during times of crisis."

I did. Steph put aside her own issues, no matter how significant, to help others heal. "Let me know if you hear anything," I told Rob.

"While you're snooping around, can you put these bottles back into the shed?" Rob motioned his foot toward the remaining Wipr jugs. "Lock the door on your way out. And watch yourself. Aaron has cameras everywhere."

I took his warning and grabbed two bottles as I went to the shed. Rob was convinced Aaron was harmless, but I wasn't so sure. Aaron may not have pulled the trigger, but he was definitely involved with Leah's death. And perhaps Mackenzie's as well.

As I entered the shed, I saw shelves lined with mint-green Wipr boxes. A single bulb hung from the ceiling, swinging in the airy draft, spotlighting thousands of dollars' worth of product collecting dust. My eyes watered from the fumes that were permeating the seals. LuminUS was toxic, and I would bet my last twenty bucks that Wipr was worse, despite its claims of being "derived from 99.9 percent natural ingredients." The Monroes' sudden pivot to Wipr made sense now—I'd bet anything it was their exit strategy. They must have known it was only a matter of time before the toxicity of LuminUS came out and the company went under, taking them down with it.

I was placing the bottles on the floor, my sinuses burning, when I noticed a dollop of green fluid on the ground near the back corner. It trailed across the concrete floor, the slime leading to a coffee canister under the lowest shelf.

At the base of the container were tiny bubbles corroding a hole through the tin. The source of the leak, I realized. This was odd. Why would Aaron be storing Wipr chemicals in a separate container, one that was hidden? Careful not to touch it with my bare skin, I pulled my sleeve over my hand and used my knuckle to pop open the plastic lid.

"No!" I gasped.

Floating in the thick mucus-like solution was a pocket-size revolver. Its wooden grip was stained green, the veneer buckling from the acid. I didn't dare touch it. Aaron put this here, I realized. He scrambled to hide the murder weapon before the police came. But why would he ask Rob to help him clean up? Why would he encourage him to use Wipr products, knowing what was hidden in the shed?

Then I realized—he *wanted* Rob's fingerprints all over the shed, just in case his attempt to frame Jenny didn't pan out. In case he needed to frame another innocent person. He must have texted Jenny from his dead wife's phone, luring her to his home. He must have called the police immediately after, knowing that when his buddy Mike got there, he'd take Aaron's word for it, and Jenny would be arrested on the spot.

It had all gone down before Jenny even got there. Aaron had shot his wife. Aaron, who used his community standing as a shield, who thought he was above consequence, and who was now . . .

At Steph's house!

I knew I had to act fast. As I ran down the streets of the development, redialing Steph's and Rob's numbers again and again, I felt it in every cell in my body.

Steph was in danger.

Chapter 25

The run from Leah's house to Steph's house took me eleven minutes, which by Boston Marathon standards is a piss-poor time, but was my personal best. I really regretted letting Bre drive me to party—if I'd just taken my dad's car, I wouldn't have had to spend the whole night sprinting all over Clearfield. Pouring sweat and weighed down by Leah's mohair sweater, I could hardly breathe and was hunched over with cramps when I pounded on her front door.

"Steph! Are you—" I gulped in a lungful of air. "Are you home?"

No one answered.

My worst fears began to rear their ugly heads. Was I already too late? Was I about to find my best friend's body? I hadn't dared call the cops on my way over, fearing that Chief Briggs would show up and let his buddy slither away yet again. It was all down to me.

I knew the code to get in: 0621. Her wedding anniversary. When I let myself into the front hall, I heard voices coming from the kitchen. No raised voices—just a normal conversation.

I ran into the back of the house and saw Steph and Aaron sitting across from each other at the kitchen counter, holding mugs of hot coffee. They looked startled to see me, but otherwise seemed relaxed. No blood, no weapons—but that didn't mean Steph was safe with him, either.

I was too emotional to take the cool and calm approach, so instead, I yelled at Aaron. "Get away from her!"

"What's wrong with you?" Steph asked, her brow crinkling, sounding more concerned than accusatory.

I approached her and tried to pull her away from Aaron and out the back door, but she planted her feet and wouldn't budge. "Come with me. Trust me," I pleaded, but Steph didn't move. "We need to leave."

"What are you talking about?" Steph said. "I'm not leaving. The boys are sleeping upstairs, and Aaron and I are talking about Leah." Her face softened. "Drew . . . something terrible has happened."

"I know," I panted. "I know Leah is dead, and it's even worse than you think. Listen—"

"We're trying to figure out how to best honor her," Aaron interjected. "Maybe you can help. Do you think she would have preferred pink peonies or stargazer lilies?"

"Are you fucking kidding me?" I exclaimed. "You're choosing funeral flowers for the wife you *killed*?"

A heavy silence fell over the kitchen, broken only by the sound of my heaving breath.

Maybe there was some better, smarter way to approach the situation, but my patience had run away, taking my tact with it. Watching Aaron look all innocent, adjusting the collar of his crisp blue dress shirt, gray eyes wide in consternation, made my cheeks grow hot.

"Drew!" Steph scolded me, slapping both hands down on the counter to express her displeasure.

"It's all right," Aaron said. "I know Jenny was your friend, and that it's difficult to accept she's a murderer." He spoke to me in a serene voice, as though he were ministering to his flock. But I wasn't one of his sheep.

"I found the gun," I said. "In your shed. Nice job trying to dissolve it with Wipr acid, but it didn't work. Guess that shit is all smoke and mirrors. Just like LuminUS. And just like you." I stood defiantly, angling my body in front of Steph's as I watched Aaron's face change. He took off his glasses and pinched the cartilage above his nose, letting out a long sigh.

I expected a denial—for Aaron to laugh in my face, or call me crazy, or threaten to call the cops or sue for slander. Instead, in a meek voice, so quiet it was nearly a whisper, he said, "I didn't want to do it. I loved her."

Another heavy silence fell over the room. I looked at Steph, hoping to see in her face that she believed me now. I could see the confusion in her eyes turn to fear, then to anger.

"What are you talking about?" Steph asked, her voice wavering. "Are you saying that *you* . . . killed Leah?"

"That's exactly what he's saying! Which is why we need to go. Right now." I put my arms around her shoulders, leading her around the island and toward the back door. This time, she moved with me.

Aaron sprung toward us, blocking our path. "I can't let you leave." His voice shook. He still held out his coffee mug, the molten liquid steaming. It was two against one, and Steph and I were unarmed. I had no idea if Aaron was carrying a weapon.

I needed to keep him talking.

"Why did you do it? Are you getting paid by LuminUS, too?" I asked Aaron, ignoring Steph tugging on my arm, pleading with me to be quiet. "Are you another one of their conspirators?" I watched Aaron raise his brows and cock his head, the mug quivering in his hands. "That's right," I continued. "I know all about LuminUS paying off Leah, Steph, and Mackenzie to promote their shitty brand."

Aaron scoffed. "That's a lie. LuminUS wasn't paying for our life-style—we made our money fair and square. Leah built her downline and her empire herself. Leah lived and breathed the company. She bled LuminUS blue, for God's sake."

That wasn't true. She bled regular red blood, I thought, picturing her body face down in her pool.

"But she knew about the deals Dixie made with Steph and Mackenzie, didn't she?"

Aaron said nothing.

"Is that why you killed her?" I pressed. "Because she was going to tell everyone that LuminUS was a fraud? That they had to prop up their own consultants to make them look successful? Or was she was going to come clean about how harmful the products are?"

Aaron stayed silent.

"If you're telling the truth, and Leah really did make a fortune through LuminUS, then why do *you* care if the truth comes out?"

"Don't you see?" Aaron burst out, the coffee in his mug sloshing onto the floor. "They would call us frauds. Scammers. We'd be a joke to the community." He took a step closer, eyes alight with frustration. Steph pulled me back a few steps in response. I eyed the hot coffee in his mug, ready to duck and tackle Steph if he decided to throw it in our faces. "If anyone found out two of Leah's best downlines were plants, we'd be through. The only reason anyone joins is because of the prestige of having Leah as their upline. Without that trust, her downline would fall apart, my congregants would leave, my church would go under, and I'd have nothing. Not even Wipr."

His face contorted as though he was about to cry. It seemed genu-ine. Aaron was waging a battle within himself. He didn't want to hurt us, but he would if he had to. He would barrel through any obstacle that came in between him and his image. "But now she's gone," he whispered. "If I couldn't save her, I can still save myself."

Steph whimpered from behind me. The hand she had clenched tightly around my forearm was shaking. Aaron kept stepping closer. With every inch he pressed forward, we shuffled backward, moving as one. Steph was hardly able to stand from shock, much less help me attack Aaron. I needed to stall him while I thought of another plan.

"Did she know about the poison in the products too?" I asked. "How LuminUS killed all those women?" If I could eat enough time, someone would come to our rescue, right? Rob had to come home eventually—especially after the slew of urgent messages I left him. I only hoped the boys upstairs would stay asleep in their beds.

"We knew they were harmful, yes. And I knew it wouldn't stay under wraps forever," Aaron said. "Eventually LuminUS would close up, marred by negative reviews, or, worse, a full exposé. It was only a matter of time before someone found out about the ingredients."

"Ingredients?" Steph squeaked.

"Heavy metals. Lead. Mercury. The stuff's loaded with them," I told her. "LuminUS is killing people and the Monroes knew all along."

"We had no idea when we first joined!" Aaron protested. "My wife was just a distributor, like all the rest of you—she had no idea until her LuminUS ladies started dropping like files. It's Dixie you should blame," he said, eyes narrowing. "But we had a plan. I asked Mike to seal the autopsies to buy us more time. We were going to leave LuminUS long before they shut down and focus on Wipr. By the time the truth came out, we would have cut ties long ago. No one would blame us for the company's failings. And with Leah's abilities, Wipr would be an instant success. We would move on and never look back."

"Did you kill Mackenzie?" Steph asked in a weak voice.

Aaron took another step forward. There was sadness in his eyes, but also rage. He was readying himself for the unthinkable.

"No. Leah did. Mackenzie threatened to go public about being a plant, but we needed more time. Wipr is only just getting off the ground. If it all came out before we were ready, we'd be ruined. Leah did it for us. She did it for me! But the guilt destroyed her."

"Don't come any closer," I warned. "Rob will be here any minute."

Come on, Rob, I thought. *Stop pounding cheap light beers and come home.*

"Now you see why I can't let you leave. Leah's gone. That wasn't part of the plan, but her death won't be in vain. If I let you tell the world, she died for nothing." Sweat rolled from his temple and down his neck. "You see why I had to do it, right?" he pleaded with me. "She was going to tell everyone. The guilt over what she did to Mackenzie was killing her inside. It all came to a head after Jenny smashed up her party. She said she wouldn't involve me in her confession, but it wouldn't have made a difference. Her confession would open too many boxes, create too many questions. Before long, the spotlight would be on me and my church, and I'd be dragged down with her."

He took another step forward.

I moved us another step back.

"You don't have to hurt us," I pleaded. "I can see how you were forced to make a bad decision, but it doesn't make you an evil person. You can make it right, put an end to this nightmare. Don't add another death to the list. You can let us go."

Aaron paused. For a moment, I thought he was calming, allowing the smallest sliver of his rational side to take over.

I was wrong.

"I won't lose it all!" he screamed as he swung the full coffee cup. I ducked to my left, pulling on Steph's arm, but she didn't move in time.

"*Argh!*" she cried out. The mug slammed against her brow, shattering with an ugly crunch. The pieces crashed to the floor, the hot liquid splattering along with it. Steph steadied herself as Aaron grabbed her throat, digging his fingers so deeply into her skin that they turned white.

I threw myself on Aaron, hitting and scratching him, yanking at his arms, even sinking my teeth into his skin, but he was strong and broad. I was no match for him. I had no time to think. Steph's face was turning purple. Blood vessels in her eyes burst. Her breath was making an awful rattling sound.

I turned toward the counter, frantically searching for a weapon. I grabbed the closest item I could find: LuminUS's makeup-setting face spray with a refreshing citrus blend and a vitamin C boost. I knew from experience that the essential oils it contained burned like hell.

With both hands, one thumb on top of the other, I spritzed madly right into Aaron's face.

He let go of Steph with a shout and covered his eyes with both hands. "My eyes!" he hollered, blindly stumbling backward into the kitchen.

"Run!" I yelled to Steph, hooking my arm into hers and dashing out the door.

We ran. She coughed, hacking as air flooded her bruised windpipe. Her eyes were cloudy and bloodshot, but we ran.

I didn't let her go. Not for a single second.

From the CCPD Twitter Page

May 2018

ALERT: #CCPD is investigating an aggravated assault in the Cortland Ranch development. Suspect has been apprehended. Minor injuries reported. Investigation is ongoing. #ClearfieldCounty

BeetleBally_69: herd it was the priest. betya he was doped up two. scumbags.

FlowersInHerHair_127: What is happening over there?! We should cancel school ASAP!!! Think about the children!

Kama_Burns_52: Ask me how I make $2727.00 every week working from home! 🏡
No experience or computer required! Get paid weekly. Stop dreaming and start earning TODAY! 💰💰💰

BeagleAuntie725: Thoughts and prayers 🙏

Chapter 26

"Want another cup of coffee?" I asked Steph, even though the Styrofoam cup she balanced on her lap was nearly full. The bandage across her eye was beginning to ooze and would need a replacement.

"It's hurting my throat," she rasped.

"You're not supposed to be talking. How about I get you some tea instead?" I glanced toward the break area. An old Mr. Coffee hissed steam. Beside it stood a bulk-size can of ground coffee. No tea bags, but there was a faucet and a microwave. "Or how about some hot water with . . ." I doubted there was a lemon anywhere. "Sugar?"

"Ew," Steph said.

"Yeah, I know. We should be out of here soon. I'm going to top myself off." I had been saying we were going to be leaving soon for the past four hours. Yet there we sat, in the police station, hour after hour, on stiff, plastic chairs that could be easily hosed off in case of the occasional drunken perp with a full bladder.

We had been questioned separately to make sure our stories matched. Steph was provided with medical attention first. A ring of purple bruises wrapped around her throat. She was given a neck brace to keep from moving too much and reinjuring the tender area. The lump above her eye swelled her lid shut, but it didn't need stitches. The ER doctors concluded her injuries were minor enough to forgo a hospital stay. She was given an ice pack and a Tylenol. I came out of the ordeal without a scratch, but was given a Tylenol and one of those crinkly silver blankets by the paramedics anyway.

After Aaron attacked Steph, we ran as far as we could before finding the first house whose lights were on. Steph pounded on the door as I rang the bell, and it wasn't long before Mr. and Mrs. Thomas opened their door to find two sweaty girls, one yelling over the other, "We need help right now call the police there's a murderer oh my God help!!"

I didn't feel safe even when the Thomases let us in and reset their door alarm. I didn't feel safe when the police showed up, knowing the chief was in cahoots with Aaron. I didn't feel safe when Aaron was handcuffed and taken into custody, assuming he would sweet-talk his way out of the situation and be free to finish the job.

As I poured coffee into my empty cup, I wondered if I would ever feel safe again. As far as I knew, Aaron couldn't weasel his way out of the situation. Steph had security cameras in every room of her home, equipped with microphones. Aaron's attack and confession, from start to finish, was captured in high resolution and backed up on a private cloud server that even Chief Briggs couldn't access.

But who else was involved? LuminUS was ingrained in Clearfield. It had invaded and spread like an invasive species, destroying everything in its wake. LuminUS ladies were everywhere, hidden in plain sight.

They were your hairstylists, librarians, teachers, nurses, nannies. The mom at your kid's soccer practice who brought the tree-nut-free, peanut-free, and gluten-free brownies? She could be a LuminUS lady.

The woman in front of you in the checkout line at Target, buying scented candles at 50 percent off? Yup, a LuminUS lady. How about your coworker who calls her cats her fur babies and plays Christmas music starting November 1? That's right, folks. A LuminUS lady. Dixie's army of women tasked with spreading the good word of LuminUS outnumbered us.

And what would Dixie do when she found out about the arrest? Worse yet, what would she do when she found out Steph and I had every intention of going public—security footage and all? She had an army of lawyers and enough money to make our lives hell. And who were we? Just a failed journalist and a stay-at-home mom with crippling debt.

I wasn't completely dismissive toward LuminUS. How could I be? I'd learned there was one good thing about its products: thanks to LuminUS cheaping out on their face mist and using artificial chemicals for their citrus blend instead of pure oils, Aaron had suffered serious damage to his eyes. The chemicals caused second-degree burning, which led to swollen corneas. His right eye got most of the damage. Doctors weren't sure how long it would take for his vision to return, or if it ever would.

"Ms. Cooper?" Officer Reeves walked up beside me. She was more squirrely than when I saw her last, her gaze darting around the room although she was addressing me.

"Are we free to go?" I asked.

"You sure are. We need your signature on a few of your statements, and you can be on your way."

I was so desperate to leave the station that my seedy hotel room seemed like the Four Seasons. All I wanted to do was take a scalding hot shower and change into leggings and a new T-shirt. I was still wearing Leah's sweater around my waist. Multiple times throughout the night, I considered tossing it, but it wasn't mine to throw away. Meanwhile, I had developed the stench of someone who exercised in heavy wool.

Officer Reeves handed me a clipboard and pen, watching me as I signed. She rocked back and forth on her police-issued leather boots. I could tell she wanted to talk. I doubted she was permitted to interview those involved in high-profile cases, and, by Clearfield's standards, a beloved local minister arrested on aggravated assault charges was as high profile as it got.

"Do you know what happened to Leah? How she died, I mean," I asked. At my question, Officer Reeves lit up. I had given her the opening she was craving.

"Well," Officer Reeves began, taking a quick look around to make sure no one was listening, "I can't say much, of course."

"Of course," I assured her.

"But, Leah was shot. Once. In the back of the head."

Back of the head? I wondered. It explained the halo of blood and why I hadn't seen the wound. It must have been covered by her hair as it floated in the water.

"Has Aaron confessed?" I asked, having already told the detectives numerous times what Aaron had said. He hadn't directly confessed to Leah's murder, in the sense that he didn't say the exact words "T'was I who killed my wife!" but he may as well have.

"No. He hasn't. He's being questioned, but isn't saying a thing without his lawyer."

"What about Jenny Fitzsimmons?" I asked, handing back the clipboard. "Is she still being charged?"

"For now. It's a formality until we get a confession or more proof that she didn't pull the trigger. Between you and me"—she leaned in and cupped her hand at the side of her mouth—"it won't be long.

Especially since you found the murder weapon."

I looked over at Steph. She was using a pencil to scratch the skin on her neck beneath the brace.

"What's taking them so long to test the gun?" I asked. Jenny was in a cell somewhere, wrongfully accused and worrying for her life, while Aaron was waiting on his high-priced attorney, thinking he was going to slip out of the situation as he had slipped out of all the others. He was a snake and always would be.

"It's covered in some sort of slime. We won't get prints, but the serial number should be easy enough to match to Mr. Monroe—once we clean it enough to get a good read."

"Reeves!" Chief Briggs called from his office. "We're not paying you to gossip!" He had the reddened, glassy face of someone on the verge of a heart attack.

Knowing Aaron, he would throw Briggs under the bus with him. There was no loyalty amongst thieves. No captains going down with the ship. When cornered, Aaron would kick and scratch, making as many deals as he could to save his own skin. If that meant tattling on the chief of police, so be it. Officer Reeves scurried away to file my paperwork, and I sat back down beside Steph.

"Steph!" Rob came in and wrapped his arms around his wife. She nuzzled her face into the side of his neck. "I've been trying to see you for hours! They wouldn't let me past the front desk until you were cleared."

I allowed the two to reconnect. Rob stroked Steph's hair and winced at the sight of her injuries. Over a decade spent together, and the love between them wasn't lost. It was stronger than ever. After a few minutes of hushed conversation, Rob grabbed my attention.

"You saved her," he said. "I can never thank you enough." He brought me into a group hug which didn't last long, because Steph cocked her neck too much and yelped in pain.

We laughed together, in happiness and relief, with tears pooling in our eyes.

"I should have fixed things before it got this bad," Rob told Steph.

"You didn't know," Steph said. "I kept everything so hidden. I was ashamed. But I should have been honest instead of holding it in and then fighting with you."

"I knew enough," Rob said as Steph furrowed her brow. "Okay, maybe not *all* of it, but I knew that something was wrong with that fucking company. I should have been there for you instead of blaming you. I'm just so glad you're safe. Whatever the fallout is, we'll figure it out. Together."

They held each other until Steph asked, "Can you give me and Drew a second alone?"

He nodded and stepped back.

"I've been wanting to say this for a while now." Steph hung her head as much as her brace would allow. "I am so sorry. This is all my fault. I should have never gotten you involved with LuminUS." Steph cleared her throat. I wanted to interject, to tell her to rest her voice, but she was intent on communicating words she had held on to for too long.

And I couldn't deny I wanted to hear her apologize. Our last conversation had been a massive fight, and I was still angry that she roped me into LuminUS, despite knowing it was a money pit. "Why did you recruit me?" I asked. "Was I just an easy mark?"

"I was desperate," she said, her eyes filling with tears. "I wasn't thinking clearly. Any new member in my downline was another step toward getting out of LuminUS's deal and saving my family. It's all I thought about, day in and day out. 'How many new women can I find to grow my numbers?' No one was safe. No matter how little you had or whether you'd hit rock bottom, if you were over eighteen with access to a credit card, you were my target. Given the chance, I would have recruited Mother Theresa. I hate myself for it. But of all the disgusting things I did, targeting you is my biggest regret. Besides making the initial deal with Dixie—the devil herself."

We sat back on the bench. Both our energy levels were dwindling, and Steph's pain medications were making her sway. But she continued. "The sick part is that I still thought there was a chance of success with LuminUS. Even after I found out they made the same deal with Mackenzie, I thought that maybe, if we worked hard enough, and the company grew bigger, we could make real money. Then I could pay our debts, reimburse LuminUS for everything they spent on me, and you would have enough to help your dad, and we could ride off into the sunset. How stupid was I?"

"Not stupid," I told her. "Brainwashed, absolutely. But not stupid."

Steph tilted her body, resting her head and stiffened neck on my shoulder. "Will you ever forgive me?"

"Already have," I said. "I know how it feels to be trapped—willing to step over anyone to claw yourself from the cage you're in. It's why I agreed to join LuminUS even though it went against everything I believed in. Altering photos, cold messaging anyone I could with blatant lies, wearing sequin minidresses—I lost sight of who I was, and I know you did too."

"I don't know who I am anymore."

"Don't worry about that now. Let's enjoy this moment, knowing that the truth will come out and that Aaron is busted," I said.

"You have no idea how happy I am that this is over," she said.

△ △ △

Within the week following Aaron's arrest, the evidence began to add up. (Officer Reeves may have been a massive gossip, but it sure was nice to have her as an inside source.)

After the murder weapon was tested, it was determined it belonged to Aaron, no surprise there. No prints could be pulled thanks to the Wipr gunk, but the serial number matched Aaron Monroe. Gunpowder residue was found on his shirt while none was found on Jenny. It also helped that the Monroes had the same security camera system as Steph. Aaron had attempted to erase the videos, but was so technologically inept he only moved them to a separate folder. The actual shooting wasn't on camera, due to the angle, but it was enough to prove that although Jenny had been in the house, she hadn't done anything.

Jenny was finally released, and Aaron was accused of first-degree murder and attempted murder. He was pleading not guilty, claiming Leah's murder was somehow self-defense. I eagerly awaited the trial in which he would have to prove he shot his wife in the back of the head to protect his own life.

Disappointingly, Chief Briggs and the coroner didn't even get a slap on the wrist. Briggs denied everything, claiming nothing Aaron said could be believed. "How can you trust a man who brutally murdered his own wife?" I never found out how Briggs was able to convince the coroner to fudge the records, but I assumed Briggs either lied to him, bribed him, or threatened him. I only hoped the truth about their involvement would come out during the trial.

I met with Jenny once she had time to process what had occurred. She had reconciled with her husband and moved out of town to get some space from everything. We decided to chat as she walked her new puppy around the park.

"He's super cute," I told her. The dog was a six-month-old rescue.

A boxer mix she named Douglas.

"Paul thought it would be a good idea to get a dog. I've always wanted one, and he figured it would give me something to take care of," she explained. "I thought about getting another hamster, but Douglas is more active."

"It works for my dad," I told her, thinking of Captain Milton.

"He's eaten my wireless headphones and a shoe. But I can't stay mad at that goofy face." She bent down to scrunch Douglas's wrinkles. He wagged his tail and tried to jump on her chest. Jenny had put on some weight and was looking healthier. "He's also tried to get into an old bottle of LuminUS night cream, but I caught him in time."

"You don't want him getting into that stuff. Who knows what's in it."

The toxicology reports hadn't been unsealed, but JB had filed an official lawsuit against LuminUS. Media had jumped on the story, especially after the news of Aaron killing his wife. JB's legal team was working on getting products tested and putting in motions to unseal the reports.

Many of the victims' husbands were on board. It would be a chance to justify their intuitions that their wives hadn't overdosed. With the legal pressure, media coverage, and support of families, it was only a matter of time before the truth came out.

As we walked past a couple walking their dog, Jenny gingerly tugging on the excited Douglas's harness. She shared what had happened that night at the Monroes'.

"The ironic part is that I went over to apologize. Leah texted me to come over so we could talk things out. As much as I hated Leah and what she had done to me, I still felt badly about my actions. I shouldn't have thrown bottles at her or ruined her dinner party."

I nodded, not telling Jenny what chain of events her actions had precipitated. Aaron had claimed Jenny's outburst was Leah's breaking point. She had been wrestling with guilt for some time but seeing how hurt Jenny was, and knowing she had ruined yet another life was too much for her. She resolved to come clean that night about LuminUS and about what she did to Mackenzie.

"The dinner party was a sham anyway. Who cares if you ruined it?" The dinner party was a front for another of the Monroes' many scams. It was discovered the Bread of Christ charity had donated only $2,600 worth of food and supplies in 2017, despite having raised and claimed taxes on a total of almost $100,000. The charity was no more than a money-laundering scheme. Between LuminUS, Wipr, the fake charity, and the entirety of the Monroe Ministries, they were professional con artists making millions off of donations and revenue from the people they'd duped.

The one thing Aaron didn't lie about was how much they earned with LuminUS. Leah had joined early on, thanks to her connection with Dixie. She was at the top of the pyramid: one of the lucky few who had enough women in her downline to do the heavy lifting for her.

"When I got to her house, the front door was open," Jenny continued. "I went around back and that's when I saw her body. I tried running away, but that stupid house is so big, and I got lost. Aaron caught me, locked me in the pantry, and called the police. I now know the text Leah sent came from Aaron. He needed a scapegoat, and I was the easiest target."

"You're lucky he didn't kill you," I said.

"The only reason he didn't was because he knew he could pin the murder on me."

"Do you think Mackenzie's murderer was premeditated?" I asked. I'd been wondering this for days. Had Leah really meant to kill Mackenzie? The push may have been purposeful, but Mackenzie plummeting down eleven stories may have been accidental.

"I don't know," Jenny said. She stopped walking, allowing Douglas to sniff a dandelion that he then attempted to eat. "I don't think I want to talk about this anymore. It's too much. I want to watch Douglas grow up and never think about LuminUS ever again."

"I understand."

We did a loop around the man-made pond in the center of the park. Douglas chased after two wood ducks who were trying to enjoy their morning paddle. Jenny spoke about her plan to start taking classes at the community college in the fall. She wanted to be a phlebotomist.

"They're always hiring at the medical center. Plus, I think blood's kinda neat," Jenny said. She had always been obsessed with slashers. Her room in high school was covered in vintage movie posters showing masked killers and women running away in fear.

"Sounds more promising than LuminUS."

"I know, right? Can you imagine getting a stable paycheck on a regular basis? And being paid for the hours you put in? It'll feel like a dream come true," she said.

I was glad to hear Jenny back to her cynical self. She was wearing a wig while her damaged hair grew back, but she had chosen a shade that matched her natural deep brown.

"What about you?" she asked. "Now that you're out of the direct sales game. Are you gonna move back to New York?"

I hadn't thought about my next move, other than writing about what happened. Steph had insisted I move back into the apartment above her garage until they figured out another place to live. I didn't need much in the way of convincing. Saying goodbye to the Thunderbird Inn was one of the best moments of my life.

When my time wasn't spent with Steph, who began every conversation with an apology, I sat on my bed and wrote. My earlier hunches about a story were correct. Between my firsthand experience and the drama of the events that unfolded, I knew that if I could craft the exposé properly, it would be a career maker. Never being the patient sort, I sent an early excerpt to a few editors along with a proposal. I wanted to be the first to break the entire story. Some of the pieces had been reported on, like Leah's murder and Mackenzie's death, but there was no story yet that made the connection between the murders, all the other dead downlines, and JB's lawsuit against LuminUS and its unethical practices.

Each of my emails was met with a resounding "Yes!" and a "Let's schedule a call to discuss." Finally, I was attracting interest. I had started to forget what the word *yes* looked like.

"What are you going to do with the LuminUS stuff?" I asked Jenny. "Steph has a garage full of it. She doesn't know what to do. It's just sitting there."

"I thought about selling it to make up some of the money I lost. But I can't. I don't want anyone to have it. I'll probably flush it down the toilet," she said.

We finished our loop. Douglas rolled onto his back and pretended to play dead so he wouldn't have to go home.

A woman in a matching neon-green sports bra and leggings jogged by, nearly slapping me with her long, blond ponytail. Her phone peeked out from the top of her hip pocket. I recognized the case immediately: metallic blue with a silver lotus.

Chapter 27

After everything that went down, once some of the dust began to settle, Steph and I figured we deserved a night on the town—revisiting old haunts and repeating inside jokes we hadn't heard in years.

One of our stops was the alley behind what used to be Bill's Corner Deli. It was where I had my first kiss. Bill Junior, son of Bill Senior, who owned the deli, asked me to help him dump the grease cans into the sewer. They were supposed to be properly disposed of, but neither of the Bills cared much about environmental protections. Bill Junior planted a wet one on my lips when I wasn't paying attention. It took me by surprise, and I yelled, "Gross!" and ran away to Steph's house, where we rinsed my mouth with dish soap. Bill Junior was cute, but I didn't appreciate the barrage. It didn't help that he was wearing his butcher's apron, having just carved a hog, and was covered in smears of fresh blood. For years, I associated kissing with the sweet, metallic smell of pig's blood. Likely the reason I didn't eat meat past high school.

"I didn't kiss anyone else until I was in college," I said.

"I remember," Steph said. "Tyler Lawrence tried to make his move at Heather Simpson's party, and you practically kneed him in the balls."

"He would have deserved it. What sort of guy thinks it's okay to layer puka shell necklaces?"

"I think they were shark teeth," Steph corrected.

"Even worse."

Walking down Main Street felt like a ghost tour. As we shared old stories, ones I hadn't allowed myself to think about until then, I saw phantom versions of our old selves. I saw past the busted windows and poorly drawn graffiti and could see how things were before everything changed.

It would have made me painfully melancholy if not for Steph's company. She still wore her neck brace, which her family had signed. I signed DREW WAS HERE '18 in bubble letters, adding a Cool S symbol for good measure. She moved with the grace of an unoiled Tin Man, which had become a point of frequent, playful teasing. Despite the injuries, both physical and mental, Steph's spirits had improved. She was finally free—of LuminUS and the secrets she was forced to keep.

It wasn't the smooth road to freedom she imagined. She had never expected it would include the death of two friends and an attempt on her own life. But the relief of no longer having to hide was so strong it outweighed the darkness in her past.

"I think we should get a drink," Steph said. We stood in front of the Rusty Nail Bar. A sign on the door read SORRY, WE'RE OPEN, and a neon sign flashed BEE in red letters. The R had burned out.

"I could go for a bee," I said.

"M'lady." Steph pretended to tip a hat as she opened the door and motioned for me to enter.

We were immediately hit with a cloud of cigarette smoke. The

Rusty Nail was one of Clearfield's last remaining dive bars. It would likely be the town's last remaining business, surviving the wave of bankruptcies, because there's no stronger business model in any recession than a bar that serves $2 well drinks. It was one of the few remaining neighborhood bars in New Jersey where you could enjoy a drink and smoke indoors. They had circumvented the law by claiming they were a casino, since there was one poker machine that they kept in the corner next to the men's bathroom. It hadn't worked for years. Patrons used it to hold their beers while they used the bathroom.

It was Friday night, and the place was crowded. We found a spot at the bar in between two men who were both struggling to keep their jeans at their waistlines.

"Crack kills," Steph whispered.

We ordered whiskey sours, figuring the sour syrup would be strong enough to hide the taste of cheap whiskey.

It wasn't. We pretended to gag as we drank, and stuck out our tongues to air out the tartness. A man tried to get past and bumped into Steph, spilling his rum and Coke onto her shoulder.

"So sorryyy," he slurred. "Let me buy you cuties a drink."

We accepted and ordered two more whiskey sours before a woman with a teased updo behind her zebra-print headband pulled him away by his belt loop. She yelled at him the entire walk back to their seats.

The speakers blared. The Rusty Nail had a stage area, where a stocky man sat on a stool and held a microphone to his lips. His polyester shirt was unbuttoned down to his diaphragm. A gold crucifix necklace was nestled between tufts of chest hair.

"Please tell me it isn't open mic night," Steph said.

"Nope. It's karaoke Friday," the bartender told us, having overheard our conversation.

"Oh no," Steph and I lamented in unison.

The hairy man started the chorus to "Forever in Blue Jeans," turning the Neil Diamond song into a croon. He scanned the room, making sexy eyes at every woman he saw, hoping one would reciprocate.

We dubbed him Dean Fartin. Our level of maturity plummeted as our alcohol intake increased.

"Should we sign up?" Steph asked, despite knowing my aversion to singing in public. I had the voice of a cat in heat.

"I'd rather go to a LuminUS conference," I said. I wasn't sure if Steph was at the point where we could joke about the ordeal. One of my coping mechanisms was using humor as a deflection. Steph wasn't the same way. She pushed problems away, pretending they didn't exist. In her mind, if it wasn't said out loud, it wasn't real.

I didn't need to worry. She threw her head back and laughed before saying, "Ow," and rubbing the brace. "We should have a drink to celebrate never needing to throw another LuminUS party ever again."

"Fine, but I can't do another sour. My tongue is on fire."

Steph ordered for us. "Something light," she told the bartender, "like a Long Island iced tea."

"How about an orange juice with vodka," I offered, wanting something less sugary.

"You said nothing sour. That's citrus!"

"Citrus saved your life," I reminded her, thinking with relish of the moment I'd sprayed the citrus concoction into Aaron's eyes.

Steph put her hand to her chest and closed her eyes as though she were taking a solemn vow. "You're right. To citrus!" she said, and lifted her empty glass.

The bartender was used to dealing with drunkards, so he ignored our crazy tribute and made two screwdrivers.

"I put two extra lime wedges on the rim, since you two seem to really love citrus," he told us. He laid down two napkin squares and placed the drinks on top.

"To citrus!" we cheered again, clinking our glasses.

"I'd much rather be forever in blue jeans, babe . . ." On the stage, Dean Fartin finished his song, stretching out the last word as he eyed an older woman who had a deep tan and the skin texture of a piece of beef jerky.

My phone buzzed: an email from JB.

"Check this out," I told Steph. I leaned in so we could both see the screen.

"No way," Steph said. "Open it!"

JB had forwarded the toxicology and lab reports with a message that read, "Thought you'd like to see these. Don't share with anyone!" Her team had finally succeeded in getting the autopsies of the dead women unsealed.

The file was huge. "Download, damnit!" Steph yelled at my phone. She tapped the screen as if she could threaten it with violence to move faster. She no longer sported long acrylics and was back to using a clear coat of regular polish. Her real nails were brittle and yellowed from the supplements and years of acrylic.

It finally opened, and the screen filled with pages of medical jargon and numbers, none of which made sense at first glance.

"I can't read this," Steph said, squinting.

I moved the phone closer to my face and tried to will myself to sober up enough to decipher the medical language.

"Tests ordered were a postmortem urine screen, blood alcohol screen, and novel psychoactive substance screen," I said out loud. I scrolled through each report. One after the other showed a negative result for the full panel of drugs. The only positive results were for caffeine and alcohol, though the levels were low.

"It's like we thought," I told Steph. "No drugs."

"What about Mackenzie?"

"She's not included here. She died in Utah. Out of Briggs's jurisdiction. I don't think they even did a toxicology report since it was an accident."

"It was a murder," Steph reminded me.

It sometimes surprised me how easy it was to forget Leah had killed Mackenzie. Leah was shot in the head by her husband and left to float in a cloud of her own blood. As much as she was complicit in LuminUS's misdeeds, I still thought of her as a victim, too. I would never claim she was a good person, but Leah had felt guilt over causing Mackenzie's death, leading her to try to confess, which was more than Aaron could say. He hadn't killed without remorse, but his guilt wasn't strong enough that he would take the blame for his actions.

Steph dug around in her purse for lip balm. Much like her downgraded nails, she had sold her luxury purses and now toted a more modest faux-leather bag she bought at Marshalls for $25. She pulled out a packet of SkeleSlim stuck to the side of her water bottle.

"I keep finding this shit everywhere. It's like glitter," she said. "What else do the lab reports say?"

"Way ahead of you." I was already midparagraph in the summary section of the results for the exact product Steph had fished from her purse. "Holy shit! It's worse than we thought."

"Worse than arsenic? Or dried human bones? Or the venom from brown recluse spiders?" Steph asked. We had occupied our time thinking of the most outrageous ingredients LuminUS might have used, creating outlandish scenarios, like Dixie using the hearts of virgins and chanting satanic verses over factory assembly lines.

"Shockingly, worse. Besides lying about their listed ingredients— like this packet that has no collagen or biotin, but *does* have a shit ton of caffeine—it also has trace amounts of . . . wait for it . . ." I drummed on the bar top. "Radium."

"What!" Steph shouted.

"This is crazy." I reread the same section to make sure what I saw was true. "It makes sense. The hair loss, weight loss, mood disorders . . ."

"And the glowing skin."

I continued reading. "BeautyBoost has the most, but it was also found in SkeleSlim. Along with . . . oh my God." I gagged.

Steph grabbed the phone. "Tapeworm eggs!" She clenched a hand to her stomach. "I'm going to be sick."

"Here." I handed her my cocktail. "Drink up. The vodka will kill the worms."

"Is that true?"

"I don't know, but it will at least make them sleepy."

"Not funny!" she said, and punched my arm.

We googled how to treat tapeworms in humans. Steph made a doctor's appointment for the following afternoon and asked the bartender if he had warm milk and castor oil, because we read it could be a holistic remedy.

Eventually, Steph calmed down. If she was growing a worm baby, there was nothing to be done until the doctor's appointment.

Steph ordered a shot of pure vodka. "The cheapest one you have," she told the bartender. "Moonshine, if you have it. I want it to feel like rubbing alcohol burning every inch of my esophagus."

I ordered a classier drink: pinot grigio with an ice cube. If nothing else, my experience with LuminUS had warmed me to the stuff.

We listened as more people sang. Steph watched until she couldn't take it anymore. "You know what?" she said. "I'm not going to let this worm get me down. We're here to celebrate, and we are going to celebrate! Let's go!" Steph grabbed me and led me to the stage, pushing aside Dean Fartin, who was preparing an encore.

"Please, no," I pleaded. I was properly drunk, but it wasn't enough to make me comfortable with singing in front of a crowd. Even if that crowd was even more drunk and not paying attention to us.

"Come on! You know it. You'll love it. We're doing this!" Steph said.

It took two notes for me to recognize the song she chose: the colossal hit from our New Jersey lord and savior, Jon Bon Jovi.

"Was 'Sweet Caroline' not available?" I joked.

Steph ignored me and sang the opening lyrics about how Tommy and Gina are struggling to get by despite it being tough, so tough.

I joined in, doing more talking than singing.

Letting go of the events of not only the last month, but years, Steph set herself in the front of the stage and began changing the lyrics. She performed like a woman possessed, pumping a fist into the air as she belted:

They say, you've gotta give us all you've got
It doesn't make a difference if you believe it or not
They'll tell you lies
And promise you a quick buck
Don't give it a shot!

Woah, you'll never get there!
Woah, LuminUS is full of hot air!
They'll take your cash and use it for themselves
Woah, LuminUS is biological warfare!

I knew the words to the original song but not Steph's rendition, especially with the added beats. I stepped back, allowing her to have her moment. She played air guitar during the instrumental bits. I joined in on those, and we rocked out, backs touching.

Quickly, the crowd took notice of our performance. Phones raised into the air, and videos began recording. I thought they were making fun of us. I didn't care. It didn't stop me. And it didn't stop Steph.

Woah, you'll never get there!
Woah, LuminUS doesn't care!
Drink their shakes and you'll lose your hair
Woah, LuminUS doesn't care!

As she sang the chorus, other women began to join in, especially during the line about LuminUS not caring. They too pumped their fists in the air.

I saw how connected the crowd was to Steph. With her musical venting, she had touched a common thread amongst the women in the audience. She and I weren't the only ones burned by LuminUS. Clearfield was slowly learning the company had betrayed them, and the army of women were rebelling.

When the song finished, chants continued.

"LuminUS doesn't care! LuminUS doesn't care! LuminUS doesn't care!"

Steph and I joined in. Videos continued to record.

From "The Pyramid Has Crumbled: The Rise and Fall of LuminUS"

First published in *Vanity Fair*, July 2018

Within the framework of these companies lies an intersectionality between girlboss feminism and hustle culture capitalism. Early in my stint at LuminUS, one of my friends accused me of being—or should I say, accurately noticed—blind to the issue. But my eyes are open now.

Each "girlboss" is selling more than oils or leggings or weight-loss shakes. She's selling the idea that if you sign up to join her team, you too can achieve the quality of life she has. And who wouldn't want her life—the house, the cars, the handbags, the Chanel? She can do it all, cooking, cleaning, getting everyone ready for church, taking care of a husband who no longer works (thanks to her business!) and her *X* amount of children.

See the problem?

MLMs advertise an empowered woman with terms like "boss babe" and "She-E-O," all while implicitly encouraging a subservient, domestic image. The woman is both the breadwinner *and* the homemaker, and neither one trumps the other on social media. She's seen taking the kids to soccer practice (while wearing her plumping mascara), baking cookies for the husband when he comes home from work (without a single chip on her set of press-on nails), and sitting down to work on her business after everyone's been put to bed (curled up under a puffy blanket and clutching her collagen tea).

Beyond the pyramid structure of their "businesses," these women live in another: God at the top, then husband, then kids, then, if she's lucky, at the bottom, her.

hapter 28

"Ready, Thelma?"

"Sure am, Louise."

I pushed the final box of LuminUS into the U-Haul. Steph pulled down the door and hooked the lock in place.

Clearing out the garage was the final step of Steph ridding her life of LuminUS. She had to give up the house, which she did so willingly. Not only was it being rented, under her name, but she had no control over the interior decor.

"Did you believe I would choose to own a sign that read 'Life's too short, lick the spoon'?" she asked. "I can't wait to never see another rustic painting of a pastel beach scene again."

Since none of the furniture belonged to the Murphys, they didn't have much in the way of boxes. They were moving back to Clearfield into a three-bedroom cottage-style house with a melon-colored door. Steph didn't want to stay in Clearfield County, but Rob's business was doing well, and she didn't want to separate the boys from their friends or pull them out of school.

The new house was also rented. Steph planned on buying once

their finances stabilized, but for the time being, they were lucky to even get the lease agreement. LuminUS had put all the contracts in Steph's name, but not her husband's; her credit was screwed, but Rob's wasn't. The new house and new car (a used Subaru hatchback) were both under his name.

"I feel like I don't own a single thing," she told me. "Suddenly, I'm completely reliant on Rob. I feel like there's been a shift in equality, and we're not on the same level anymore. Not that he treats me any differently. In fact, our marriage has never been better. I'm no longer stressed and obsessed. We've been spending more quality time together without having to take photos of everything."

They had also signed up for marriage counseling to rebuild trust between them. They could hardly afford it, but both felt the expense was worth it. "I just can't be more grateful he forgave me for concealing so much from him," Steph said. "It's more than I deserve."

I reminded Steph it wouldn't be long before she was again contributing to the household. She had signed up for the fall semester at the community college in the nursing school program. In two years, she would become a registered nurse and transfer to nearby Stockton University to get her bachelor's of science in nursing. Her ultimate goal was to work in the neonatal care unit.

Steph had also sued LuminUS. A five-inch tapeworm had taken up residence in her large intestine, and she had enough radiation poisoning to show up on a test. She would need yearly monitoring for cancers, but according to the doctors, it was more of a precaution than real concern.

The tapeworm had died after a series of anthelmintics. Feeling the cramps of it passing and seeing its segmented body in the toilet was the most disturbing moment of Steph's life, and I had to promise on my dead mother's grave that I would never mention it—to her or another soul—for as long as I lived.

LuminUS had settled the lawsuit out of court with the agreement that Steph sign another NDA, forbidding her to speak about her experience with the company.

"You should hold out," I told her. "This story is exploding, and you're at the center of it. You could help me with the book and get a cut."

Steph refused. Taking the payout was the right move for her family. It was the only way she could afford to keep her kids in school. Banking on book deals and exclusive interviews was too much of a gamble, even if her karaoke performance had gone viral. Many women in Clearfield had been burned by LuminUS, and they had shared the video, along with their own supportive comments.

LuminUS had been settling out of court as often as possible and throwing their NDAs in the faces of anyone willing to take their new deal. Despite having taken advantage of women throughout the eastern United States (LuminUS hadn't spread much in the West, where the Mormons had their hands full with their own MLMs), they were still using dirty tactics to convince ex-distributors they'd be better off taking a lump-sum payout.

They tried it with me. I received multiple calls and emails from the LuminUS legal team. I didn't have a tapeworm or radiation in my system, but Dixie knew I was there when Aaron snapped.

I refused. There was no way I was going to sign an NDA. I couldn't be silenced. I had a whole lot to say.

My article, "The Pyramid Has Crumbled: The Rise and Fall of LuminUS," was bought by *Vanity Fair*. I was still working on final edits, but it was scheduled for the July edition, bumping one of their originally scheduled features about how studios were buying and selling canceled TV shows.

News of the forthcoming article had traveled rapidly in media circles. It didn't take long before I was offered an exclusive book deal with Penguin Random House, ripe with a fat advance that would allow me to move back to New York.

"I'm going to miss you," Steph told me at least once a day.

"I'm moving down the street," I would remind her.

"But it's not the same. You won't be above my garage." She pouted, pushing out her lower lip as far as it could stretch.

"I'm *so* sorry you'll have to walk an entire five blocks."

I wasn't moving back to the city. Not yet, anyway. I rented a house near Steph: also a cottage, but it had two bedrooms, and the door was barnyard red. Clearfield was a slow-moving town where I could write in peace. It was also close to my dad. I offered to give him my spare bedroom, but he refused. "It won't be long before I get on your nerves," he told me.

I yielded, but not without paying for him to move into a new apartment building. He fought me on it. "First month's rent is already paid for," I said. "If I cancel the lease, I'm forgoing first and last month's rent and the security deposit." My dad couldn't stomach unnecessary fees, so he agreed. He, along with Captain Milton, settled into a one bedroom at the Parkhouse Condominiums, where there were no rats, but there *were* granite countertops and a Jacuzzi.

"Your skin's looking much better," Steph told me as she eyed my face.

"I should have seen a dermatologist ages ago." With my face soon to be in the press, attached to an article and a book, I made an appointment with a dermatologist. No mystery pills or serums with cutesy names this time, but cold, hard medicine. I was put on a regimen of prescription retinols, niacinamides, and oral medications to control my sebum levels. With consistency, it would work, and I was already seeing improvement.

"This is it, huh?" Steph asked as she started the truck. It rumbled to life, spewing clouds of exhaust. "My last haul. Once we leave the driveway, I'll never have to come back here again."

We drove past the emptied garage and onto the street. Steph rolled down her window and stuck out her middle finger. "Fuck you, LuminUS," she shouted.

△ △ △

A man greeted us at the gate to the city dump.

"Proof of residency," he instructed.

Steph handed him her license. He wrote on a clipboard.

"Are you disposing of any tires, appliances, paint products, batteries containing lead, or any other hazardous items?"

Steph and I shared a look.

"No," she said.

"Proceed forward."

We drove past the gate and further into the landfill. "You're sure none of this stuff is toxic?" Steph asked.

"The stuff we have back there? I'm sure. The radium and hard metals were only in BeautyBoost and SkeleSlim. And we got rid of those a while ago."

After the news broke that there were radioactive ingredients in LuminUS products, a safe disposal site was set up for any distributors and consumers who wanted to responsibly rid their homes of the dangerous items. The program was a raging success. They received more items than they knew what to do with. The latest gossip was that the supplements and powders were being transported to New Mexico, where they would be buried within concrete tombs in the desert.

Good riddance, I thought.

For the nontoxic products, Bre had a GOOB sale, which was MLM lingo for going out of business. She wasn't the only one with the idea. Hundreds of distributors had set up their own GOOB pages. Nothing sold, and she was forced to give most of it to Goodwill. At least she would get a tax write-off. Much like the disposal sites, Goodwill had been inundated with LuminUS products. They tried selling them for a dollar a piece, then fifty cents, then they threw them out.

Completely unfazed by the scandals, Bre had already joined two more MLMs. One was selling press-on nails and the other was Platinum Pump, the fitness program that sold "custom" workout routines and hot-pink two-pound weights. I wasn't sure if she took the payout, but she wiped any mention of LuminUS from her post history. She was a regular feature on a subreddit devoted to calling out influencers who lied about photo editing—she claimed she was a size XXS thanks to Platinum Pump. Her filler had migrated, creating a lumpy mustache above her upper lip line. She swore she was going to get it dissolved, but in each reel, it continued to expand.

Steph unlocked the truck's back door, and we started unloading. Box after box was sliced open and tilted, allowing the bottles inside to stream out.

"It's time to be amongst your own kind!" I told the bottles as I poured them onto the heaps of trash. Garbage deserves to live with other garbage.

The job took an hour. By the time each box was emptied, we had worked up a sweat and an appetite.

"What do you want for dinner?" I asked.

"Nothing green apple, chocolate mint, or ginger peach."

"Mexican it is."

We got back into the truck. Behind us, the pile of metallic blue bottles glistened in the setting sun.

We both rolled down our windows and flipped the bottles the bird before breaking into a chorus of "LuminUS Doesn't Care."

From "The Pyramid Has Crumbled: The Rise and Fall of LuminUS"

First published in *Vanity Fair*, July 2018

Why did she do it? Why did Dixie knowingly poison people?

The easy answer is greed, and yes, greed was a major part of it. But as someone who witnessed her in action first-hand and saw the darkness within, I think she was evil.

What kind of person would undergo chemotherapy and think, "Sure, my bones were weakened beyond belief and my lung tissue is so scarred I will never be able to take a full breath again. But, hey, chemo did clear my blemishes and I lost a bunch of weight! If only I could bottle this experience and sell it!"

I've witnessed evil. It had its hands wrapped around my best friend's throat. It drove desperate families in my town further into financial ruin. It ruined marriages, friendships, lives. Dixie was evil because she danced over the bodies of dead women in her Louboutin heels.

Members of LuminUS's leadership team revealed her future plans were to phase out the radium. An anonymous source told me, "[Dixie] had wanted the formulas to change once the company penetrated deeper into the West. Early users were posting their results left and right.

So much so that it was being called a miracle weight-loss supplement. Dixie knew the potential side effects. We all did. When she was pressed on it, she kept reminding us it wouldn't be long before the formula changed. 'Don't worry,' she would say. 'LuminUS has every intent to transition to an all-natural blend in the upcoming quarter. Besides, keeping the one we have is becoming too expensive.'"

LUMINUS

From the LuminUS Income Disclosure Statement

Published by court order, 2018

LuminUS Industries is a direct selling company offering skincare products, although we are in the process of branching out into other lifestyle products, including makeup and apparel. We offer consultants, known as LuminUS Ladies, the opportunity to build their own businesses. Our mission is to reach as many women as possible to spread the benefits of our proprietary formulas.

Consultants earn commissions on each product sold. Other income opportunities include recruitment bonuses, which increase as consultants rise through the ranks of LuminUS. All details are outlined in the Compensation Plan.

In 2017, the average annual earnings were as follows:

National Vice Presidents: $303,202

Regional Managers: $77,444

Area Managers: $6,102

Independent Consultants: $204.25

Annual earnings do not include outside expenses that a consultant incurs while operating their business. Examples of these include, but are not limited to: office supplies, cameras, computers, shipping, packaging, self-maintenance (e.g., fashionable clothing, makeup, facial fillers, hair bleach).

Sixty percent of consultants who joined in 2017 became inactive during the first year after joining. If a consultant does not make a sale within their first three months of joining, they are considered inactive and can rejoin at a later date so long as they pay the start-up fee again.

No refunds on unsold products or start-up fees will be given.

LUMINUS

From: Daily Affirmations to Attract Success

LuminUS Training Document

I will allow myself to dream without limits.

I am making money doing what I love.

I attract positive people.

I love LuminUS.

Reading Group Guide

1. *Death in the Downline* dives into the strange world of multi-level marketing schemes, or MLMs. What is your personal experience with MLMs? Have you known someone who was part of one or been part of one yourself? Have you watched any documentaries about them, such as *LuLaRich* or *Betting on Zero*?

2. Some of the over-the-top moments in the book (like the LuminSANITY conference) are based on real aspects of various MLM companies. Were there any moments that surprised you or prompted you to do your own research? Do you think the author's portrayal of these organizations is fair?

3. Drew gets involved in LuminUS in large part because of economic precarity. What are some other reasons someone might get involved in an MLM?

4. The LuminUS ladies are selling a lifestyle as much as a product, showing off expensive cars and perfect houses—while some of them are secretly drowning in debt. What about our culture encourages this kind of behavior? Do you think social media plays a role?

5. Do you empathize with Steph's position, or do you feel that she is complicit in the damage LuminUS caused to the people in her downline?

6. Steph's husband calls LuminUS a cult. Do you think that MLMs can reach cult status?

7. The book explores several complicated relationship dynamics. What do you think it has to say about female friendship and the power dynamics between uplines and downlines? Have you ever had a friendship like Drew and Steph's?

8. Were you surprised when the murderer was revealed? Did you have any theories that were proven right or proven wrong?

A Conversation with Author Maria Abrams

Death in the Downline **offers a look into the strange, sometimes sinister world of multi-level marketing schemes, or MLMs. What attracted you to this subject?**

I've always been interested in cults and their dynamics, specifically how members become recruited and indoctrinated. And what's even more interesting than a cult? A cult that peddles essential oils or lipsticks, with Facetuned women as the leaders. People expect cults to be run by religious fanatics in white robes, but they never imagine that the ordinary women in their mommy groups might be part of one. It might sound extreme to compare MLMs to cults, but if you compare their structures and social dynamics, it's hard to tell the difference. I followed MLM news and lawsuits and current and previous distributor stories for years before writing *Death in the Downline*.

Do you have any personal experience with MLMs?

You can't throw a nickel without hitting someone who has experience with MLMs. I've had friends and family who have ended up in MLMs or accidentally purchased from MLMs in ignorance of their nefarious structure.

Luckily, I've never been asked to join an MLM. The people I've known in MLMs loved the products and wanted to share them as gifts without any pressure to purchase. You'll still find a dozen MLM essential oils in my bathroom that I received as gifts from an in-law. (Side note: I use the oils in my diffuser; don't ever ingest that stuff!) I will say that I once used a topical muscle-pain-relief

MLM oil that worked so freakishly well, I questioned what sort of illegal ingredients it contained.

What was the weirdest or most surprising thing you found in your research for the book?
There were many instances when I wrote something I thought was so outlandish that it would be purely comedic or satirical, but then found an *actual* social media post nearly identical to what I wrote. The most egregious were posts using deaths in the person's family or their children's illnesses to sell more product. I saw a post by a mother sharing a photo of her young daughter in a coma, plugged into multiple machines at a hospital. She bragged that she had spent the past two days with her daughter—*and*, of course, helping women secure their MLM starter kits. There was even a promo code to save 20 percent!

Members of LuminUS join or are drawn deeper into the scheme for a number of reasons, such as economic precarity. What are some of the reasons you feel people are drawn to MLMs?
MLMs are experts at targeting people and convincing them to join. They use recruitment tactics that are nearly identical to those of cults. The "marks" are often stay-at-home mothers who might be feeling lonely, struggling to make ends meet, or desperate to have something of their very own. They are told they can still spend the day with their children, but also make money on the side. All they need is their cell phones! MLMs make it sound easy and risk free.

Then, the love bombing begins. Other members shower the new recruit with compliments and encouragement. The new member feels like part of a supportive group of other women in similar situations. There's also an authoritative figure (usually whoever's near the top of the pyramid) who doesn't allow criticism and demands loyalty. All standard cult tactics. It's fascinating but frightening to dissect how MLMs are so successful at recruiting.

There's a big focus on female friendship in this book. What inspired that? Do you think that part of the appeal of MLMs comes from the social aspect?
Absolutely! Many MLMs call themselves "tribes" and claim that by joining, you'll be joining a "tribe" of tight-knit women. Social media posts from those in the MLMs show girls' trips in tropical places and gorgeous women dressed up at conferences and at group dinners. I can see how many would be drawn to that instant support system.

Female friendships often suffer or even break down because of MLMs. You might see a friend falling down the MLM rabbit hole and try to warn them, but get pushed away because MLMs forbid their members from spending time with "negative" people. Or maybe you begin to hang out with someone who you thought could be a close friend, just to find out that they only ever saw you as a sales target. Friendships can also become strained when a distributor is so desperate to succeed that she bombards everyone in her social network with constant sales pitches, driving them away in the process.

What was the inspiration behind the seemingly picture-perfect lifestyle you designed for the LuminUS ladies?
Part of the MLM guidebook is selling a lifestyle. Distributors want people to see their posts of the big house with the fancy car and

the luxury purses so that anyone viewing them feels that they could also have that life *if* they signed up for the MLM. But what you're seeing on social media isn't real—the big house might have multiple mortgages, the fancy car may be leased, and the luxury purses might have put the owner in debt.

What would you say to a person who thinks they're too smart to be sucked into an MLM?
No one is too smart to join an MLM. I've known doctors who have fallen for MLMs. MLMs prey on weaknesses, which we all have. Friends, financial independence, a purpose, freedom; whatever you feel you're lacking or wanting, they'll target it. They're so good at psychological and emotional manipulation that intelligence isn't even a factor.

I consider myself intelligent. I have a master's degree, graduated with honors, and can write entire books. But could I have fallen for an MLM before I read the subreddits and saw the documentaries? One million percent. I would have failed miserably since I'm the worst salesperson, but I would have joined.

Plotting a mystery novel can be difficult—you want to keep readers turning the page. What was your process like?
I like writing as though I were watching a movie in my head. I see the scenes unfold and hear the dialogue spoken. This approach might not work for other genres, but it lends itself well to creating a page-turner. My scenes often end where a shot in a movie would cut, at a moment of tension. I also leaned heavily on my wonderful editor.

What's next for you?

I loved writing this book, especially leaning into satire and comedy. I can't say too much about the manuscript I'm working on now, but it's definitely going to be in the same vein: a darkly funny mystery novel about female social networks, but, this time, with a supernatural twist.

I'm also an unapologetic fan of trashy reality television and I think that that as a backdrop, or a house renovation show, would make an excellent, snarky murder mystery.

Acknowledgments

This is a book that could not have been written without the help of my team. Rebecca Gyllenhaal, my wonderful editor, brought this book to life. To the talented people at Quirk: Ivy Noelle Weir, Christina Tatulli, Kate Brown, Kassie Andreadis, and Scott MacLean. And, of course, a huge thanks to my agent, Lane Heymont, for his advice and encouragement.

On a personal note, thank you to my husband, Steve Goodman, for helping me come up with character names when my brain is mush. Thanks to Linnea Lang for always having a kind word about my writing. Thanks to my family and friends: Robert Goodman, Christine Alexy, Glen Lang, and Samantha Coppola.

Next, thanks to my furry and amphibious pets who have sat with (or at least next to) me as I wrote.

I already dedicated the book to them, but I'd be remiss not to thank my parents, John and Dorothy, for their continued support and love. You'll never know how thankful I am for you both. A posthumous thanks to my grandparents who I miss daily.

Lastly, I wouldn't be an author without the support of readers, librarians, booksellers, other authors, and teachers who cultivated my love for reading and writing.